Pillow PRINCESS

Part 2

Avery Goode

Life Changing Books in conjunction with Power Play Media
Published by Life Changing Books
P.O. Box 423 Brandywine, MD 20613

"Library of Congress Cataloging-in-Publication Data;
www.lifechangingbooks.net

13 Digit: 9781934230541

Dedication

This book is dedicated to all of my readers and true supporters. I couldn't do this without you.

• •

*A*cknowledgments

Right now, I am extremely grateful to God for blessing me to complete this novel. I remember thinking back to the day I told people I wanted to write and so many of them laughed in my face. They told me I was on some "other" ish and I needed to hang it up. I'm so glad that I didn't. They doubted that I would finish one novel and now the Lord has blessed me to finish 3. Look at God!

Big thanks go out to my family and friends. We are a crazy bunch but love one another dearly. I'm not going to name all of you again because you know who you are but my thanks spans far and wide.

Thank you to my wonderful and EXTREMELY PATIENT publisher and everyone from Team LCB who made this possible.

A special thanks to Laneika Cratic who gave me the title for Pillow Princess and then told me what it meant. Thank you for sharing your stories with me so openly and honestly. You are amazing and I am so glad that we met!

To the Daniels family who welcomed me and my crew into your lives and allowed us to become a part of your family no questions asked. We needed the love that you all offered so freely and I thank you so much for it. Melinda, you blessed me with a brand new computer when I thought I was going to have to write at the library every day using their computers. Shawn, you made sure that it was top notch for me. You guys rock! Randi, your loving words and prayers brought me through many nights. Knowing that you guys were rooting for us to succeed made a huge difference. Thank you for simply being the obedient children of God that He called you to be.

Janelle Grissom whose open lifestyle choice and crazy selection of girlfriends help me come up with the Psycho Dyke idea in the first place.

A hero's thank you to my grandfather, Willie Runnels, who transitioned in 2014. He taught me to keep on going even if I didn't feel like it and he gave the best hugs ever! I love you GrandPa and I will never forget the talks we used to have every time I came home.

E. Lynn Harris, who before he died, told me that I was crazy and needed Jesus after I ran this idea by him and told him what I planned to put in my book. He was an amazing author and a Goode friend.

Finally, I would like to thank everyone who had the audacity to succeed even when others told you that you wouldn't. Their disbelief is a catalyst to propel me forward. This is only the beginning!

Lots of Love,

Avery Goode XOXO

Instagram: @thegoodscribe

Chapter One
Reasons and Regrets

At first there was a light drizzle of rain and then the Atlanta sky opened up. The rain fell in sheets and it was beginning to get dark outside. A very gloomy day, perfect for a funeral. Charmaine put on a black-linen, Ralph Lauren pants suit and pulled her shoulder length hair back into a ponytail. She didn't dare bother with makeup because she was crying so hard it would be ruined before she made it out of the house. The sound of the thunder mimicked the sound of Charmaine's breaking heart and she was overcome with grief.

"I can't do this. How am I supposed to live without my love?" Charmaine cried.

Up until the DJ started speaking, Charmaine had forgotten that the radio was even on. There was a commercial break and then a man began to sing a capella. "How do I say goodbye, to what we have?" The song made Charmaine feel even worse so she changed the station. That song wasn't any better. "I miss you, I'm talking to you, baby. I miss you." She didn't want to hear Aaron Hall either. The next station was playing an up-tempo 90s jam so she left it there. She went into her walk-in closet to find her heels and when she came back, the song faded off and another began to play. "Unbreak my heart, say you love me again. Undo this hurt that you caused when you walked out of the door and walked out of my life. Uncry these tears; I've cried so many nights. Unbreak my heart. My-y-y heart."

*"What the fuck is going on with Atlanta radio today?"
Charmaine cried angrily. She walked over to the Bose radio,
picked it up off her nightstand and threw it across the room. It
shattered into pieces upon impact and hit the floor. Fuck that
radio, she thought, wiping her tears. She was already feeling bad.
The last thing she needed was sad love songs that made her feel
worse.*

*Charmaine sat down in the wingback chair and curled up
into a little ball. She placed her head on her knees and cried. As
the volume of her cries increased, so did the sound of the rain. The
one person she loved the most was gone. Donnie Stone was not a
perfect woman but she was perfect for Charmaine. Theirs was a
love like no other. Regardless of what they went through, they always found their way back to one another. Donnie was fine and
sexy, so of course there were other women. They may have had
Donnie's body, but Charmaine had her heart. Until that bitch
Symone came along.*

*Before Symone entered the picture, Donnie would fuck
around with other bitches but she never set up house with any of
them. But there was something about Symone that Donnie could
not resist. From the time she first called Symone's radio show, she
was hooked. Once they met in person it was all over. Charmaine
started seeing Donnie less and less every day. Their calls were not
as long and the texts were infrequent. And then one day, Donnie
didn't call at all. Charmaine was losing the love of her life and it
was all Symone's fault.*

*This is why Charmaine decided to eliminate her from both
of their lives. Symone posed a threat to Charmaine and she
couldn't handle that. The night that she cut the brake line on
Symone's Range Rover, she was beyond angry and hurt. Her plan
was fool proof. She followed Symone on many occasions and was
aware of her driving habits so Charmaine knew that she would be
speeding to work. Symone worked early morning hours and without a doubt would hit traffic by the time the brakes gave out. An
accident was inevitable. As fast as Symone was known to drive,
Charmaine counted on death and destruction. But she didn't count*

on Donnie being in the car.

"Baby, I'm so sorry. I love you so much. I never, ever meant to hurt you. Forgive me. Please."

The clock on the wall chimed twelve noon, interrupting Charmaine's thoughts. If she didn't hurry, Charmaine was going to be late for the funeral. Tears blurred her vision and she could barely unlock the door to leave when it was time to go. Driving was out of the question. Fortunately, she had the good sense to hire a driver for this sad occasion. The rain caused some delays and Charmaine ended up fifteen minutes late. When they pulled up in front of the church, mourners were going in, following the navy and chrome casket that held her girlfriend, Donnie. Charmaine shook her head in disbelief as she joined in the procession.

Seated on the first and second rows was Donnie's family. Charmaine was supposed to walk in with them but because she was late, she couldn't. She ended up sitting on the second row on the opposite side of the church but she had a clear view of the immediate family. Damon, Donnie's brother, was very distraught. Everyone knew of the close knit relationship that he and his sister shared. Next to him was their father. He laid his head on his son's shoulder and wept.

The preacher got up and opened the service with a prayer and then read Psalm 23. Loud cries and wailing moans filled the church when the choir got up to sing. The remainder of the service was a blur to Charmaine. She sat in the pew and rocked back and forth, crying all along. Two men in black suits came up front and began to remove the flowers off of the casket. One of them flipped a latch on the side of the casket and slowly opened the lid.

"Oh my God! My sister!" Damon yelled. "Why her, Lord? Why? Jesus, please. NO!"

Charmaine looked across the church at the family, while locking eyes with Damon. She felt his pain and could not believe this was really happening. How did he find the strength to identify the body and pick out a suit for his sister? It was almost as if she was living a real life movie. The look of despair they held compounded the guilt that Charmaine felt. All she could do was turn away and let the tears fall that she held at bay. The funeral direc-

3

*tor asked everyone to stand, as it was time to view the body. The
ushers started at the back row and one by one, made their way to
the front. Charmaine wasn't ready for this, but nobody was. Donnie was young and full of life. She had the rest of her life ahead of
her and Charmaine had taken that from her and her loved ones,
disrupting everyone's life.*

*Friends and family passed her on their way to pay their
final respects. Charmaine recognized many of the women as
bitches that Donnie had cheated with. A few of them were pillow
princesses; lesbians who thought they were too good to give pleasure, only desiring to be on the receiving end. Like their mouths
were too good to touch another woman's pussy, whatever. Seeing
them made Charmaine's blood boil. Then a woman with crutches
hobbled down the aisle, escorted by a tall man in an Armani suit. It
was Symone and her ex-boyfriend, Keyon.*

*"It should have been you, ho!" Charmaine screamed an-
grily, lunging at Symone who almost fell down.*

*"Fuck you, bitch. Donnie was mine. If she wanted to be
with you, she would've. Nobody wants your psycho dyke ass,"
Symone snapped.*

*"This ain't the time nor place for this bullshit," one of
Donnie's cousin's said, holding Charmaine's arms back. "Donnie
wouldn't want y'all doing this shit here. Get y'all act together."*

*Reluctantly, Charmaine and Symone retracted their claws.
No amount of arguing, fussing or fighting would bring Donnie
back. A few more rows of attendees made their way to the casket
and then it was finally Charmaine's chance to go view the body.
Wobbly, unstable legs carried Charmaine closer to the body of her
girlfriend. Once she got near the casket, she gently leaned against
it to get her bearings. Taking two small steps, she inched near
Donnie. Without thinking, she eased her arms underneath Donnie's
head and brought the corpse close to her.*

*"I love you, baby. I love you so much," she cried. Onlook-
ers gasped in disbelief as Charmaine kissed on Donnie's stiff lips.
"I'm sorry. You hear me, baby. I'm soooo sorry." Curious whis-
pers circulated amongst the people, wondering exactly why Charmaine was so sorry. An usher rushed to the funeral director to tell*

5

him what was happening at the front of the church. The director and usher rushed up front and together they pried Charmaine off of Donnie's body so the viewing could continue, while carefully escorting Charmaine outside with the rest of Donnie's family.

"I...I'm sorry, Damon. Just didn't know this would be so hard."

"None of us did, Charmaine," Damon said, hugging his sister's ex-girlfriend. "I wanted to thank you for helping me cover the funeral expenses. We wouldn't have been able to put Donita away this nicely if it wasn't for you."

"No thanks is necessary, Damon. I loved Donnie, you know that. She was all that I ever wanted and needed. I just wanted to be the same for her."

"I know that she did a lot of dumb shit, but in her own way, she loved you very much."

"Yeah, I know," Charmaine said through a stream of tears.

The funeral staff rolled Donnie's casket out and loaded it into the waiting white hearse. The driver of the first limo held the door open so the immediate family could get in.

"C'mon, Char. You can ride with us. You're family."

"What about Symone?" *Charmaine asked Damon, really to insure her good standing with the family. It was no secret that Damon couldn't stand Symone. Charmaine just wanted to know if his feelings had changed. They hadn't.*

"Man, fuck that bitch. I asked her to help me with some of the costs and she told me she would. I called her a last week to talk about it and she said she was in the middle of something and would call me back. Shit, I'm still waiting. Then she got the nerve to show up at my sister's service with a nigga in tow? She ain't shit to me!" *Damon said.*

It was messed up that Symone would come to the funeral with a man that she left for Donnie, but Charmaine didn't care about that slimy chick or the man she was with. This was about Donnie and she was definitely looking down at all the people who showed up for her.

There were four limousines in all and once all of the family was loaded and the police escorts were in place, they traveled to-

wards Donnie's final resting place. Inside the limo, Charmaine, Damon, Damon's wife Stefanie and Donnie's father, Daniel, strolled down memory lane. Even while they grieved, they were able to conjure up good memories of Donnie that made them all smile and even laugh. Charmaine desperately wanted to join in but guilt wouldn't let her. Donnie's family had to bury her today and it was all Charmaine's fault.

"Our final words will come from Donita's brother, Damon," the preacher stepped aside so he could speak.

"My sister was many things to many people. But to me, she was my Bop. That's the name I gave her when she was young 'cause she was always in my stuff. I would tell her to stop and since she couldn't talk very well yet, she would repeat after me and say 'bop'. Well, the name fit her and she's been my Bop ever since. Good, bad or indifferent, I loved my sister. I know many of you did as well. Bop, we're all here. Pops, Steph, even Charmaine. She's looking real pretty too, Bop."

Charmaine couldn't even muster up a smile.

Damon continued, "We know you're smiling down on us. Watch over us like we know you will. One day, we'll meet again. Until then, we love you." Somehow Damon managed to say all of that through tears. His voice cracked a few times but he made it. Charmaine cried uncontrollably. This was the worst day of her life. After Damon spoke, the preacher prayed over the casket. This was it. Per Damon's request, Donnie's casket was to be lowered while they were in attendance. It was almost over. The gravediggers began to turn the crank that helped lower the casket in the cold ground.

"No, don't!" She yelled at them and lunged at one of them, trying to grab his shovel. Damon grabbed Charmaine and held her close as she cried.

"Charmaine, don't act like this. You have to be strong," Damon admonished. "She's dead, Charmaine. We gotta let her go, now," he whispered.

"I can't. She was all that I had. Baby, please come back to me," she cried, pain ripping through her heart. "Donnie, no!" Charmaine yelled, as she awoke in a cold sweat.

Chapter Two
Hindsight is 20/20

Symone was lying on the floor begging Donnie to stop kicking her. Donnie picked up her right leg and with all the strength she could muster, she stomped on Symone's leg. Over and over, she stomped on her girlfriend like she was killing bugs. Symone was balled up in the fetal position doing her best to protect her head.

"Look at me, bitch! " Donnie commanded. "You see dis shit here?" Donnie pointed to her left arm that was in a cast. "This shit yo' fucking fault. Yo' bitch ass almost got me killed. Stand yo' punk ass up!"

Donnie didn't wait for Symone to get up on her own. With her good arm, she grabbed Symone's shirt and lifted her like a rag doll. She spun Symone around to face her and with the butt of her cast she began to hit Symone in the head. Symone used both of her arms to try and shield the blows that were being inflicted upon her.

"Why are you doing this, baby? Please stop!" Symone pleaded.

"Say something again and I'll kick those fuckin' teeth out ya' mouth!" Donnie yelled angrily, taking a swig of the Jack Daniels bottle that she held in her hand. She was drunk. Again. Since the accident, Donnie had been popping Oxycodone pain pills like they were Tic Tacs and chasing them with hard liquor. She was out of control.

"Baby, please!"

"Please what, ho? Slutty ass, stupid ass heifer!"

"Don't do this," Symone cried.

"Do what? Huh, bitch? Did yo' ass do what I said when I told you to have the brakes on ya' fucking SUV fixed? Fuck no! So why in da hell should I listen to you now?"

"I took the truck in. I promise I did. The mechanic said they were fine," she said, trying to ease away from Donnie's grasp.

"That muhfucker will say anything 'cause yo' bitch ass is prolly sucking his dick."

"I'm not cheating on you. I love you. You know that."

"I'on know shit other than I'ma stay black and eventually die."

Symone was almost out of Donnie's reach when her intoxicated girlfriend grabbed her by the collar of her dress and pushed her up against the wall with the cast across Symone's neck.

"I can't breathe."

"Da fuck I care for? Did you care about me when you almost killed me? Huh? Did you?" Disgusted, Donnie spat in Symone's face. "I get it, though. Yo' ass think you better than me."

"No!" Symone yelled out. Donnie elbowed her in the stomach, causing her to double over. The cell phone Symone had been clenching tightly was now exposed.

"Yo ass running around here, texting muhfuckers like you single and shit. Like my ass ain't done shit for you. You prolly got texts from some nigga now. Matter fact, gimme dis got damned phone!" Donnie snatched the expensive iPhone, walked over to the balcony and sent it careening down to the sidewalk. A man, walking his dog, looked up to see what was going on.

"Mind ya' fuckin' bidness, honky!" Donnie stepped back into the condo and was silent for a moment.

Scared, Symone just stood near the wall, trembling in fear.

"After all the shit I done did for you and this is how you wanna treat a nigga like me? You's an ungrateful ho. I swear on my life, you is."

Symone didn't respond. She knew that it was best to just be quiet. It seemed that every day since the accident, Donnie beat her mercilessly. It didn't matter what Symone did or what she said, Donnie would wild out on her. Tears poured out like rain down Symone's face. Inside, it felt like she was dying. The Donnie she fell in love with had disappeared. Symone could tell by the look in her eyes that she was a different person.

Although she did sustain a broken arm, the doctor said that Donnie could work. Not long hours, but part-time. She didn't want to do that. All she did was sit around the house, pop pills, drink, play video games and fuck Symone. Symone was carrying her battered and bruised body to work every day as the radio host of her very own show, 'Symone Says' and here was Donnie, hardly bathing anymore and wearing the same clothes for days on end. Gone was the clean cut stud who dressed to impress. That person was replaced by someone who reminded Symone of Eddie Caine, Jr. on *The Five Heartbeats*. *This cannot be my life*, Symone thought, wiping tears from her face.

"Did I tell yo' bitch ass to move?"

Donnie punched Symone in the back of her head with a closed fist. She hit her so hard; Symone was seeing stars. Then Donnie wrapped a fist full of hair around her hand and pulled Symone's head back so that she was facing her.

"See, it's disobedience like this that keeps me kicking yo' ass. Now you done pissed me off. Assume the motherfuckin' position." Donnie used her good hand to unbuckle the belt on her pants and slide them, along with the boxers, down past her waist. Once the boxers were down, the strap-on that Donnie wore sprang up like a real dick.

With tears in her eyes, Symone got down on her knees and began to suck the strap-on dick. Even though the member wasn't attached to Donnie's body, Donnie moaned in pleasure as if her beefcake was real and she was getting head just like a real man.

"Wait, don't be so rough," Symone pleaded to Donnie, who was trying to shove all nine inches down Symone's throat, without care.

"Fuck that! Yo' bitch ass wanna act like a monkey, you gon' be treated like one. Take this shit, you nasty bitch. I hate yo' ass for making me angry like this." The angrier she got, the harder she

10

thrust, until she made Symone gag.

"That's what's up. Now you 'bout to learn, for real, how monkeys get down." A couple more hard thrusts and Symone vomited her lunch on the floor at Donnie's feet, getting nasty chunks of food on her lover.

"Get your monkey ass down on the floor and lick this shit off of my feet!" Donnie yelled.

"I'm not going to do that, Donita. That's nasty," Symone protested. Donnie whacked her across the face with the back of her hand and kicked Symone in the stomach.

"Yes the fuck you will, or else, I'll plug that iron up and burn your ass again. This time I'm gon' burn your face."

Symone knew that Donnie wasn't playing. A month ago, she and Donnie were having an argument while she was ironing a blouse for work. Donnie came over and snatched the iron out of Symone's hand and placed the triangular tip of the iron on Symone's upper thigh. She never told anyone about that and the scar couldn't be seen very well. The mark was beginning to fade with the relentless use of cocoa butter and bleaching creams. As much as she didn't want to do it, she didn't want her face burned either, so she leaned over and began licking the vomit off of Donnie's feet. The very taste and texture of the throw up made Symone want to regurgitate all over again. It took everything in her to keep from throwing it all back up but the thought of another beating had her slurping it up.

"Stop! Now clean this shit up, go brush your teeth and run me some fuckin' bath water."

Symone did as she was told, without hesitation. Tears streamed down her face as she sat on the side of the tub checking the water temperature. She missed Keyon so much. She missed running the bath for his sexy, chocolate ass. She would always end up in the tub with him, riding him just like a surfboard. He was not the best fuck she ever had but he was gentle and a perfect gentleman. He really loved Symone, too. He never made Symone do anything so degrading and never would even think about half the sick shit Donnie did to her.

The day of the accident, she was supposed to meet him for

a breakfast date. Even though they were just meeting so he could borrow some money, she had planned to put the wheels in motion to get him back. Hindsight was a bitch. If she knew back then what she knew now, her life would definitely not include daily beatings. Had she known Donnie would be like this, she would have stayed with Keyon's lying ass rather than Donnie's abusive one. As much as Symone wanted to leave, she couldn't and she didn't. Symone couldn't explain it, but Donnie had a strong hold over her. She knew that their relationship wasn't healthy, but Symone didn't want to be alone. She would rather have a wanna-be man, than no one at all.

Donnie walked naked into the bathroom with her strap-on flapping around. She was eyeing Symone like she was piece of meat and Donnie was a wild animal.

"Bring yo' hoe ass over here and give daddy a kiss." Donnie leaned in to kiss Symone but stopped before their lips touched. "Wait, did you brush your teeth like I told you to?"

"Yes."

"Come here then." Donnie traced the outline of Symone's lips with her tongue roughly and then slowly, before sliding it in. She moved it in and out, rubbing it over Symone's tongue, the inside of Symone's mouth and over her teeth. Symone was the least bit turned on. Donnie's tongue trailed down the front of Symone's neck and she bit hard at Symone's cleavage, causing Symone to wince in pain.

Donnie tore the clothes off of Symone and forced her to lean over the side of the tub. Donnie knelt down behind her and fingered her pussy roughly. Unclipped fingernails scratched Symone's lips and the soft lining on the inside of her womanhood. Donnie didn't care. One finger, then two, then three and four, penetrated Symone.

"Shit, this pussy is wet! Just how I like it. Spread ya' legs and open wider for me," Donnie commanded.

Symone moved her legs out a little but Donnie wanted more. With both hands, Donnie parted Symone's ass cheeks and pushed her plastic dick inside of Symone's anus.

"Ow! Donnie, please, don't!" Symone yelped in pain. She

felt like her asshole was tearing apart. She was pinned against the bathtub on her knees and couldn't move. There was nowhere or way for her to escape. Donnie didn't care that she had entered Symone's ass dry, without lube. All she cared about was her own satisfaction.

Donnie pumped hard and reached around and grabbed one of Symone's breasts and pinched the nipple hard, going for blood. She leaned over and bit Symone's back, leaving small teeth prints in a trail.

"Ah," she groaned through gritted teeth. "This feels good!" Donnie pulled out of Symone's ass and plunged into her wet pussy.

"It never takes much to get you wet. That's how I know your pussy was made for me." She began fingering Symone's ass until Symone's body involuntarily responded in pleasure. She then slapped her ass for coming too soon.

"I'm going to cum, oh shit!" Donnie exclaimed, holding Symone's head down, pushing her face in the water.

"Take this big dick in this wet pussy," Donnie pumped vigorously.

Donnie lifted Symone off of the floor, turned her around and sat Symone on the vanity. Before shoving her dick into the now tender pussy, Donnie put her entire hand inside of Symone and fisted her aching pussy. Symone was being stretched to the limit with Donnie's thick arm inside.

"I feel ya leg's trembling. Cum for me again, you nasty bitch."

Symone's legs were indeed trembling, but from pain. There was nothing pleasurable about what was taking place. She just wanted the sexual assault to be over and done with. Silently, Symone begged for it to stop. As if she read Symone's mind, Donnie snatched her hand out, slid the man-made dick inside and went to work again. A few short strokes later, Donnie came. She pulled Symone off of the cabinet and dragged her to the bedroom, flinging Symone onto the bed.

Symone watched as Donnie quickly dressed and skipped the bath she'd just run for her. Donnie's cell phone vibrated. She picked it up and replied to a text message.

"I'm going out. Where yo' wallet?" Donnie demanded, rather than asked. Not waiting for Symone's response, Donnie walked to the chaise and snatched up Symone's Birkin bag. "Damn shame how much this purse cost. Muhfuckers could eat for a year." Normally Symone would ask where Donnie was going but lately, she didn't give a fuck and Donnie wasn't going to volunteer the information either. Once she got in Symone's SUV, a 2014 black Porsche Cayenne, she made a phone call.

"What's up? You home? Cool. A nigga 'bout to ride through there. See you in thirty."

More like an hour later, Charmaine opened the door and stood there, staring at Donnie with disgust.

"What?" Charmaine was not happy.

"Awe, don't be like that, Lucky Charms. You my woman and as a result of all this madness with the accident, I realize that we were meant to be together. Now come over here and give Daddy a kiss." Thanks to the cameras that Charmaine had planted around Symone's house, Charmaine opted out of kissing Donnie on her mouth and presented Donnie with a kiss on the cheek.

"Oh, it's like that?"

"Yeah, something like that. You were at another bitch's house, living with her like ya' married and shit and then you get in an accident. How you think that made me feel when the cops called me to tell me what happened? I' on know why you got me listed as your next of kin anyway. It needs to be your brother."

"You're my wifey, that's why you're my next of kin, Char. I love yo' ass, girl. Can't you see a nigga like me is beggin'?"

"Nah, what I see is a nigga lying. You can't love me too much, you're still with Symone. Even after she almost got your ass killed. Nah, from the looks of it, she's the one you really love," Charmaine finished scathingly, like she didn't have shit to do with the wreck.

"On some real nigga shit, I'm putting some shit together so that you and I can ride off into the sunset and shit. Ya feel me?"

"I guess. How you gon' do that?"

"You let me handle all the details. All you need to worry your sexy ass head about is where you want us to buy our home to-

14

gether."

"I hear you talking. We'll see."

"Yep. Now all I wanna see is your pretty pussy in my face. Get ready."

Charmaine smiled and walked over to the sofa, stripping quickly before sitting on the edge. Donnie, who stayed dressed, got on the floor in front of her and sniffed Charmaine's womanhood.

"I'on know how your shit always smells like peaches. That shit drives me crazy."

"You're so silly. Who knew that when we met at Crenshaw Plaza four years ago, that we'd be here right now? I'm so glad that you talked me into moving here to be close to you. And now I am a real Georgia peach."

"'Let's see if you still taste like one." Donnie made lazy circles around Charmaine's clit and licked it like a lollipop. "Hell, yeah, fucking turning me on. You taste just like peaches," she said, inserting two fingers into her sopping wet pussy. "Get up on your knees." Charmaine did and faced the back of the sofa. Once she was in position, Donnie licked Charmaine's asshole, making her tongue stiff so she could put it in. Satisfied moans and groans escaped past Charmaine lips.

"Mmm, ah. Oh, yes. Suck me, baby. Yes, that's it." The more Charmaine moaned, the more intense Donnie licked and fingered her. "Ah, babe, right there. Don't stop! Yes! I'm 'bout to cum!" She sang out. After the orgasm, she collapsed on the sofa. "Damn, baby. It's been too long."

"Sheeit, daddy missed you, too. But uh, I got something for you," Donnie said, pulling out a long black box. "It's just a token of my affection for you."

"A Cartier tennis bracelet? Nice. Does Symone know about this?"

Donnie laughed. "Nah. I got one of her credit cards and been using it. She just pay the bill on them joints. Don't even be looking at the charges and shit. I told you she got money."

"I'm surprised you're being so honest with me about your girlfriend."

"I told you, Lucky Charms, a nigga is turning over a new

leaf. This bracelet is only the beginning. Next is gon' be that ring on your finger."

Charmaine just smiled a fake smile and looked down at her ring finger. Yes, she wanted a ring, but no longer from Donnie. She was becoming immune to Donnie's bullshit. Things between Donnie and Charmaine went left and would never get right since Symone was still an issue. Charmaine laughed and turned on the Bose radio that she dreamt about destroying and scanned each station. Not finding anything she liked, Charmaine sang her own tune to herself.

I'm making a list, checking it twice. 'cause all these bitches are naughty not nice. Charmaine's wrath is coming to town. I see you when you're fucking. I know that you're a fake. I know when you have fucked my girl and I'm gonna make you pay. So, you better watch out, you better not pry, watch who you are fucking with, I'm telling you why. Charmaine's wrath is coming to town.

Chapter Three
Like Mother, Like Daughter

Charmaine walked into the Savannah hotel like she was a superstar. A silk Pucci print scarf was wrapped around her head and a pair of large framed Tom Ford shades covered her eyes. Her only luggage consisted of a Louis Vuitton garment bag and a matching make-up case. She always traveled in style.

Charmaine, or rather Zabria was accustomed to the finer things in life. The life of Zabria and Charmaine were worlds apart even though they were the same person. Zabria shopped at places like Hermes but her alter ego was limited to places like TJ Maxx or Ross. It was better to keep Charmaine's persona low-key.

Before walking into the hotel, Charmaine's phone rang. It was the last person she wanted to talk to, Donnie.

"Hello," Charmaine answered, rolling her eyes.

"Hey, babe. What you doing?"

"Taking care of some business. What's up?"

"Not shit. Just thinking about my Lucky Charms. Shit, when you coming home? A nigga like me is missing you."

"Oh, yeah?" She knew Donnie was lying. "I miss you, too."

"You know I love you, right?"

"Yeah, sure. Look, I'm about to walk up to a counter and don't wanna be on the phone. That's rude. I'll call you back in a few." Not waiting for Donnie to respond, Charmaine hung up the phone.

"Welcome to the St. Regency. We've been expecting you. The name on your reservation?"

"Zabria Moreland."

"Welcome back, Ms. Moreland. It's been a while."

"Yes. But you all will see more of me going forward. I had a lot of business to take care of but I'm getting back on track."

"Good to hear. We've put you in your usual suite. Here are your keys. If you need anything, please dial zero. Valet will bring you your claim ticket once your car is parked. Enjoy your stay and thank you again for choosing the St. Regency."

It felt so good to be back in a place where she could finally be herself. To be around the one person who really knew her and loved her and knew all of her secrets. Her mother. Over the last few years, Charmaine learned that one of the hardest things to do in life was to pretend to be someone else. But she had been Charmaine Franklin for so long, she was actually beginning to think that's who she really was. Yesterday, after Donnie left her house; Charmaine broke down and started crying. She saw that her life was imitating her mother's and she really didn't want that.

Charmaine Franklin, who was born Zabria Charmaine Moreland, in Beverly Hills, California, was an heiress of sorts. She was the only child of a white man whose father invented the first motorized wheelchair. This left her father, Zachary, with a billion dollar inheritance when her grandfather passed years ago. Her mother, a beautiful black woman, won over fifty awards in Hollywood and New York for make-up transformations. She also created the first prosthetic face mask that was used in the Star Trek series.

An interesting couple they were. When she was little, Charmaine was mechanically inclined just like her father and he used to call her his Tinker Bell, named after the Tinker toys she played with daily. She could put a 1,000 piece puzzle together by the age of five and she knew how to disassemble VCR's and put them back together by age eight. Her grandfather, who spoiled her rotten, thought that she was a genius.

She also took after her mother. Applying make-up and creating different looks came naturally to her. Her mother, Melissa, would take her to movie sets with her where she worked as an assistant. With make-up techniques constantly changing, Melissa was always learning something new. Whatever she learned, she taught Charmaine. Charmaine could contour a face long before contouring became popular. There was nothing that Melissa could do that Charmaine couldn't. The only difference was that Melissa did it better and with a finesse that Charmaine admired.

Charmaine's parents were married, briefly for eight years, and divorced by the time she turned five years old, due to irreconcilable differences. After Charmaine and her mother moved out of the family home, her father remained there, dated here and there, but never remarried. Her mother, Melissa, moved on. But not with another man. She told Charmaine that Zachary was the only man for her. Instead, she started dating a manly looking woman, named Jean Joiner. When Charmaine first saw Jean, she thought that she was a man. That's when she learned about studs and fems. She was ten years old and this was a lot for a little girl to take on, especially without the protection she always felt from her father.

Jean looked just like Hill Harper and carried herself just like a man. They hit it off immediately. The three of them did things together as a family all the time. But Zachary didn't like the fact that his daughter was being raised by a Lesbian. Every time Charmaine came to Savannah, she would think about her parents and the life she had in California.

Where did I go wrong? She thought. Charmaine hopped off the bed and went over to the vanity to remove the make-up off her face. She pulled out a small bag of cotton balls and an organic solvent that removed any type of make-up, including pancake, which is what she wore. Once the pancake make-up was off, she washed her face with an oatmeal scrub and rinsed her glowing skin with warm water. She grabbed the plush towel off the rack and patted her face dry.

"Welcome back, Zabria," she said to the reflection in the mirror.

Charmaine turned her face to the left and the right, remembering the real woman inside and behind the mask. The Charmaine who people saw daily had shoulder length black weave, a caramel complexion, a small contoured nose, big brown eyes and full pink lips. Between the dowdy clothes and simple make-up, she looked more like a thirty five year old woman instead of the twenty five year old she actually was She was five-eight and shapely, weighing in at about 165 pounds. Thick in all the right places; cute and simple but could stand to tighten up a little. Her looks were unassuming and easily forgettable which is what she was going for. The Charmaine that she was looking at now was naturally light-skinned, with a thin, straight nose, bluish- gray eyes and sandy-red hair. Her lips, height and weight were the same.

Charmaine couldn't count how many times she and Donnie had fucked but Donnie never paid attention to the fact that her body was a little lighter than her face. But that was normal with black people. The skin exposed to sun was darker than the skin always covered by clothing. Donnie couldn't have cared less. All Donnie cared about was pussy, money and weed. And sadly, Charmaine knew it. She was swimming an ocean for a woman who wouldn't even cross a puddle for her. Since she had been with Donnie, Charmaine had assumed so many different personalities and looks that she almost forgot who she really was. She had been lying to herself and to Donnie. There was no way that she would be able to explain it.

"I can see it now," she said to the mirror. "Hey, babe, how was your day? Oh, mine? It was great. By the way, I've been lying to you for a couple of years. My first name is Zabria, I'm mixed, my daddy is rich as fuck and my mother is in the loony bin. Shit, he'd probably beat my ass like he did Symone's ass yesterday. When I watched that shit on tape, I actually felt bad for the hoe. Nah, I'm good. Some things are better left unsaid."

Feeling down, Charmaine pulled her cell phone out of her purse. She dialed three digits, 213, and the rest filled in.

"Hello," the proper sounding man said.

"Hi, daddy. It's me."

"Bria. How's my Tinker Bell doing?"

"Not too good. I'm in Savannah."

Charmaine's father understood what that meant.

"Awe, sweetheart. How's your mom, doing?"

Charmaine told her father that she hadn't visited her mother in a while and how she felt guilty about it. Her dad reassured her that it was okay. Hearing the depression in her voice, he changed the subject.

"How's school?"

"Good, dad. I'm making all A's."

"That's my girl. I'm proud of you, Tinker Bell."

Charmaine exhaled. Her father wouldn't be so proud of her if she told him everything she was doing in addition to going to school.

In fact, he'd be furious. Zachary thought his daughter's sole purpose for coming to Atlanta was to attend Emory Medical School, not to chase after a woman. A woman who didn't even know who Charmaine really was. All he knew was that his daughter was pursuing her dream of becoming a surgeon. Something she had wanted to be since she was a little girl.

"Thanks, Dad. I'm proud of you, too." She said, thinking of how far her dad had come and how happy he was now with his new lady.

"Do you need any money, sweetheart?" He was always offering his riches, to which Charmaine declined, as she felt he did enough for her already.

"No, daddy. You deposit five grand in my account every month. I don't spend even half of that."

"I know. You're the only rich kid I know who knows the value of a dollar."

"Money doesn't grow on trees, dad. Gramps taught me that."

"Yeah. You need to call him. He *is* getting old."

"I spoke to him yesterday after school. He and Grams are in Hawaii living like retirees should. I'm gonna lie down now but I'll definitely call you after I see, mom. I love you."

"I love you, too, Tinker Bell."

Charmaine hit end on the cell phone and fell asleep as soon as her head hit the pillow. That night, she dreamt the same dream she always did when she came to Savannah, about her mother and Jean.

22

Charmaine remembered it like it happened yesterday, Jean and her mother, Melissa, started arguing all the time because of Jean's cheating. Melissa started wearing disguises to follow Jean when she went out so she would have solid proof of Jean's whereabouts. They would argue, fuss and fight all the time until one Christmas Eve; Jean packed her bags and got ready to leave. That morning, Charmaine woke up, hoping to open a few Christmas gifts before breakfast. She walked into the living room and Jean and her mom were yelling and physically fighting. Jean picked up her large Army issued duffle bag and headed towards the door.

"You are not going to leave me, Jean. I need you!"

"No you don't, Mel. You want me. There's a difference. But I don't need or want you. This arguing is for the birds. Have a nice life."

Melissa ran to the door and blocked it. Jean yelled for her to move out of the way. Neither Jean nor Charmaine saw it until it was too late; the butcher knife that Melissa had. Jean didn't realize she had been stabbed until blood started coming out of her mouth. By then it was too late. Jean's body dropped like a leaf. Melissa casually washed the knife off, came into the living room and just sat there. Charmaine called her dad instantly, who in turn called the police and vowed to get to her as soon as possible. Because of his wealth, Zachary was able to get the D.A. to sweep the murder under the rug. They lessened the charge to self-defense and transported her directly to the psychiatric ward. Jean had been in and out of jail and it didn't matter one way or the other that another black woman had died. The day Jean died was the last time Charmaine had heard her mother speak. She was fourteen years old.

The next morning, Charmaine arrived at the hospital, in a good mood. Christmas was just around the corner and she came bearing gifts. When she went to the nurses' station, everyone who knew her spoke a warm hello.

"Hey, Ms. Bria. We've missed you."

"I've missed you guys, too. How's mommy?"

Debbie, the charge nurse came over to Charmaine and hugged her.

"Hey, baby girl. Your mama ain't the same. She's lost a lot

of weight 'cause she stopped eating. Last month, during arts and crafts, someone left some scissors on the table and she got a hold to 'em and cut her hair. It's a hot mess, child. We tried to call you to see if you wanted us to try and fix it, but you changed your number. We couldn't reach you."

"I'm sorry. My ex-boyfriend wouldn't leave me alone," she lied.

"No worries. We called your dad and he said to fix it but your mama would freak out every time we got close to her so we just left it alone. Just be prepared, okay? She ain't what you remember."

That was a gross understatement. Melissa Moreland looked like she weighed 100 pounds, soaking wet. The small t-shirt she had on was draped on her like a curtain. When Charmaine hugged her, Melissa's rib cage was visible through the shirt. The haircut Melissa had given herself looked like a lawnmower got loose on her head.

In some spots the hair was long, while in others, it was cut down two or three inches. Melissa's once beautiful skin looked sallow. Her big brown eyes had no spark and her teeth looked they hadn't been brushed in years.

"Hey, mommy" Charmaine said softly, after she removed her arms from her lifeless mother. "I'm sorry I haven't been here in a while. Please forgive me. I love you, mommy." Charmaine became a little girl every time she was around her mother. She just wanted to please her mother and never disappoint her the way Jean had.

"The charge nurse said you cut your hair. Guess you got tired of combing it, huh? I understand. I just had my hair weaved again, so I totally get it, mommy. My beautician keeps asking me why I wear a weave since I have good hair. I told her there's no such thing as good and bad hair. People are a trip, huh, mommy? So much has happened since the last time I came up here. Let me tell you all about it."

Charmaine got comfortable and began slowly, "It was this one chick that Donnie was messing with who was a model. mommy you should have seen her, she had long black hair like an

Indian. *Had* being the operative word. I disguised myself as a cable guy and got into her house and switched her hair conditioner with Nair. Now that trick's head is smooth as a baby's bottom." Charmaine laughed out loud. "I broke into another chick's car and planted old fish, chicken and maggots and put glue on her head rest. When she got in the car, her weave was stuck to the seat. I killed her cat, too. Put that mangy thing in the trunk," Charmaine let out another giggle but the thought of killing caused her to get serious. "I've done something bad, mommy. I killed one of the broads that Donnie messed with. Sad thing is that I don't even know why. It was just something about her that rubbed me the wrong way. Just like Symone. She's Donnie's new bitch. I want her dead more than I want my next meal. She's going to get hers though. Mark my words."

Melissa didn't acknowledge Charmaine's presence, at all. She stood by the window making circles on the glass with her index finger but listened as her daughter told her all of the dastardly deeds she did since the last visit.

"Mommy, can I brush your teeth? I don't want them to fall out, okay? After that we'll have some lunch. They said you're not eating either. C'mon, mommy. Come with me."

Charmaine lightly grabbed her mother's hand and led her over to the sink. Her mom didn't protest which was a good sign. Melissa allowed Charmaine to brush her teeth and wash her face. Charmaine put a clean nightgown on her mother that fit and sat her in the wheelchair she purchased for her.

"You wanna eat lunch in the dining room and get out of your room, mommy? Let's go for a walk."

The two of them exited the room and went to the patient dining room. The nurses smiled as Melissa and Charmaine passed by. Many of them had tried to get her out of the room before but were met with combative resistance. Fresh air was an important component of anyone's good mental health. Once they arrived in the dining room, the orderly brought over two trays for them to dine. Charmaine scooted her chair next to her mother's and fed her. Melissa ate everything on the plate. After the dining room, Charmaine walked her mother through the gardens.

25

"Look at the pretty flowers, mommy. Do you remember the flowers you and I planted in California? They grew so pretty. Grammy said they're still going strong."

Charmaine stopped rolling and set the brakes. She walked around to face her mother and kneeled down next to her.

"Mommy, do you remember? Do you recognize me?"

Melissa didn't respond. She just looked down at her hands and scratched the back of her left hand with the right one. Charmaine exhaled and resumed, pushing the wheelchair. She took her mother back to her room and polished her fingernails and toenails.

"Every girl needs a good mani-pedi. Isn't that what you used to tell me all the time? It's a travesty to go around with feet that look like the monster on the cover of that book, *Where the Wild Things Are.* You used to read that to me all the time."

Charmaine got a brush out of the nightstand and started brushing her mother's hair.

"Your hair is so soft, mommy. Do you remember when I was a little girl and you used to brush my hair like this? You told me that I was your little caramel drop. I miss those days. Don't you?"

No reply from Melissa.

"Mommy, I had a dream about Jean last night." She wasn't sure how her mother would respond.

Melissa jumped up out of the wheelchair and started to go crazy. She walked around the room at a fast pace, knocking things over and running into the walls. Charmaine tried to hold her but Melissa broke free from her grasp. Two nurses rushed in, one holding a syringe with a yellowish substance in it and the other with a woven strap.

"I'm sorry," Charmaine said. "I brought up a name from her past and set her off. I didn't mean it."

"It's okay, baby. We're used to it. The doctor said she has Schizoaffective Disorder along with Bipolar Disorder. Do you know if anyone in your family suffered from any type of mental illness?" Before Charmaine could answer, her mother broke free from the two nurses who held her.

"Melissa? Melissa! Calm down. Grab her, Tessie." Char-

26

maine cried like a baby, watching her mother in such despair.

The other nurse, who was built like a small linebacker, put both arms around Melissa from behind and sat her down in the wheelchair. The charge nurse put the white, woven strap around Melissa, strapping her into the chair, wiping the injection site down with alcohol and administering the shot.

"She'll settle back down, in a minute, baby. Awe, don't cry, sugah. God'll take care of your mama. Just keep praying for her."

"You said mental illness is inherited?"

"It can be. But don't worry your pretty little head. You don't have anything to worry about."

That's what you think, Charmaine thought.

The nurses left the mother and daughter alone. Melissa sat quietly in the wheelchair and Charmaine started back brushing her hair.

"I'll be right back, mommy."

She went to the nurses' station and asked for a pair of scissors. Charmaine went back to her mother's room and cut her hair even so she wouldn't look as maniacal as she just displayed.

"Mommy, I dare not tell you *all* the mess I've done since I last saw you. All I will say is that you and Daddy would be very disappointed in me. I think I've inherited more of your traits than I care to admit. I think I may have the same disorder, but I will be okay, right? If I pray, mommy, do you think that God will hear me? I'on know if He wants to entertain a sinner like me. I'm horrible mama, I'on know if I did the right thing flying you out here to be close to me just so I could be close to Donnie. And I put her before you. I'm sorry, mama. Daddy sends his love. He's still not dating anyone. You must have a platinum pussy, though, because daddy said you were it for him and he wishes things were different."

"Let's get you into bed. I see you over there dozing off. Daddy's going to fly here soon to see you. I'll be back on Christmas Day, okay? I love you so much, mommy."

"I love you, too," Melissa whispered. Charmaine jumped back, not expecting to hear those words and looking into her eyes for more but nothing came out. Charmaine broke down in tears and allowed herself to savor the moment. She hadn't heard her mother's voice in almost ten years, so this came as a complete shock. Charmaine felt satisfied and hoped the next visit included more of her responding.

Avery GOODE

Chapter Four
Who Do You Love?

Keyon's kisses were sure-fire panty droppers. The way his tongue caressed and explored Domynique's mouth tenderly made her want to come up out of her clothes. He fondled her breasts through the sheer nightgown as he continued to kiss her, while picking his dream woman up and placing her on the bed, standing up. Then his tongue parted Domynique's lips so he could explore further. Even with her standing on the California king-sized bed, she was still only a few inches taller than Keyon's six-feet-nine inch frame, leaving her breasts right at his mouth.

Nimble fingers removed her gown, revealing the firm, perky D-cup breasts.

"Is it just me or are your breasts bigger?"

"It's just you," Domynique replied, a bit nervous.

Keyon used his teeth to gently bite on Domynique's neck and breasts, then used his velvet-like tongue to lick her nipples.

"Mmmm, yes Baby." Domynique slid the long gown down past her hips. She wasn't wearing any panties. Keyon kissed and nibbled down her slim stomach. He placed his tongue on Domynique's nether lips and began to tease the swollen pair with his tongue.

"Oh my," she gushed, stumbling. "I need to lie down." Without waiting for Keyon, she eased down, careful not to move his mouth off of her sweet spot.

He wrapped his lips around Domynique's clit and used his hands to remove his t-shirt, while simultaneously pushing his lounge pants down to his knees.

"Shit," he said, having to stand up and move away from her long enough to remove the clothes. "Now, where was I?"

He placed his tongue deep inside, licking Domynique's walls and nibbling the hard nub between her pussy lips. Domynique moaned and pinched her nipples in sheer pleasure.

Keyon buried his face in her wet pussy, feasting on his woman until her legs began to shake. He knew she was on the verge.

"I'm cumming, baby. Ooh wee. Oh, yes," she panted. Domynique's breathing was heavy and her heart was beating fast. She was hot and ready just like a Little Caesar's Pizza. Without removing his tongue, Keyon added two fingers to her wet pussy and slid them in and out slowly.

"Lemme take care of you," she offered. Although Keyon didn't want to stop eating her out, he wanted what she had to offer. He lay at the top of the bed and allowed his lady love to come sit on his face so that they were in a 69 position. Because Domynique was a virgin until she got with Keyon, she didn't know much about giving head other than what she had learned from YouTube and porn videos but she was going to give it her best shot. At twenty six, Domynique's sexual experiences were limited to whatever she and Keyon did in their bedroom. He was unselfish in his lovemaking and was always giving to Domynique, because she loved him so much, she wanted to reciprocate.

She took him into her mouth slowly and used her small hands to massage his stiff meat. The tutorial videos said to make the dick wet for easier massaging and she did. She gripped his dick with her mouth as hard as she could and sucked up and down. She used her hand to knead his balls. They were heavy with his seed and she wanted to drain him dry. Keyon finger-fucked Domynique's pussy and then lubed one finger and her ass with lubricant, gently sliding a finger in. She pulled her mouth off of his dick and eased up until she was sitting upright on his face.

"I want you inside of me" she said timidly.

31

Keyon placed his hands on her ass like they were basket-
balls and moved Domynique from his mouth to his dick. She slid
down his hard shaft, her sexy ass facing Keyon. Up and down, she
rode him like a mechanical bull. His left hand massaged
Domynique's ass again and the index finger on his right hand
played with her clit.

"Damn, Domynique your pussy's tight."

"Umm, huh," she moaned.

Lost in pleasure, she grinded and grinded and he pumped
harder. He spun her around and watched her titties bounce up and
down. It didn't take long for Keyon to reach his peak and she was
coming again, too.

"Ahhh, shit," was all that escaped his mouth as he erupted
inside her and she collapsed on his chest. The sound of heavy
breathing and rapidly beating hearts was the only noise in the
room. Keyon pulled the blanket up over the both of them and they
lay there in silence. Domynique rested comfortably in the crook of
Keyon's arm. A pillow was situated between the two of them. She
had put it there purposefully to keep him from noticing too many
changes in her body. Her breasts were fuller and her nipples were
ultra sensitive and there was a small pooch forming in her lower
abdomen, all signs of the pregnancy she was hiding.

"Is that gonna happen every time I get up for a drink of
water?" Domynique giggled.

"Yep," Keyon said, rubbing her bottom and staring into her
eyes.

"What'cha thinking about?"

"You and how wonderful you make me feel. In and out of
bed."

"It was good, huh?"

"Like Maxwell House Coffee, it was good to the last drop."

Domynique fluffed her pillow and looked into Keyon's
light brown eyes. She was in love with Keyon and prayed that he
felt the same about her but she dare not ask him. Not yet anyway.
She still was not sure of this entire situation and it all came about.
She was sought out and still found it a little strange but it was com-
forting to be sought out by a sexy, rich, brown-skinned man.

"You're beautiful, you know that?" Keyon said admiringly.

"Thank you. I feel the same way about you, looking like Montell Jordan's brother." They both laughed. Domynique loved looking at Keyon. His caramel brown skin, full lips, and light brown eyes were a sight to see. She rubbed her hand over his smooth cheek before kissing him on it.

"Babe, I gotta ask, why were you in a homeless shelter when Watson found you? I searched high and low looking for you after the video tape. Of all the places we looked, that's the last place I thought I'd find you."

"I didn't have anywhere to go. I had no job, money, no family. I was on my own."

"At one time, I had a good job at Saks, and I helped style a so-called movie producer. He told me that he was casting for ATL Part 2."

"Ugh, why? The first one was barely any good." I had to laugh at his reaction.

"Hush. That's my movie. Anyway, he said, since Lauren London was busy, I was the next best thing and asked me to come read for him. Apparently, people think we resemble each other."

"Nah, y'all don't just resemble one another, y'all damn near twins. Being the same cute, lil' ass height, too, makes you her double. The only difference is that you have all this real hair on your head. Most broads can't even *grow* a quarter of that and you over here lookin' like Pocahantas."

"That's what the guy said. Anyway, he handed me his card and told me to call him to set up a reading and so I did. When I got to his studio, all he wanted to do was have sex with me. I grabbed my shit and ran as fast as I could up outta there. Shortly after, my sister died and I was left in a downward spiral, homeless and running the streets."

"Damn. Tell me about your parents," Keyon said.

"Well, my father, James, is a short, round Dominican and Italian mixed man who owns a landscaping company. Well, he did. Honestly, I don't know what he's doing now. Anyway, my mama, Netta, said I got my hair from him." As if on cue, Keyon stroked her long, waist-length tresses while Domynique continued.

"Netta's short, too. She's a light-skinned beauty who looks like Sally Richardson. She has perfect skin, straight teeth and not one stretch mark after giving birth to two beautiful daughters. Unfortunately, she thought that me and my baby sister, Britain, were inconveniences. Once I was old enough to be left home alone, I was. After Brit was born, I had to balance school and taking care of an infant. Netta would stay out all night. Sometimes days and weeks at a time. Trust, I wasn't surprised to come home and find all of Netta's belongings gone. She took everything that she thought of value. Except me and my sister."

"You call your mother by her first name?" Keyon thought that was crazy but he was raised by two parents so he had stability and a solid foundation growing up.

"Yep. That's the way she wanted it. When people saw us together, she would tell me to say I was her little sister if they asked who I was."

"What? Your own mother denied you?"

"Every chance she got, babe. She used to tell me, repeatedly, that I was the reason that she couldn't keep a man. I think she hated me."

"Why didn't you go live with your dad or other relatives?"

"If that was an option, I would have. I had no clue where to find my dad and Netta screwed over so many people that when I needed them, all they could think about was the wrong she did to them. My mother's sister told me that if Netta was a whore I probably was too and she didn't want me near her new husband."

"What the fuck?"

"That's what I said."

Keyon sat up, exhaled and pulled Domynique near him.

"Domynique, I need to tell you something. Things I should have told you a long time ago."

"What is it?"

"Um, after I got the tape, in the mail last September, I wanted to find you. At first I was angry with you but the more I watched it, the more intrigued I became. There was something about you in that tape that made me want to know who this mystery woman was. It was like love at first sight for me. You know I

34

hired Watson to help find you. He never even told me how he found out your name," Keyon stopped talking.

"Face recognition software."

"What?" Keyon was baffled.

"Watson told me he used face recognition software. Something about the CIA and FBI were the only ones who knew about it and if he told me too much he would have to kill me."

Smiling, Keyon spoke. "Yeah, that sounds like Wat. Anyway, when he found out your name, he started to look for your parents, thinking that you may have gone with them. He found your dad, James, and spoke to him."

"Watson talked to my father? What did he say? Did he ask about me? Where is he? Wow, I haven't spoken to my father in over twelve years. I wanna see him. Jesus! Did he find Netta, too? Even though she left me, I'd like to see her. Find out how she's been. Ewe, is she still with Deano? I can't stand him. Forget him though, I just wanna see her."

"Domynique," he said softly. She kept talking.

"Keyon, you just don't know how happy I am to know you found the parental units."

"Domynique, stop!" He said forcefully. She quieted immediately.

"Your dad does want to see you. He said he loves and misses you. Deano, your mom's boyfriend was killed in a robbery in Waco, Texas in 2002."

"Damn, Deano. Can't say I didn't see it coming. He was probably trying to sell dope and pimp hos out in Waco," she rhymed, then got serious.

"Babe, your mother...she...," he hesitated.

"She's in jail again?"

Keyon cleared his throat. "Your mom died, Domynique."

"What did you just say?" She asked in stunned disbelief.

"Netta died in 2003 of Pneumonia. She had full blown AIDS."

The room was quiet. Keyon barely took a breath during that moment, waiting to see how she would react. A few minutes passed and finally Domynique spoke.

"I knew it. I was just hoping my gut feeling was wrong. Damn. I told her to use protection like I was her mother," she whispered.

"Are you okay? You're awfully calm for a person who just found out her mom died." Keyon was beginning to rethink this whole Domynique deal. What was he so attracted to? The sex was out of this fucking world but it would not last forever.

"I'm fine. But Keyon, I haven't had a mother my entire life. Your mom's been more of a mother to me than Netta ever was. Your mother knew, didn't she?"

"Yeah. I went to her and asked what to do. Why you ask?"

"After I first arrived, she told me that she'd be honored to be my mother, whether we were together or not. I fell in love with Mama Carolyn right then."

"All my family loves you, Domynique. You fit right in."

"Yeah. I finally have a family."

"Uh, do you wanna go to Texas and get a headstone for Netta?"

"No. Netta died the way she lived, in anonymity."

"What about a headstone for Britain?" Domynique missed her little sister, terribly.

Domynique rose up off his chest "Do you really mean that?"

"Absolutely."

"Oh, wow, baby. I would love that. Thank you so much!

"I care about you, Dom. I got your back."

"I know you do," Domynique said, kissing his lips, reigniting his fire. An hour later, after the couple had finished round two, showered and dressed, they prepared to go downstairs for breakfast.

"Do you smell something?" Domynique asked, who's senses where heightened due to her condition. "That smells like weed."

Keyon led Domynique out of their bedroom. At the bottom of the stairs, Keyon's grandmother, Lillian Steele, stood there smoking a tightly rolled joint. She lived on her own but was always visiting.

36

"Domynique, come over here and give me a hug."

"Is she the only one you see, Gran?"

"Spoiled ass. I was gonna hug you."

"Mama, I thought you were going to stop smoking?" Carolyn reprimanded, walking over to join the group. Michael's mom and dad would be there a while since their home was dismantled by Big.

"Well, you thought wrong. This is that bubonic chronic. It's good for my glaucoma, too."

"You don't have glaucoma, G-Steele," Keyon said, coming into the kitchen.

"Whatever." The older lady put her headphones on her ears to tune Keyon out.

"I ain't got no type, nah…bad bitches is the only thing that I like."

"What is your grandmother listening to?"

"Ear Drummers, Domynique. She got her hands on his new music. Gran is gangster."

"How do you feel though, Dom?" Keyon asked her, concerned that she hadn't become emotional in any way.

"I'm good. God is a keeper."

"I'm here for you, whenever you're ready to talk."

"Thanks, babe."

Domynique walked over to the stove and began helping with breakfast. It was still hard for her to fathom waking up in the Buckhead mini-mansion. The home boasted seven bedrooms and eight and a half bathrooms, an indoor gym, a music studio, an in-law suite complete with kitchen and a bowling alley in the basement. Keith, Keyon's father, walked over to him and grabbed Keyon's shoulder. He was the spitting image of Keyon, with salt and pepper hair and a beard. Caroline was regal and classy and reminded Domynique of Michelle Obama.

"Morning, Son. Your mother and I have something we need to talk to you about."

"Morning, Pops. What's up?"

"Well, we've been talking about your debt and how we can help. We prayed and God came through in a mighty way. The insurance company contacted us and said that we'd be getting a check in a few days. We wanna bless you with it."

"Mom, Dad, as much as I appreciate the offer, I can't take your money. That's the money you need to rebuild your home."

"Not really. A few years ago, your mom bought this ugly painting from a garage sale. Turns out it was an original Rembrandt worth millions. They're only sending us a portion of the estimated value. The rest will be paid out in a few months. Your mom bought an almost priceless painting from a garage sale for ten bucks. Ain't that some shit? I still can't believe it myself." "You serious, pops? Which painting was it?"

"The one your father hated with the women in the pink dresses," his mother answered. "It was the Les Demoiselles d'Avignon."

"The Young Ladies of Avignon," Domynique said.

"You speak French?" Keith Steele asked with his head cocked to the side.

"Yes, pops. Spanish, German, Japanese and Jamaican Patois," Domynique boasted.

"Whoa. Keyon did you know this?"

"Yeah. I did."

"Oooh wee. You got yourself a good'n here, Son." It was easy for the Steele's to love Domynique because she was so sweet and genuine. They knew of her plight in life and sympathized with her. They admired the fact that even though she had hard times, she was a survivor.

"Thanks, dad. She's great." He looked at Domynique lovingly.

"Keyon, the check is two million dollars."

Keyon made it a point to tell Domynique everything. One of the mistakes he feels he made with Symone was keeping things from her. Although this was personal business, it also involved his family and Dom was family. .

Keyon coughed, "Two million? Ah pops, I can't take that. It's too much."

"Son, pride always comes before destruction. That's how you ended up in this mess in the first damned place. Take the

38

money, but if it's okay with you, we'll need to stay in the basement a little longer or until we get our rebuilding settlement."

"Hell yeah, for two million dollars y'all can stay as long as you want."

"I don't know about all that, son. Cary and I need our privacy."

"I hear ya', pops," Keyon chuckled. "Thank you so much. I *will* pay you back. I promise."

"Don't you worry about that, baby," his mother hugged him. "Just pay this animal off and as long as you live, do not borrow a damned thing without talking to us about it first! Agreed?"

"Yes, ma'am." Keyon looked at this watch. "I'm going to work out for an hour or so, then I have a conference call. What y'all getting into?"

"Well," his mother began. "Gran and my daughter-in-law and I," Carolyn said, winking at Dom, "are going Christmas shopping and your dad is going to hold our bags. You can join us after you handle your business."

"Sounds like a plan. Dom, I have something for you."

Keyon walked over to the built in desk in the kitchen. He picked up an envelope and handed Domynique a platinum American Express card with her name on it. She stood there speechless. Keyon knew that his finances were uncertain, considering he was in debt with Big, but he wanted this to be the best holiday for Domynique because fooling with Big this could be Keyon's last one.

"Keyon, you shouldn't have. I didn't expect this." Domynique was in shock.

"Don't be silly. You're my lady and I can't have you out here with no money."

"Now, that's the shit right there," his grandmother said. "Take care of your woman, my nig."

"Oh, lord," Keyon said, rolling his eyes. Together they all cleaned up the breakfast dishes and then left the house. Keyon got a good workout in and then completed his conference call. His company, Man of Steele records was blowing up. He was about to launch an international office and was very excited. He did want to join his family but he was sweaty all over again and went to shower. He stepped out feeling rejuvenated and refreshed.

Keyon thought he heard a bump downstairs but blew it off when he didn't hear it again.

After wiping his face with the towel, he was was totally caught off-guard by a very familiar but crazy woman. He didn't even hear her come in. She made him want to go off right then and there but he kept his cool, knowing how crazy Symone could be. He wasn't sure what was running through her mind ever since she started seeing a stud so he played off nervousness.

"What the hell? How did you get in here, Symone?"

"Hey, baby. I thought you could use some company."

"I asked, how did you get in here?"

"I still have a key, remember? Aren't you happy to see me?"

"It's good to see you. Now, what are you doing here?"

Keyon was still angry with Symone for not believing that he was telling her the truth about being set up. She was the last person he wanted to see.

"If you ever responded to my texts and emails or returned any of my calls, you'd know."

"I've been busy. And right now I'm busy, too. I'm meeting with my family shortly."

"Awe. I was hoping Ms. Kitty could get rescued by the Man of Steele again." Symone dropped the Burberry trench coat she was wearing and revealed her nakedness. Slowly, she walked over to Keyon in black leather Giuseppe stilettos and removed the towel from around his waist. His dick sprang to life when the air hit it. Keyon let her put on her performance because he knew if he stopped her, she would become embarrassed and possibly do something she would regret.

"Hmmm, Man of Steele is very happy to see me. Let me show him how happy I am to see him. You miss me, baby?" She said to the hard dick before wrapping her hot mouth around the en-gorged head. It felt so good to her to suck a real dick again, not that plastic shit Donnie forced down her throat. Donnie didn't know Symone was there trying to rekindle a spark between with her ex. She thought Symone was at the gym.

"Ah, shit!" Keyon said, throwing his head back in pleasure, forgetting that it wasn't Dom sucking him off. Symone licked up and down the shaft, getting it wet and sucked lightly on his nut sack until his legs began to shake.

"Mmmm, mmmm," she hummed. Her head bobbed up and down and her hands squeezed and twisted from the base of his dick up to the head, increasing his pleasure. Before long, she was making slurping and sucking noises that caused Keyon to get even harder.

"I know you missed this, baby. These lips were made for this dick."

For a moment, Keyon was lost in the pleasure of the fellatio and forgot about Domynique and his family. Abruptly he pulled back, causing Symone to fall forward.

"What are you doing? I was just getting started."

"No, you're done. We're done. This can't happen."

"Come on Keyon, we're both adults. We can do whatever we want."

"You have a woman, Symone, or did you forget?"

"What does she have to do with this? I wanna please you. Don't you miss me, Keyon?"

"Symone, I'm with someone now."

"What? You moved on fast. Did you have her waiting in the wings?"

"I know you didn't just say that and you were living with your stud a few weeks after you left me."

"We weren't fucking, though."

The day that Keyon and Symone received the damning video was devastating. His was delivered to his office and her's to their house. By the time he made it home, she had packed and was ready to leave him. Donnie just happened to be a very good friend, at the time, which Symone turned to in her time of need.

"But you are now."

"Baby, I made a mistake. It's you I want. I still love you, Keyon. We can work things out."

"I meant what I said. I have someone. I'm happy."

"Oh, really? Well, you can't be too happy or else your dick wouldn't have responded the way it just did."

"Any man's dick'll get hard when a woman sucks on it. Look. You gotta go. I have to meet my family."

"Like that?" She pointed to his hard on.

"It'll go down and if it doesn't, I have Five Finger Felicia."

"Humph. I guess. Call me when you're ready to cum in this hot pussy." At that point, Symone was becoming more and more embarrassed, willing to try anything to get him back.

"Goodbye, Symone."

So, you're just going to dismiss me like that after all that we've been through? She yelled angrily. "Fuck you, Keyon! I'm going to let you have your little fantasy for now, but I know you'll be back," Symone rolled her eyes at started to walk off.

"Goodbye, Keyon."

"Oh, Symone?"

"What?"

"Gimme my keys." He had forgotten she had a set. He made a mental note to change all the locks just in case she made a copy.

She rolled her eyes but left the keys on her way out. Keyon wrapped the towel back around his waist again and walked downstairs to make sure she had left. His heart was beating fast at the thought of cheating on Domynique. He didn't want things with Domynique to end before they had a chance to begin. Admittedly, things were moving fast between Keyon and Domynique but he was happy with the way things were going. Keyon had just secured the lock when his cell phone on the sofa table vibrated. He walked over to see who it was. Big. He was the menacing loan shark who Keyon had borrowed money from to expand Man of Steele. Bile rose in Keyon's throat as he opened the message.

"I c u juggling 2 dime pieces & I ain't mad atcha. In case u can't come up w/ da 4 mill. I'll take the one who looks like Lauren London off ya hands & we'll call it even. WTF I'll take the 1 who looks like Rudy Huxtable 2. U know how much I like choices so I'll let u decide. Don't 4get. January 5th. 5 pm. 4 mill."

Keyon, forgetting he was only in a towel, ran outside on his porch. He looked down the street and didn't see one car out. Where the hell was Big watching him from? One thing Keyon knew for sure was that he needed to pay this maniac and soon. Because if he didn't, someone was going to die.

Chapter Five
My Little Secret

Devine was caught between a rock and a hard place. Literally. At the moment, he was lying with his ass pressed up against Charles' very hard dick, waiting patiently for his man to enter him. Two big, strong hands gripped Devine's ass cheeks and spread them apart. The tip of the penis settled right at the lubed opening.

"Ahhh," Devine moaned as the thick meat slid in. Although Devine and Charles had been together many times before, there was resistance each time they made love. The girth of Charles's dick was enough to have him stretched out for the rest of his life, but Devine had that snap back.

"I love you, baby. I love you," Charles said, pumping in and out. It had been a minute since the two of them had been together and Charles wanted to savor each moment in case Devine got angry and cut him off again. Devine was fed up with Charles playing games. One moment they were hot and heavy then the next they were cold as ice. Charles knew that he had hurt Devine when he told him that he was engaged. And to a woman at that.

It took a small act of Congress for Devine to even meet with him but once Charles explained to Devine what was going on, the truth this time, then Devine became a little more agreeable.

"Ooh, yes baby, give it to me right," Devine begged, sucking Charles's fingers when they grabbed his shoulder. Charles's was trying to pull Devine into him as far as he could go. This was their third round since they had met up that afternoon.

"Awe fuck, I'm cumming," Charles said through gritted teeth.

"Oh, baby, yesss! Me too!" Devine sang.

A cool breeze from the ceiling fan wafted over the men's hard bodies and Charles pulled the covers up over them after they came down from their orgasmic high. Gently, Charles kissed Devine on his left shoulder and held his lover close to his body.

"So, lemme get this straight. I'm not to tell anyone, not even Jynx about what you just told me? You know she's my best friend, don't you?"

"No, Babe. In due time, she'll find out. But right now, I just want to enjoy us for a while before the world intervenes."

"Okay. You know she's my bestie and I don't normally keep secrets from her but I agree with you on this one. She'll find out in due time."

"I love you, Devine. I'm not trying to hurt anyone here. I just…I just wanna be happy for a change."

"I know, love. Me, too. And believe me, I understand you on that. But…"

"But what, D?" Charles asked, concerned.

"I'm confused as to how she *doesn't* know."

"Well, there have been a few near misses but the family is very protective of our secrets. I'm telling you, some secrets are going to be buried with us and never spoken of again."

"If you say so," Devine said, perplexed. "Listen, I promise you, when the time is right, everything will come to the light.

"From your mouth to God's ears," Devine said.

The cell phone on the night stand vibrated. Devine looked at Charles to see what he was going to do. Charles lay in bed without budging.

"Aren't you going to get that?" Devine asked.

"The only person I wanna talk to at this moment is lying here in my arms."

"What if it's important?"

"Nothing is as important as you, me and this moment right

here."

"I hear you, love."

"Now, let's see if we can't set a few more records. Climb on top and get ready for the ride of your life."

● ● ● ● ● ● ● ● ● ● ● ● ● ● ● ● ●

Jonathan wasn't answering his phone and Jynx was getting worried. She sensed some preoccupation with her man and really wanted to talk to him about her concerns. Since they got engaged, she noticed some visible changes in him. He was not as open as he once was and when she asked him questions, he sounded pissed off when he answered. Rather, if he answered. It was almost as if he wanted to say 'Bitch, mind your business', but he never did.

He was still a compassionate lover and he still made sure that she reached her peak even before he reached his. On a few occasions, Jynx believed that Jonathan had faked orgasms just to end their lovemaking sessions. Tears sprang to her eyes, thinking about him. Jonathan was the man of Jynx's dreams. More than anything, she wanted to be his wife. Unfortunately, she didn't think that was going to happen. She hated to admit it but the writing was on the wall. Jonathan was cheating on Jynx.

Avery GOODE

Chapter Six

Betrayed By Love

Charmaine was still while watching Donnie and Symone. As much as she wanted to stop, she couldn't. Not right now anyway. She had a score to settle with Symone. Other than watching Symone and Donnie argue and fight over the past couple of days, not much had happened. She did overhear Donnie's brother Damon talking about remodeling his house so Charmaine knew that she was going to have remove the monitors from the attic of his home.

Damon was going to fix the house up and flip it so that he could buy his wife Stephanie her dream home. She sat and waited for Damon and his wife to leave so that she could go in and quickly get her things out. Fortunately for her, her monitors were lightweight and she was able to put them in banker's boxes and move them quickly.

Charmaine was in disguise as usual. This time she was in a rented cargo van and she was dressed like a delivery man. Fortunately though, Damon lived in the kind of neighborhood where everyone kept to themselves.

One more trip and she would be done. On her last trip up to the attic, she remembered to take care of the special contents in the white bucket in the far corner of the room. Charmaine went over to it and lifted the lid.

"Jesus!" She said as she stumbled backwards, gagging her

way to the cabinet in the other corner. The smell of decomposition was heavy but not as strong as it would have been had there been a whole body there. Charmaine pulled out a bag that contained medical gloves, lemons, limes and grapefruits then cut them open, placing them in the bucket to squelch the stench. Then she scooped out a handful of vapor rub from the jar and rubbed it on the inside of the lid before resealing it. She hoped that would mask the smell.

"There, that should hold for a couple o' weeks. I'll be back to change it." She hoped her idea worked to hold the odor back a little while longer.

Before she left for the last time, Charmaine decided to stop in Donnie's room. It felt like ages since she had physically been there and she still had flashbacks of all their divine love making.

The room was as clean as a baby's bottom. Damon wouldn't allow his sister to leave it any other way. Charmaine opened up the door to the walk-in closet and with the exception of one Six Flags t-shirt, it was empty.

What the hell? She wondered what the fuck was going on and her head began to spin.

She checked the drawers and they were empty, too. There were no shoes under the bed, just empty boxes. Donnie had moved out completely.

Wow. This shit is fucked up. Charmaine's head was going a mile a minute

Charmaine needed to talk to Donnie. She needed answers. Just as she picked her box to head out, she heard a knock at the door.

Who the hell is that?

Creeping quietly across the hardwood floors, Charmaine made her way to the front door and looked out through the peep-hole.

Damn, your ass is fine, Charmaine smiled, looking over the unwelcomed visitor. *Boy, you better be lucky I'm trying to escape from this house unseen, or else you'd be in big trouble.* On her way back from her visiting her mother, Charmaine decided that she'd give her and Donnie's relationship one more chance. If it worked out, fantastic. If not, she was leaving women alone and dating men again. *Bitches really ain't shit but hoes and tricks*, she said to herself.

The handsome man wrote something on the back of the card he held and slid it between the screen door and door handle, then left. When he was off the porch, Charmaine crept back to Donnie's room, which was at the front of the house and peaked out of the window. The man got into a navy blue, Crown Victoria. He was a cop.

I wonder what he wanted with Donnie, Charmaine mumbled to herself. After removing the card from the door and reading the back of it, Charmaine put it in her pocket. She must have thought Donnie up because no sooner than she had gotten in her car, Donnie sent her a text.

I need to see you, Lucky Charms.

Charmaine smiled at the nickname that Donnie had given her so long ago. Lately, she didn't use it much when talking to Charmaine. Hell, she didn't use any name because she was virtually non-existent in Charmaine's life, these days.

Knowing that Donnie was coming over, Charmaine decided to leave the few boxes in the trunk and run in the house to shower before her girlfriend came over. It had been a hot minute since the two of them made love and Charmaine was horny as hell.

She sprayed a clean linen scented Febreeze on her already clean sheets and lit some candles all over the room. The sun was setting and Charmaine closed her room darkening drapes to set the mood. There was a knock at the door and Charmaine immediately became moist at the thought of Donnie's tongue entering her. Dressed in a negligee and matching robe, she walked to the door.

"Good evening, my love," she said, greeting Donnie with a passionate kiss, handing her a glass of Cristal.

"Now that's how you greet a nigga, babe. Stand back and lemme look at your sexy ass."

Charmaine stepped back and spun around so Donnie could admire her. She had gone through great pains to look good for her and really wanted the evening to be special. Tonight, Charmaine was going to lay her feelings out on the table and tell Donnie that she wanted it to be just the two of them. Fuck all of the other bitches and everything. She wanted them to have a fresh start. Whatever happened in the past was the past.

"Thanks, babe. I got this just for you. It cost almost $300."

"Shit, you could have saved that money and gave it to me. I'd rather you came to the door naked." Donnie said, brushing past Charmaine.

"I have a bottle of Cristal chilling in the bedroom. Follow me, baby." Donnie did not mind following Charmaine, at all.

They got in the room and Charmaine sat Donnie down in the recliner next to her bed. She got down on the floor and removed Donnie's Timberland construction boots and thick socks. Placing her feet in her lap, Charmaine picked up some warming oil and began massaging Donnie's feet. Donnie leaned her head back in the chair and absorbed the relaxing massage. .

"Take your clothes off, baby," Charmaine instructed.

As expected, Donnie was wearing her strap-on when she stood up and took all her clothes off. She never left home without it on. Charmaine knew that Donnie even wore it to church.

"This is a new one, I see."

"Yeah, it is. Brand new. Never been kissed either."

Taking the hint, Charmaine crawled over to Donnie, who sat back down, and began sucking the large rubber dick. Donnie started moaning and groaning and forcefully rubbing the back of Charmaine's head.

"That's it. Take this hard dick down your throat." Charmaine looked into Donnie's eyes and saw a rage she had not seen before. She suspected it to be from the pills she was popping. Charmaine watched her pop Oxy's, smoke weed and drink all day from the monitors placed in her home.

Lovingly, Charmaine kissed, licked and sucked to Donnie's pleasure, only aiming to take care of her woman.

"Get your ass in this chair!" Donnie demanded. Charmaine noticed her change in attitude. One minute, she was loving and the next she could be hostile. She knew Donnie could be crazy but this was becoming more extreme.

Donnie parted Charmaine's legs roughly over the chair

armrests, sniffed her womanhood and rubbed her nose against Charmaine's clit. Charmaine cried out as Donnie teased her then began licking her with her hot tongue. Donnie licked up the front of Charmaine's vagina, up her belly and then her breasts. She took a hard nipple between her teeth and gently bit down on it, hoping to hurt Charmaine in a good way.

"Let's go to the bed," Donnie said, pushing Charmaine down on the plush bed.

Charmaine kneaded her breasts while Donnie sucked on Charmaine's neck and fingered her.

"Turn over and get on your knees."

Obediently, Charmaine complied.

"I love the way your pussy looks when my fingers slide in and out."

Unable to speak, Charmaine just moaned in pleasure.

Donnie leaned down and licked Charmaine's pussy from behind. It was hard to balance her with one arm so she flipped over to lie under Charmaine. Using her knees, Charmaine rose up and down, like a butterfly flapping its wings. Donnie made loud slurping noises as she sucked on Charmaine's sloppy, wet pussy. She twirled her tongue around Charmaine's clit and then flicked her tongue back and forth.

"Mmmm, Ahhh, Unnn." Charmaine let out pleasurable cry.

She took her middle finger and thumb, wetting them inside Charmaine's hot cavern. Donnie's middle finger, slid easily into Charmaine's ass and her thumb massaged her clitoris.

"You like that, baby?" Donnie asked, already knowing the answer.

"Yeah, uhh huh. I'm so wet right now, baby. I love you daddy," she moaned.

"I want that ass, baby."

"Take it, baby," Charmaine told her, tooting her ass in the air.

Donnie reached to the side and grabbed the KY Jelly and lubed her dildo. Slowly, she eased in her hot box.

"Push that ass out, baby. That's it. Make it easy for me to get in."

With the entire eight inch dildo impaled inside, Donnie began to move back and forth, rubbing Charmaine's clit. Charmaine heard a buzzing noise just before Donnie placed a lipstick sized vibrator on her clit. On the verge of an explosive orgasm, Charmaine's legs began to quake and her breathing was erratic. Donnie stopped pumping and lay down, bringing Charmaine's pussy to sit on top of her dildo. Suction noises and slapping skin was all that they heard. Charmaine's ass cheeks clapped like they were applauding the performance. Charmaine's back arched as Donnie went deeper. Charmaine responded by grinding down hard to feel the fullness of Donnie's manmade dick.

"I'm cumming, daddy. Drink this juice!" Charmaine yelled, jumping up and sitting on Donnie's face. Donnie's tongue pulled every bit of juice from Charmaine's body, leaving the woman spent and satisfied.

"That was amazing," Charmaine said lovingly.

"It really was, Lucky Charms."

"You want some more champagne? I'll go pour us some. I left the glasses in the kitchen."

Charmaine wasn't gone five minutes but by the time she walked back in the room, Donnie was fully dressed.

"What's going on here?" She asked, confused.

"We need to talk, Lucky Charms." *Donnie never really had time for a heart-to-heart so what was different this time*, Charmaine thought.

"Okay, you talk first. I have something to talk about, too," she said, handing Donnie a champagne flute. Charmaine was trying to keep her cool but she could not believe how serious Donnie's tone was. One minute ago they were fucking and the next, as serious as a job interview. Charmaine wasn't sure what was going on.

"Sit down, Lucky Charms, chill out. I have something I need to say," she began. "It is not easy for me to get out so I need to take it slow."

Mistaking her nervousness and apprehension for a possible proposal, Charmaine sat down, excited. "Okay, love. What is it? You can tell me and *ask* me anything?"

"You and I have been friends for a long time." Charmaine took note of the word 'friends' when they were clearly so much more than that, but she allowed Donnie to continue, uninterrupted.

"We had our ups and downs, good times and bad ones. But for the most part, it was pretty good. Over the past few weeks, I felt myself growing up. Changing if you will and I noticed that something was missing from my life."

"Oh, yeah and what was that?"

"Stability. I want the life that my homeboy, Nick, and his girl, Tasha have. A home. Family."

Charmaine got more excited about the implications of their conversation. And still she didn't interrupt.

"This isn't easy for me. You know how much I care about you and value our friendship." There goes that word 'friend' again. "But I am going to have to end things right here, right now, because *I'm going to ask* Symone to marry me."

The smile turned upside down on Charmaine's face.

"I'm sorry, what did you just say to me?" She couldn't have heard her correctly.

"I said, that I'm asking Symone to marry me."

"I heard what the fuck you said the first time! How in the hell are you going to come over here in my house and tell me that you're gonna ask the next bitch to marry you when I have been here for you through thick and thin? After all the shit you don' put me through, this is how you choose to end things? You have got to be fucking kidding me right now!"

"I know it's hard right now, Lucky Charms but you need to lower your motherfuckin voice." Donnie knew Charmaine was a nut bag and wasn't surprised at her lack of understanding.

"I ain't doing shit!"

Donnie responded by slapping Charmaine, who fell across the bed.

"Symone is my soul mate."

"You told me the same shit. Your ass is a liar, Donita. You said you loved me."

"Love you? Bitch, I can't stand your crazy ass! The only thing good about you is your pussy. You can't cook. You stupid as fuck and you ain't got shit. I need a woman who is educated with income potential. Not some broke bitch that terrorizes my lovers. Yeah, you didn't think I knew about that shit, did you? Dumb ass, maggot ass, bass mouth bitch!"

"GET! OUT! OF! MY! HOUSE!" Charmaine yelled.

"Gladly. You ain't gotta worry 'bout me coming back either. Whatever shit I got over here, you can burn it or give it away. I'on need it."

Hurt, Charmaine picked up the champagne flute Donnie drank out of and threw it across the room. This was the ultimate betrayal for Charmaine. After everything that Charmaine had done for Donnie, this is the way her girlfriend chose to end things.

The anger that coursed through Charmaine's body had her veins popping out of her neck. They were huge, like earth worms. Hot tears ran down Charmaine's face and blinded her as she walked to her basement door near the back bedroom. Someone was going to have to pay for this and since Angela was the only one there, she was the unlucky candidate. A sleeping Angela was jarred awake by the sound of the heavy metal door banging hard against the concrete. The look she saw on Charmaine's face made her scared. She had never seen that type of rage before although she thought she had seen all Charmaine had to offer. Tears started coming down her face and she prayed that she was anywhere but right there at that very moment.

"I dunno what da fuck you crying for. You're not the one who just got dumped! No, you're the one who was begging, saying, "Put it in me, Donnie. Harder baby, more, yes that's it'!" Charmaine mocked.

"I didn't do anything. I swear I didn't know she was with you. She told me she was single. She said that I was her main girl." There was no need for Angela to be bound and gagged all of the time, as she was located so deep in the basement, nobody could hear her.

"Shut the fuck up! You wanna fuck? Well, I got something for that ass!"

Charmaine grabbed Angela's right foot and buckled a brown leather strap around it then pulled it to the right post of the king-sized brass bed and fastened the strap around it. She repeated that for the left side and when she was done, Angela laid spread eagle on the bed, naked.

"Please, whatever I did, I'm sorry. I'm very, very sorry."

"I know you're sorry, hoe. Y'all bitches are always sorry after you get caught. Now shut the fuck up."

Roughly, Charmaine started kneading Angela's breasts and pinching her nipples until she cried out in pain. Then, Charmaine licked each nipple and beyond Angela's control, they hardened. She was getting turned on by the rough sex and Angela felt ashamed. Charmaine grinded her pussy against Angela's and bucked wildly when the throbbing ache between her nether lips intensified. A guttural moan that started in the pits of Charmaine's belly escaped past Charmaine's lips and she threw her head back as she came.

Not satisfied, she got into the scissor position with her hostage and scooted towards Angela until their pussy lips touched. Charmaine parted her lips and then Angela's until they were flesh to flesh, clits touching. Tiny pulses of electricity coursed through Angela's body when Charmaine lightly rubbed her clit against hers. Up and down, round and round, in slow motion, it felt so good to them both. Charmaine was leaning on her elbow, grinding her clit until she felt another explosion coming on. Then a sticky wetness ran down the two women's thighs.

Angela was out of breath. Having come twice, she thought that maybe Charmaine was done also. Oh, how wrong she was. Charmaine crawled between Angela's thighs and began suckling her clit until Angela was worked into another frenzy. The more Charmaine licked, the wetter Angela became. Charmaine fingered the woman in bondage with two fingers, gradually adding another until Charmaine's whole fist was pumping and pounding into the other woman. All of this, she learned from Donnie so she thought Angela would love every minute and from the looks of it, she was. So, she turned it up a notch.

Her anger returning, Charmaine said, "You want something in you bitch? Well, I got just the thing." Angela felt herself stretch as something hard and ice cold was shoved into her vagina.

"What is that?" She demanded frantically. But Charmaine didn't answer her, loving the fact that her ten inch metal vibrator was lodged in Angela. Instead, Charmaine sat on Angela's face and told her that if she didn't eat her pussy until she came, Charmaine was going to put a bullet into Angela's temple. Angela ate her out like her life depended on it. Because, now it did.

Charmaine left Angela in the bed, in desperate need of a shower and in pain from the 12 inch glass dildo she stuffed inside her. Charmaine would be back to deal with her later.

An hour later, Charmaine was in her room, throwing clothes around. She didn't think she had ever felt emotional pain like this. It felt physical, although nobody had laid their hands on her. Charmaine slid down the wall and slumped over, lost. She felt that she was betrayed by Donnie's love. Now both Donnie and Symone were on Charmaine's hit list. Wiping her tears, she began to pick the clothes up. A gray business card fell out of the pocket that Charmaine had worn earlier. Clearing her throat, Charmaine dialed the number on the card.

"Detective Blair, I have some information you can use."

• • • • • • • • • • • • • • • • •

Jynx was lying across the bed with a black silk nightgown and matching kimono reading a magazine when Jonathan walked in. He was tired and worn out from the workout he had just had.

"How was your workout at the gym baby?" Jynx asked seductively.

"It was cool. I lifted some uh, weights and played a little ball with my boy," Jonathan said, kissing her on the forehead.

"Mmm, you smell good. You showered already? I thought you hated bathing at the gym?"

"Uh, yeah. I had to. After I left the gym I met up with Keyon at the office to go over a few tour details for some of the artists."

Jynx noticed how Jonathan failed to look her in the eyes when he spoke. He was lying about something.

"Hmm, well since you're already clean why don't come over here and sit next to me."

If he hesitated, Jonathan knew that Jynx would go in on him with questions so he went and sat down on the bed next to her. No sooner than he sat down did Jynx's small hands travel up his legs to his manhood and began rubbing it. Tired or not, his member sprang to life just like Jynx planned.

"I've missed you, babe," Jynx said, pulling the string on the sweat pants and tugging them down his hips when Jonathan lifted up to make removing them easier.

"Damn! I've missed you too," Jonathan moaned when Jynx placed her hot mouth on his dick. "That's it, baby. Get it nice and wet."

Jynx slobbered on the hard meat and massaged it with her jaws and hands. She made slurping sounds with her mouth and smiled when he moaned in pleasure. Her small hands gripped him firmly and stroked him up and down. A few more slurps and strokes and Jynx felt Jonathan's thighs tighten. He was on the verge of cumming.

"Huh uh, I'm not ready to come. It's my turn to please you."

Jonathan moved Jynx to the head of the bed and spread her legs wide. She wasn't wearing any panties. He sniffed her womanhood and he scent drove him crazy. Gently he placed his lips around her clit and he began nibbling it.

"Oh, my," she moaned pleasurably.

He licked her clit like an ice cream cone and then she felt his tongue go inside of her. He was fucking her pussy with his tongue like it was pink little dick.

"Mmmm," Jonathan groaned between her legs. He was lapping her pussy like a dog, hungry for more. The more he licked, the wetter she got.

"Baby, I'm getting ready to come," Jynx purred.

"Come down my throat," he said, only taking his mouth off of her for a minute.

Within seconds, Jynx was coming in her mans mouth. So many questions were running through Jynx's mind as Jonathan repositioned her to doggy style. Why did he shower before he came home? He hated the gym shower because he thought dudes were looking at him when he got out. And why did he lie about meeting with Keyon? She had spoken to her cousin earlier and he and Domynique were home watching a movie. What was going on with her man? Jonathan didn't give her the chance to ponder any longer because he positioned his dick at Jynx's wet snatch and thrust into her.

"Ooh, Jon. You do me so right."

Jonathan licked two of his fingers and began rubbing Jynx's clit. The electrifying sensation caught her off guard and she had to put her hands on the bed in order to stabilize herself. He pumped rhythmically as Jynx exercised her pussy muscles around his dick. She pressed her head down into the pillow and tooted her ass in the air so he could thrust deeper.

"Oh, gawd," Jonathan grunted as he felt his volcano preparing to erupt.

"Huh, baby," Jynx moaned.

Jynx felt her body began to release. Her breasts tingled, the hairs stood up on her back and neck and finally her pussy began to contract with a powerful release. Jonathan filled his woman's pussy with his cum, mixing it with hers, creating a beautiful mess. Spent, the two of them got under the covers and rested in one another's arms.

"That was amazing my love," Jynx smiled, satisfied.

"Indeed it was. You got that honey love," her man complimented.

Just as Jynx was about to answer, Jonathan's phone rang. He ignored it.

"Your phone is ringing, babe," Jynx stated the obvious.

"The only person I wanna talk to at this moment is lying right here with me."

"But it could be something important at the office."

"Nothing is as important as you, me and this moment right here."

"Awe, babe. That's so sweet. I love you so much." Jynx leaned in to kiss Jonathan.

"I love you, too. Now, climb on and ride this black stallion."

Chapter Seven

Never Knew Love Like This Before

There's no greater feeling in the world than to love someone and know without a shadow of a doubt, that that person loves you in return. After a number of failed relationships, Miracha 'Cha-Cha' Rodriguez had finally found the one. Michael Steele, executive vice president of Man of Steele Records and Keyon's cousin, had willingly and unabashedly returned that love.

Tonight, he had gone all out for his lady love. A beautiful candlelight dinner at the Sundial Restaurant, a romantic walk through Centennial Park, followed by a ride in a white, horse drawn carriage that delivered the couple directly to the front door of Cha-Cha's high- rise building made it a night to remember.

"Damn, your ass is fine," Michael said, appreciating the view of Cha-Cha's behind as she walked into the building.

"Thank you, honey," Cha-Cha said as they walked through the lobby.

There were a few women in the lobby talking and they openly gawked at Michael as he strolled through. Standing six feet, six inches, he was just a few inches shorter than Keyon. He had a low Caesar hair cut with a natural wave pattern, a trimmed goatee, lips that looked like LL Cool J's and eyelashes that were longer than most women's. His smooth, milk chocolate skin was flawless without so much as a razor bump on it. Oh yeah, he was fine.

Cha-Cha knew that they were looking at him and smiled with pride knowing that even though Michael could have been with anyone he wanted to, he had chosen her. Cha-Cha also knew that they would have something to say about her because one of the women was a neighbor of hers. The two of them exchanged words in the gym one day because the other lady thought that since Cha-Cha was transgendered; she was not a real woman and needed to use the men's locker room. The whole scene got very ugly, with lots of hair pulling and falling over gym equipment. It didn't surprise Cha-Cha that the lady spoke loud enough for her and Michael to hear.

"Damn, that's a fine ass man," the neighbor's friend said. "And she's gorgeous, too."

Cha-Cha smiled at the compliment.

"Which man is fine?" The hating neighbor asked.

"Huh?"

"They're both men."

"Girl, what in the hell are you talking about?"

"The two who just walked through? They are both men?"

"You mean that woman is a man?"

"Yep. He had an operation to make him a girl but yep, it's a man."

"Wow. Whoever her plastic surgeon was must be a genius because honey, she looks better than half the chicks I know."

Where is that damned elevator? Cha-Cha thought. Although one of the women was paying her compliments, she really didn't want Michael hearing this. She wanted him to have only great thoughts of her. She rubbed her hands all over him and tongued him down while waiting for the elevator. She wanted to keep Michael preoccupied and it was working.

"Why do you keep calling him a woman? That is a man." Cha-Cha's neighbor was getting louder and more irritated with her friend. *Why does she have it out for me,* Cha-Cha was dying to know.

"If that's a man, then I'm one, too. I 'on know why you're hating on her. You're just mad because your man looks like Shabba Ranks."

"Fuck you, Lisa."

"Whatever. You know I'm telling the truth," she laughed.

"And that ass, though. Nicki Minaj ain't' got shit on her. I wonder if it's real."

Just then, the bell on the elevator dinged.

"It is." Believe me," Michael said in a smart ass tone to the rude woman, as he and Cha-Cha stepped on the elevator.

Cha-Cha looked a bit sad.

"What's wrong, pretty lady?"Michael did not mean to embarrass her.

"I'm used to hearing shit like that. 'Specially from hatin' ass bitches. But I don't want you hearing it. I don't want you to think that you're making the wrong choice by being with me. That people are going to look at you differently."

"Look at me, Miracha. Do I look like I give a fuck about what others think about me? When people's opinion of me start paying my bills, then maybe I'll care. Until then, they can kiss my ass. I love you. Don't you know that?"

"I do now. I love you, too, Michael."

He leaned down and kissed Cha-Cha hard on her lips and kneaded her breasts through her Tom Ford, red sarong wrap dress.

"You know there are cameras on this elevator?" Cha-Cha said, backing up. She was getting very hot.

"So. Let's give 'em something to talk about."

"You're a freak."

"I know it. Is Devine home?" Michael inquired about Cha-Cha's roommate.

"Nope. He's out for the evening."

"Good. We can do it everywhere then. We're gonna break this pussy in right tonight."

"Looking forward to it."

"I know this is your first time, so I'll be gentle." Michael was giggling at the thought of virgin pussy.

"What's so funny?" Cha-Cha said.

"I ain't never done it with a virgin before. I've always wanted to say that."

"Now you and Keyon have something else in common," she said out of her slick mouth.

"Is it going to hurt? You know what I'm working with," he

said, referring to his thick and long, eight inch dick.

"I don't know. The doctor said it was going take some getting used to. We'll just have to see."

"Um, can it get wet like a regular one?"

"Doc Latio said it should. If not, I have some KY Jelly by the bed. You know that."

"Damn, my dick is hard. I wish this elevator would get there already."

"That's the woes of living on the twenty-ninth floor and having an elevator that can stop at each floor."

The elevator stopped on Cha-Cha's floor and no sooner than they got off was Michael grabbing at Cha-Cha's ass.

"It's just perfect for my big hands," he said, palming both cheeks.

"If you don't cut it out, boy. You're making me have trouble with the key. I can't stick it in."

"Oh, I can stick it in for you."

"Nasty ass. Get in here." Cha-Cha grabbed Michael by the hand and pulled him inside. Michael locked the door behind him and walked up behind Cha-Cha and kissed her neck. He locked both of his hands around her waist and gently swayed.

"This has been a very good night, Cha-Cha. Hold on, it's about to get even better."

"All right there, now."

Slowly, Michael undressed Cha-Cha and stood back to gaze at her sexy form.

"That hatin' bitch downstairs ain't got shit on you, baby. Not a got damned thing."

"I aim to please." Cha-Cha knew her body was banging. Her real measurements were 36-24-38 and the curves were all hers. She had a body sculpted by the gods. Even her perky 36-C breasts were real. When Cha-Cha was fifteen, she started taking doctor prescribed pills to combat an infection and the pills made her grow breasts. At that time, she felt she was supposed to be a woman and well after the doctors asked her to stop taking them, she continued.

Once Cha-Cha was old enough to take control of her life, she worked hard to save money for her gender reassignment surgery. No one told her how much it was going to cost and the paltry $20,000 she had saved was only enough for a few pre-operation visits which included hormones to help further develop her body. In order for her to have the actual surgery, she was going to have to either rob a bank or sell some internal organs because the cost was astronomical. Cha-Cha needed a miracle. Then one day she met a man who changed all of that for her. She thought he was the real deal Holyfield but found out he wasn't shit not too long after entering into a relationship with him so she worked very hard to keep her guard up and not fall in love. When she met Michael, she knew he was different. Her instincts told her that he was going to be a good one. So far, so good.

Michael tongued Cha-Cha and kneaded her breasts like dough. Turned on, Cha-Cha dropped to her knees and reached for his zipper. His dick sprang to life as her warm, small hands covered the head. Michael turned to putty. Cha-Cha showed him that she could handle his massive size and swallowed his stiff meat in one gulp. Michael's eyes rolled to the back of his head and his breath came in short pants. Even after Michael came in his desirable lover's mouth, he was still rock hard.

"I want you to bury this wood in my fire pit," Cha-Cha said breathily.

"Do you have any condoms?" Michael barely mumbled.

"Like American Express, I never leave home without them."

Michael sat in the chair next to the window. The curtains were drawn back and Atlanta's skyline boasted an impeccable view. The lights from the city and the holiday decorations illuminated the otherwise dark room.

"I want your ass first," Michael said.

"You got it." Cha-Cha sauntered over.

As if to sit down in the chair, Cha-Cha eased down in Michael's lap, with her ass cheeks spread apart. Michael squirted lubricant on his condom covered penis and her anal opening. Well-lubed, he positioned his dick right at the opening and helped her ease down on the length of him.

"Mmmm, baby. It feels good."

Michael mumbled something inaudibly and began his slow grind. Cha-Cha matched his thrusts and used the arms of the chair as leverage. Up, down, in and out, he pumped. Michael reached his hand around Cha-Cha's waist and rubbed on her nub. Somehow, someway, the doctor had created a clitoris that had nerves in it and excited his lover.

"Can I finger you now?" Michael asked. Cha-Cha had just received the go ahead from her doctor that *anything,* including something as small as a tampon could penetrate her pussy.

"Yes...you...can...," Cha-Cha staggered in her breathing.

"Turn around."

Cha-Cha stood up, turned around to face Michael, straddled his lap and started the rodeo all over again. She was nervous but Michael eased his friendly member in to her throbbing new oyster. Michael pushed his cock deeper and deeper in to her newly created love pocket. She placed her arms over Michael's shoulders and held on the wings of the chair. Michael kissed her passionately as he eased in and out, and Cha-Cha started grinding him with plenty of pleasure. Shortly after the lovemaking began, Michael announced that he was cumming, followed by a very excited Cha-Cha. Getting up from the chair, but without removing his member from the tight pocket it was lodged in, Michael carried Cha-Cha to the bed and placed her down gently.

"We have to do this right for your first time."

"Mmmm, hmm," Cha-Cha moaned.

Michael was still pumping while he walked and she was feeling every bit the woman she was recently created to be.

"You're beautiful," Michael said, admiringly, looking down at her virgin love machine.

"Thank you, baby," Cha-Cha blushed as she lay, facing him.

Michael slid down the bed to get a better view of the doctor's handiwork.

"Damn, it looks like you were born with this pussy," he said, before licking the nub. Cha-Cha, who had never been eaten out before, jumped from the pleasurable sensation.

"Lions and tigers and bears, oh my." They both laughed.

First, Michael licked up and down, and then he licked at an angle. Next, he made lazy circles around her clit before sliding his tongue into the hole.

"Oh, shit! This is the eighth wonder of the world. Cunnilingus."

Cha-Cha's hips bucked and grinded into Michael's mouth. She had never felt like that before.

"Michael!!! I'm cumming!!!" she cried out.

While she was in the midst of her first vaginal orgasm, Michael placed his hands on Cha-Cha's tiny, feminine waist and gently eased into her lubricated, newly installed, vagina. He moved slowly in and out, round and round. Strong hands kneaded her breasts and a hot mouth sucked on her nipples.

"I'm about to bust. Can I cum in this pussy?"

"Un huh," Cha-Cha breathed.

Michael slid out, pulled the condom off and rammed himself back in. He pulled Cha-Cha closer to him, and leaned back , taking her to another level.

"Arghh," he howled as his seed spilled inside his girlfriend.

Their sweat made them stick together as they sat, panting heavily. It took a few minutes for them to come off of cloud nine. When they did and their heart beats returned to normal, they slept like babies.

The next morning, a naked and very satisfied Cha-Cha woke up and fixed coffee and breakfast for her virile lover. Cha-Cha was happier than she had ever been. Michael treated her like a queen. She couldn't believe that a man like him would fall in love, so completely in love, with her. He knew that she was transgendered but he didn't consider himself gay, at all. When he met her, she had all female parts so technically that made Cha-Cha a woman. That was his logic and reasoning anyway. Michael Steele was a prize and Cha-Cha felt blessed to have him. She knew he had to attend a meeting and wasn't surprised when he came into the kitchen with a suit on.

"It fits you so well. You look great, babe."

"I can't believe you had a suit tailored for me. How did you know my size?"

"Fashion is my life. It's my business to know what looks good on people."

"Thank you. I feel fabulous." Michael walked over to her and kissed her passionately while reaching up her dress to finger his most favorite place in the world. He hoped like hell it would never stretch out.

They ate in silence and thirty minutes later, Cha-Cha was walking him to the elevator. They were both thankful that Devine hadn't been there so they could enjoy some quality time together. They stepped out of her condo and although she thought she closed the door behind her, the door was ajar. Michael and Cha-Cha were so into kissing and finger fucking that neither of them saw the man enter into Cha-Cha's apartment.

"Have a great day, babe."

"I will. You're working today?"

"Yep. I designed a holiday dress for one of the Real Housewives of Atlanta and we're finishing it up today." Cha-Cha was smiling and had a loving glow about her that turned Michael all the way on.

"Cool. I'm proud of you, you know that?" Michael admired her ambition.

"I do now." The elevator bell dinged. "Damn, this motherfucker didn't come this quick last night." Cha-Cha wasn't ready to let him go.

"Bye, man."

"Bye, love."

Cha-Cha floated back to her home, noticed the door was open and was thankful because she definitely did not have her key. She leaned against the living room wall with a huge smile on her face, truly happy that things were finally going her way. She went into her room and nearly jumped out of her skin when she heard the man's voice.

"It smells like you've been fucking!" he said angrily.

"Cleo, how long have you been in here and how in the hell did you get in here? You scared the shit out of me!" Just when she thought he was out of her life, she was always wrong.

"If you weren't so busy making a public spectacle of yourself in the hallway, you would have seen me."

"You need to leave," Cha-Cha said, going towards the front door.

"I can't believe you're fucking another nigga with a pussy that I paid for." Cleo grabbed Cha-Cha's arm and spun her around to face him. "You know how much I love you. I came here today to beg your forgiveness and this is what I find?"

"Get your hands off of me!"

"You whoring, bitch!" He said, jacking her up by the lapels on her robe and squeezing the terry cloth around her neck. Cha-Cha was gasping for breath. Tears sprang to her eyes.

"Cleo. I. Can't. Breathe. Please."

"How did it feel, whore? Hmm? I should strangle your ass right now! I can't believe that you would betray me like this? I swear, I will kill that bastard if you don't stop fucking him!" He shook Cha-Cha as he spoke.

There was a sound of keys jingling near the front door then the sound of a key entering the hole. Cleo dropped Cha-Cha and smoothed out his suit. Cha-Cha was coughing and sputtering when Devine sashayed in the apartment, singing a Rhianna song. He stopped short when he saw Cleo and Cha-Cha. His roommate was doubled over coughing, holding her throat.

"Are you okay, sis?" Devine rushed over.

"She's fine," Cleo answered.

"Wasn't nobody talking to you," Devine replied, snapping his fingers.

"Kill yo 'self!" Cleo laughed.

"What did this mofo just say? Ooh, honey boo-boo." Devine fanned himself with both hands. "Sis, are you okay?"

"She's fine. Just got a little sperm in her throat probably." Cleo said for Cha-Cha's ears only.

"What'chu say?" Devine didn't like this man one bit and he didn't even know him that well.

"Nothing. We will talk about this later, Miracha."

"No, we won't. We have nothing to talk about." Miracha had to find a way to get rid of his ass.

"We'll see about that."

Cha-Cha rushed to the door and locked it behind him as soon as he crossed the threshold.

"What was Cleo doing here? That man gives me the creeps."

He gave Cha-Cha the creeps, too.

"Trying to get back together. He knows that ain't happening."

"Why were you coughing?"

"Chile', I think I swallowed some dust. I was having a coughing fit," Cha-Cha lied. "How was your first night working the graveyard shift?"

"Hated it! But Jynx called and wanted to talk about Jonathan. She's upset about his lack of interest in their wedding planning. I tried to get her mind off of things and we sat up talking about her wedding dress and reception decorations. I fell asleep on her a couple of times." Devine hadn't even told Cha-Cha the secret he was keeping. He turned away before Cha-Cha saw the guilty look on his face.

"Damn. But I know how you feel. If I hear about that damned wedding one more time, I'm going to kill somebody. I'm like, get married already!"

"Me too, Sweet tart."

Devine rattled on, not realizing that Cha-Cha had tuned him out. But Cha-Cha knew Devine well since they had been friends for over twenty years. Cha-Cha knew that whenever Devine talked fast and furious, he was hiding something. She had no clue what Devine was talking about but knew he was keeping something from her.

Whatever it was, Cha-Cha knew that it had something to do with Jynx and her fiancé Jonathan. She wasn't sure what it was and right now couldn't worry about it. She could not take her mind off of Cleo's threat to hurt Michael. Was he serious? The Cleo she knew had never threatened to hurt anyone. But the man she knew then and one who came over this morning were two different people. He looked maniacal and his eyes were glazed over. Cha-Cha didn't know if he was serious or not but until she knew otherwise, she was going to act like he was.

Chapter Eight
Ho-Ho-Ho

With Christmas being just a couple of days away, everyone was out scrounging for last minute gifts. Jynx, Cha-Cha, Devine and Domynique were no exception. The three best friends still got together weekly like they did when Symone was still kicking it with them but since she kicked them to the curb, they replaced her with Domynique. The foursome had hit several malls and boutiques already and they were currently in Phipps Plaza, wreaking havoc in all of the upscale stores.

"I love shopping. Especially on someone else's dime."

"Yeah, me too, Cha-Cha," Jynx agreed.

"This is my first time doing that," Domynique chimed in. "I was so nervous when we were at Lenox that I didn't even know what to buy."

"Chile', stick with us. We'll turn you into a shopping whore just like us. Won't we, y'all."

"Thanks, Devine. You're a great friend," Domynique giggled.

"Speaking of friends, did Symone reply to either of you?" Devine asked Jynx and Cha-Cha.

"I sent about five texts asking if she was going to come today." Cha-Cha said. "She didn't even have the courtesy to reply back and say 'no, kiss my ass'. Nothing."

"She didn't reply to any of my texts either. I even left a few voice messages. I don't understand why she doesn't want to be around us anymore." Jynx said.

"Chile' she's clitmatized by that damned lesbian she's with. We've done our parts. We call, text and even go by her house. The ball is in her court. When she's ready to reach out to us, she will. Now come on, y'all, Jimmie Choo is calling my name."

The four of them walked into the designer shoe store and immediately began finding their favorites.

"Domynique, you should try these on. I can see you rocking these for Keyon," Cha-Cha said, referring to a gorgeous pair of six inch, purple suede and mesh Jimmy Choo stilettos.

"Wow. These are beautiful. But what would I wear with them?"

"Not a got damned thang, girl. All you need is your pretty ass and these shoes. Let Keyon do the rest."

Domynique burst out laughing. At that moment, Symone was walking towards the shoe store when she saw her friends laughing with Domynique.

Ain't this 'bout a bitch? How'n the fuck they gon' be out here with some random bitch and not even call me? Slimy asses. Symone was livid.

Angry, Symone pulled out her phone and sent a text to Jynx.

"I thought real friends included 1 another N their plans. Guess I wz wrong."

Jynx's phone vibrated in her pocket and she pulled it out.

"Hold up, guys. This is Symone now," she said, reading the text. "What the hell? This chick is tripping."

"What is it?" Devine asked.

Jynx read the group the text as they walked towards Saks Fifth Avenue, oblivious to the fact that Symone was trailing behind them about twenty feet. Daily, Symone was becoming more and more out of touch with reality because she didn't want to see her friends hanging out with anyone but her.

"Why is she tripping?" Cha-Cha asked.

"I'on know," Jynx said, looking down at her phone screen. *"Idk wut ur trip'n on. All of us called u. U didn't reply. If u wntd 2 b w/us 2day u wlda txt or cld. We're supposed 2 b family."*

Symone looked at the text message and rolled her eyes toward the sky.

"Blood makes you related. Loyalty makes you family. We don't have either one so I guess we're nothing."

Jynx couldn't believe what she was reading. Symone had lost her mind. She told the other's what Symone had said and they all shook their heads. Domynique didn't know what to think. Although she and Keyon had talked about what happened between him and Symone before, she only knew about Symone, the girlfriend. Domynique didn't know anything about Symone, the friend. Apparently, she wasn't good at being either one.

"Y'all know what? We could stand on the mountain top and scream Symone's name to high heaven and she'd still play like she didn't hear us. We've done this girls day out and sleepover for the past five years. Nothing has changed. Symone never takes responsibility for anything that happens in her life if it doesn't go the way she thinks it should. It is always someone else's fault. Well, you know what? I'm tired of it. I'm not going to allow Symone's nastygram to spoil my day. She can be bitter by herself." Cha-Cha thought Symone was getting stranger as time grew on, but she couldn't figure out what it was, so she brushed it under the rug.

"You're right, Cha-Cha. Let's hurry up in here 'cause I'm hungry," Devine said.

The four friends went into Saks and didn't give Symone and her angry tirade another thought.

"Oh, so Jynx ain't gon' text me back?" Symone said, sucking her teeth. "It's cool. All of 'em will be trying to kiss my ass when me and Keyon are back together." Symone watched the group laughing and talking with one another for a few more minutes. She couldn't take her eyes off of Domynique, though.

"I know that chick from somewhere," she mumbled under her breath.

Symone turned on her heels and headed in the other direction towards the Versace store. Although she really needed to go into Saks, she didn't want to run the risk of running into her so-called friends. Symone felt as if they had betrayed her but in real-

ity, Symone was losing her mind. There was a personal shopper in
Saks who had assisted Symone with the gift she ordered for
Keyon. A Rolex watch from the Prince collection. Symone was
sure he was going to love it.

Twenty minutes later, after the friends left, Symone was in
Saks paying for the watch that she ordered Keyon.

"It's good that you ordered when you did," the clerk said.
"This watch was still marked down at our after Thanksgiving pric-
ing. You've saved almost $10,000."

Thanksgiving. That's where Symone recognized the chick
that was with her friends. She was the same broad who was over
Keyon's house the day she came over and his mother wouldn't let
her come inside.

"Keyon has company." Symone remembered Ms. Carolyn
saying. The bitch that looked just like Lauren London. But that
wasn't the only place Symone recognized the woman from. There
was still something familiar about her that Symone couldn't put
her finger on.

"It'll come to me," she said, walking out of Saks into the
brisk December, Atlanta air.

Symone got into her SUV and sent a text to Keyon.

*IDK y ur not responding to any of my texts but I really
wanna c u. We need 2 talk. HMU when u get this.*

Once she arrived home, Symone sat the gift wrapped box
on the bed and began laying out her clothes. Keyon hadn't responded but she felt like he would. When he did, Symone was
going to be ready. A huge relief had come over Symone when she
got home and found Donnie gone. The two of them had been on
bad terms since the accident and Symone was sick and tired of it.
She was beginning to think that leaving Keyon for Donnie hadn't
been one of her better decisions. Donnie's lying and cheating were
still out of control and now, she was popping pain pills and drinking more. It was too much for Symone to bear.

"Soon, I'll be back in the Buckhead mansion that Keyon
bought for us so we can start our family and I will be Mrs. Steele,"
Symone said to nobody, placing her iPod on the docking bay in the
bathroom so she could listen to music while she got ready for

Keyon's call.

Symone had delusions of grandeur concerning Keyon. She was sure that once she presented him with the watch and gave him some money to help clear up his debt, he would fall back into her arms. It didn't matter to Symone that Keyon had someone else. Like Donnie, his mate was replaceable.

"We were meant to be together. I'm getting my *real* man back and once I do, I'm never letting him go again."

Symone used flexi-rods to roll her hair. Then she sat on the side of the tub to shave her legs. Because the music was turned up, Symone didn't hear Donnie stumble into the bedroom in a slightly drunken stupor.

"Shit, my ass is toasted," Donnie slurred to herself, sitting her cola bottle down.

She plopped down on the bed and closed her eyes. She drank a huge cup of coffee before she came upstairs and hoped that it would help her feel better soon. A few moments had passed and Donnie started to sit up in the bed when her hand brushed up against a box.

"What's this?" She thought and opened the box revealing the watch.

"Damn, this muhfucker is tight," Donnie gawked. She took the fake Movado watch off her wrist and tried on the Rolex. She fastened it but the clasp was too big and the watch slid down her wrist when she held it up to admire it.

"It's a lil too big but ain't shit to getting the band adjusted. My woman don' outdid herself this time." The card inside really sent Donnie over the top.

To my one true love, yesterday, today and forever.

All of a sudden, Donnie started to feel bad. Lately, she had been treating Symone like shit even though she didn't deserve it. *I didn't do all that shit I did to get her, just to push her away. Nah, Symone really is the love of my life,* Donnie thought. Happy, Donnie got up and went over to the computer. This was something for her Facebook friends to know about. Symone's laptop was already up and a window was open to the social media page already. Donnie typed in her information and her page displayed.

Just found my X-mas gift that my girl been trying to hide from me...It's a motherfucking Rolex FBF. This bitch musta cost over 10 stacks. Pics coming soon. #mychickbad.

Donnie hit the X in the upper right hand corner that closed that window when she noticed that another window was open. She stared closely at the screen and read what it said. It was a reservation for a hotel for New Year's Eve.

My babe is really going all out for a nigga like me, she thought. Donnie scanned the reservation and was about to close out of that window when she read at the bottom who the reservation was for. Symone Morrow and Keyon Steele. Donnie looked over to the bathroom and got up. She was going in there to kick that bitch's ass. Donnie placed her hand on the doorknob but right before she twisted it, she heard Symone's phone vibrate from under the pillow. She went to pick it up and saw that it was a text. Symone had put a screen lock on her phone but Donnie knew the code. If Symone was nothing else, she was predictable.

Donnie punched in the final digit and opened the message. It was from Keyon, asking Symone when and where she wanted to meet. Donnie squeezed the cell phone as anger coarsed through her body. She felt like someone turned up the temperature in her body because she began to get hot under the collar. The vein in her neck was throbbing and her blood was boiling.

Before she replied, Donnie scrolled through the thread of messages to see what Keyon and Symone had been talking about.

Stupid ass, desperate ass bitch, Donnie thought, seeing that the texts were mostly from Symone. Her girlfriend was begging this man to talk to her. *He probably only text back and agreed to meet because he was tired of her ass bugging him.* A light bulb appeared over Donnie's head and she got a great idea. She rapidly replied to Keyon's text.

Houston's tonight. 8pm. Don't be late, babe. I got a surprise for you.

Donnie waited to see if Keyon would text back but he didn't. She looked over to the bathroom and questioned why Symone was in the bathroom so long. It was hard to believe that Symone was planning to meet up with Keyon. *This was a first for*

Donnie she thought. She had been the player many times before but had never been played. *Touché', bitch.* Donnie erased the last two text messages from Symone's phone, grabbed her car keys and phone and left the condo. Once she was behind the steering wheel in her car, she placed a call to a special friend.

"Angel, it's me. I need your help again. Can I come over? Cool. I'm on my way."

As Donnie turned the wheel, she noticed something felt heavy. It was the watch. She forgot she was wearing it. *Was this watch for me or that nigga?* Donnie scowled, driving off. Hell, it didn't matter to her one way or the other. Possession was nine-tenths of the law. It was on her wrist. It was hers. A slow smile spread across Donnie's face. She had something in store for Keyon.

An hour later, Symone stepped out of the restroom feeling like a million bucks. The first thing she noticed was that the watch box was taken apart and the watch was gone. Her eyes shot to the left and saw a bottle on the bedside table. *Donnie.* Symone walked over to her computer and found the card there. Donnie must've thought the watch was hers. Feeling deflated, Symone sat down and noticed that her hotel reservation was up on the screen. *Oh my gosh, did Donnie see this?* Symone thought. *If she did, my ass is grass.*

● ● ● ● ● ● ● ● ● ● ● ● ● ● ● ● ●

The four friends sat in the floor at Cha-Cha's and Devine's place, eating, wrapping gifts and looking at old photos. Shopping wore them out and they were all glad that it was over. Domynique leaned against the sofa and exhaled in satisfaction. This was going to be Domynique's first Christmas like this. One spent with friends and family, people who genuinely seemed to care about her. While they were out shopping, they split up long enough to buy gifts for one another and Domynique took that opportunity to buy something special for Keyon, too.

"Earth to Domynique," Devine snapped.

"My bad. I was just thinking," Domynique said.

"From the looks of the smile you had, I would say you

were thinking about my cousin," Jynx spoke.

"Yeah. Something like that," Domynique blushed.

Cha-Cha pulled a huge scrapbook out and dusted it off. On the cover was written 'The Ex-Factor.'

"What's this about?" Domynique asked, opening the book and turning pages. It had pictures and mementos taped down.

"This book has pictures of some of the lovers me and Devine have had and some of the trinkets and bobbles they've given us. We look at it from time to time, thinking about how much we've changed."

"And that's not it, Cha-Cha. Now the shit we have niggas buying for us won't fit in a book. This condo, for instance, wouldn't fit," Devine bragged.

"Someone bought you a condo?" Domynique asked incredulously.

"Well, I used to date a realtor and he negotiated the price and then gave me the down payment. We broke up a few months after we moved in here. After that, every dime our paramours would give us we applied to our mortgage. Over time, we ended up paying off our bachelorette pad early."

"Wow. That's great," Domynique said, going through the photo album. She saw a great photo of the three best friend's that was taken at Centennial Park in downtown Atlanta. Domynique noted how gorgeous all of them were. In the picture, Jynx, who reminded Domynique of Gabrielle Union, stood behind Devine and Cha-Cha with a long yellow dress on. Her long hair draped over Devine's shoulder as Jynx leaned over a bit to fit into the frame. Cha-Cha sat on a park bench in front of Jynx and had on a long white maxi-dress with a big white straw hat on. It was hard for Domynique to imagine Cha-Cha as a man because she was such a beautiful woman.

"Cha-Cha, you look just like Christina Milian in this picture. Very beautiful."

"Doesn't she? Giving us face, like always," Devine agreed.

"Devine, you're looking pretty fierce, too," Domynique added. " Has anyone ever told you that you look like the guy who played Noah on that show, Noah's Ark? Curly hair and all."

"It's funny you should say that, Domynique, because Darryl Stephens, that's his real name and Devine just happened to be very good friends," Cha-Cha offered.

Who is this?" Domynique asked, staring intently at a photo. It was a picture of Cha-Cha with a dark man in a very expensive suit. He was not ugly but not much to look at. He reminded Domynique of Gary Coleman.

"Girl, he was Miracha's human ATM machine, Cleophus Robinson Abignol. We just called his ass Cleo 'cause his name was jacked up," Devine answered.

Domynique knew the man as Big. It was the same man she saw around Thanksgiving who had showed up at Keyon's homeless shelter grand opening. The same man whose goon's pulled Keyon into his car for a 'discussion'. Domynique was surprised that Keyon confided in her about the debt to Big, especially since he really didn't know her that well, but she was almost certain that he didn't know about this. Cha-Cha had been sleeping with the enemy.

Pillow PRINCESS - *Part* 2

Chapter Nine
The Big Payback

Donnie was grateful to Angel, whose mother owned a staffing agency, for getting her the valet gig at Houston's on such short notice. Angel called the guy who was originally scheduled to go in that night and told him he wasn't needed. Instead, she allowed Donnie to go in his place and use his name since this would have been the first time he worked there.

"I'on like the way these pants look on my ass," Donnie told Angel, referring to the hideous black polyester pants that were part of the uniform. "They feel like something Mr. Brown from *Madea* would wear," Donnie said, tucking her dildo in the stretchy pants. She had to do something to pay Angel back for the valet hook up so fucking her was the easy way out.

"Beggars can't be choosers, D. I went through a lot to get you this gig. You can either take it or leave it," Angel said saucily.

Donnie detected bitterness in Angel's voice. "What's with the damned attitude, Angel?"

"You really have the nerve to ask me that? You only call me when you want something, D."

"If you felt like this, why yo' ass didn't say nothing on the phone?"

Because I didn't want you to hang up in my face. Last time I helped you, we were setting the same dude up in the hotel, 'member that? I got you the gig as a bartender so you could slip ol' dude a Mickey and get him on tape fucking someone else. You said that once you got him out of the picture and was able to get a few things out of Symone, we'd be together. That was way back in September. It's been three months. Clearly, you're in love with Symone."

"We are gonna be together, Angel. I just need to handle a few things. And I ain't tripping off Symone. She can kiss my ass," Donnie lied.

"You're sure going through a lot of trouble for a woman you claim not to care about. But we'll see."

"Why you trippin' after I just put it down so hard on you? Your pussy was purring like a kitten," Donnie teased, hugging Angel.

"Whatever. Just remember, my pussy, my head and my heart are three different things and you only control one." Donnie did just eat her pussy like a bag of Cheetos, so she really wasn't trying to trip on Donnie's escapades.

Not sure what she meant by that, Donnie kept quiet and finished dressing. She used to have control over all of the bitches she fucked, but lately it seemed to be unraveling at the edges. It didn't take Donnie long to arrive at the restaurant since Angel only lived ten minutes away and there was no traffic. She arrived early so that she could park her car down the street and walk to the restaurant. There was a few valets standing around when she walked up.

"Uh, I'm looking for Todd," Donnie said, masking his voice.

"He's inside at the bar," one of the guys said.

Donnie walked in and spotted one of the finest women she had seen in a long time behind the bar.

"I'm looking for Todd," Donnie said. "But after I see him, I'd like to see you in my bed, legs spread wide, with my tongue on your clit." Donnie spoke with an unrelenting confidence.

"Damn, it's like that? I get a break in five. Meet me in the ladies room." The bartender joked, but was also serious. Neither of them knew of each other but the thought of a mid-day rendezvous was just what the doctor ordered.

"Bet. Where's Todd, though?"

"He's taking a dump. We'll be finished before he is."
Names and introductions were not important at this time, just getting in and out of the bathroom before Todd appeared was the mission.

Donnie followed the bartender to the employee bathroom that only was equipped with only one toilet, a chaise lounge, a full length mirror and a lock on the door.

"You sure can handle this with only one arm?" The bartender asked.

"I'on need hands, at all, for what I'm about to do," Donnie said, lying back on the chaise. "Come, sit here, and hold on."

The pretty bartender removed her panties and went to sit on Donnie's face as instructed. Her legs were over Donnie's shoulders and she held on to the chaise for balance. As soon as she was in position, Donnie's long tongue slithered out like a snake and rubbed up against the sensitive skin. She licked back and forth while the bartender grinded in slow circles.

"Ooh, baby. This shit feels amazing. Suck my pussy, baby. Suck it hard."

Donnie wrapped her lips around the hardened nub, gently sucked, and then added more pressure.

"That's it," the bartender panted. "Ooh, yeah," she moaned, rolling her hips.

Donnie used two fingers on her good arm and slid them inside the bartender.

"Aye, yes. Fuck me, baby. Like that. Oh, yeah, please don't stop."

The girl's pussy was soaking wet and cum was already beginning to run down Donnie's chin. She was getting nothing but extreme pleasure out of fucking a total stranger.

"I'm cumming, babeee," the bartender sang out.

In and out, Donnie continued to work her fingers. She would feel the bartender's pussy walls contracting on her fingers. The shit was turning her on. Donnie slurped a few more times and rammed two more fingers inside, then bartender's legs began to shake vigorously. Cum ran down Donnie's fingers when she pulled them out, but she continued her tongue assault until the bartender stopped shaking. Breathing heavily, Donnie repositioned the sexy bartender until she was straddling her.

"My name's Michelle. I'm Todd's wife."

Donnie looked nervous as hell and started to remove the leggy woman from her lap.

"Da fuck! You trying to get me killed?"

"Calm down. Ain't nobody trying to get you killed. I'm just trying to have some fun. Todd doesn't know how to do me like a woman can."

Donnie had a surprised look on her face.

"You thought that I thought you were a man, huh? Girl, I saw you coming a mile away and wanted you just as long. We're cool, right?"

"I guess so. You scared the shit outta me, though."

"I know. Sorry 'bout that. C'mon. It's almost eight. You know how rich people hate to be kept waiting."

The two of them exited the restroom and the bartender went back to her post as if nothing happened. Donnie was standing at the end of the bar when a tall, lanky, black dude, who looked like J.J. Evans walked up to her.

"Hello. You must be Kenneth. I'm Todd, the manager here. Angel called and told me you hurt your arm. No worries, you were just going to be greeting customers tonight anyway and learning a few things rather than driving, so it all works out. Come with me, I'll introduce you to the other fellas."

Donnie walked behind the stick figure and didn't blame the bartender one bit for seeking pleasure elsewhere. The tall man looked like his dick wasn't any longer or thicker than a tampon. Being tall with big hands and big feet was an old wives tale according to some of the women Donnie messed with. Todd introduced her quickly and then went back inside. A guy named, Bryan, was supposed to be showing Donnie the ropes, but she didn't hear a thing he said, though. Her mind was focused on one person. Keyon.

Donnie's cell phone was blowing up in her pocket. It wasn't anybody but Symone's scandalous ass. She had called Donnie crying in her voice mail, begging her to call her back but Donnie wasn't studying Symone. She'd handle her ass later. Expensive cars started to pull up to the valet stand and Donnie was on high alert. At any moment, Keyon would be pulling up and she wanted to be ready.

Thirty minutes later, she spotted him. Symone had talked about his custom painted Jaguar enough to know that it was him. Donnie stood off to the side when one of the valets walked around to Keyon's door and held it open for him. When he got out and walked past Donnie, her back was turned away from him and her head was down so he couldn't see her face. Fred, the valet who helped Keyon, got the keys and lingered up front before parking the car.

Donnie watched the valet desk closely after the driver walked back from parking Keyon's car. The valet did not the hang the keys on a hook ,yet, but Donnie needed to see where Fred placed them. A pretty white woman driving a Bentley Coupe pulled up. Her plastic breasts and silicone ass was a perfect distraction for Donnie.

"One of y'all need to get on that. You see how she's eyeing all this black meat? O' girl got jungle fever," Donnie said.

"You know what they say, once you go white, your credit gets right," an older valet added.

Since the woman was ogling Fred, they sent him over to help her. Donnie stood behind the valet desk and eased the keys off the podium, just as Fred set them down and sauntered over to the white lady.

"I'm going on break, fellas. I'll be back in an hour," Donnie said and walked off. Nobody paid Donnie any attention and they really could not care for her cockiness.

Because the keys were not on a hook, Donnie didn't know the exact location of the car. However, it was not hard to spot because of the color and the license plate that read STEELE. Donnie looked around and hurriedly got inside the car before someone saw her. She heard a car coming and slumped down in the seat. Slowly, she slid up to see if anyone was around her and then she started the car.

"Damn, you can't even hear this bitch start," she marveled

at the quiet engine. Before pulling off, she sent a text to a friend. Donnie drove down the back alley instead of going out the front way so that neither she nor the car was spotted. She drove south on Peachtree Street until she reached 17th.

This is close to where we had the wreck, she said to herself.

She turned right and kept driving until she reached an industrial park that was deserted. Donnie hit the lights and drove around one of the buildings.

It looks abandoned over here, she thought, looking at the dilapidated building. Bricks were missing and there were gaping holes in the wall. The building was already fucked up, so what she was about to do would not make a difference in its appearance. Donnie was seething with anger and destroying Keyon's precious whip made her feel a little better. She drove at a steady speed until the car collided with the building. The impact lurched her forward causing her neck to jerk.

"Shit," she screamed, rubbing her neck. *Maybe that wasn't a good idea*, she confirmed.

She popped the trunk using the button on the driver's side door and got out of the car. There was a long, black bag in the trunk so Donnie unzipped it to see what was inside. Baseball bats.

This shit just keeps getting better. There was a personalized steel bat inside that Donnie pulled out and used to start swinging at the car. Donnie was glad she had gloves to cover any fingerprints.

"I bust the windows out ya' car," she sang. "And, no, it didn't mend my broken heart. La-la-la-la-la-la-la-la-la." She hummed the rest of the song because she didn't know all of the words. It didn't matter. The song made her feel good about what she was doing. Donnie took a knife to the custom leather seats, stabbing them until the cushion filling was all over the floor. Beads of sweat began to form on her top lip. Swinging the bat and wielding the knife was a huge workout for a person with one good arm.

A set of lights were coming in Donnie's direction. She ducked down until she was sure who it was.

"Shit, remind me not to get on your bad side," the young gang member said.

"We straight, nigga. You got the tools?"

"Already," The gangster whistled for his friends and together they made quick work of stripping the Jaguar down. While one took the stereo and speakers, the other two concentrated on taking the 22-inch rims. They were done in fifteen minutes. Donnie surveyed the damage and she was satisfied.

"Yo, can I get a lift to Lenox? I've been there the whole time," Donnie said, planting the alibi in the young thug's head.

They agreed and dropped her off at the mall. She walked back to the restaurant, which was only a few blocks, and went inside. Hiding her face behind a potted plant, she spotted Keyon looking at his watch. He had been waiting almost an hour for Symone. *Dumbass*, Donnie thought. Jealousy gnawed at Donnie like a buzzard on a dead carcass and wouldn't let her rest. Keyon was everything and had everything that Donnie wanted; fortune, fame and access to some of the world's hottest women. Keyon finished his drink and threw the cloth napkin down. He was getting ready to leave.

Up front, Keyon told a valet to retrieve his car, handing him a ticket.

"It's the Midnight Grey and silver Jaguar. You can't miss it," Donnie told the valet.

The valet looked on the stand for the keys on hook 40. They weren't there. He leaned down to see if they had fallen off the hook. They hadn't. He squatted down and looked at each hook for a set of Jaguar keys. No luck.

"Is there a problem?" Keyon asked.

"No, sir. It's just that I can't locate your keys."

"That sounds like a problem to me."

"No, sir. The valet who parked your car may have slid the keys in his pocket. That happens from time to time. Allow me to locate the valet who parked your vehicle, sir."

He questioned the valets who were around him to see if they had parked his car. None of them did. The valet went into the break room where a few of them were seated. He asked them if either of them had parked a Jaguar and Fred, the guy who had parked it, spoke up. The two men went outside to talk with Keyon who was getting angrier by the second. First, Symone had stood him up, and now this.

"Mr. Steele, what's the problem?" The valet, Fred asked.

"You tell me. This dude can't find my keys and I'm ready to go. Now!"

"One moment, Sir. We will get this straightened out expeditiously. By this time, all of the valets who were on duty were outside, except Donnie who lurked inside, out of sight.

No one could find Keyon's keys. Fed up, he yelled at all of them.

"Fuck this! Take this set and go get my car. When you find the other set, call my office. My assistant will come and get them," he said, handing Fred his back up set of keys. He was glad he had put a spare car key on his key ring.

The valet walked back to the stand with his head hung low.

"Mr. Steele, I don't know how to say this but your car is not here. I'm very sorry."

"What the fuck you mean, you're sorry? Where's my car?"

"Sir, if you will please go inside, we will find it."

"Fuck that. Where's the manager. Get his ass out here, right now!"

The manager came out and did everything he could to calm Keyon down. A number of things were going through his head. Was Big antagonizing him so he wouldn't have a peaceful Christmas or did Symone do this out of revenge for him rejecting her advances? Either way, it was fucked up.

The police were called and Keyon told them what happened.

"I gave my keys to this dude right here! Now he has no clue where my car is."

"Mr. Steele, I assure you that I parked your car in spot 40. It's restaurant policy that we park all preferred guests in that area. It's under 24 hour surveillance. You can run the tape if you don't believe me." The valet was scared that he might lose his job and Donnie hoped like hell they wouldn't run that tape while she was there. Keyon recognized the look on Fred's face because he looked the same way every time he spoke to Big.

"I believe you," Keyon softened. "It's been a long day. The

police will find it. I'm sure with your video tape footage they won't have an issue. Here's my card," he handed the manager his contact information. "Call me if something comes up on your end."

One of the police offered to drive Keyon home and he accepted. The manager, who was nervous that Keyon would sue, walked back into the restaurant over to the bar where Donnie stood, talking to his wife.

Todd made his way over to tell Donnie, "I want to personally apologize to you, Kenneth, I'm so sorry that your first day involved such a catastrophe. How in the hell do you lose a car," he wondered.

The two ladies ignored him, as they were so in to one another, so he marched on to his office to watch the surveillance tapes. *Ladies will be ladies*, he thought.

Donnie stood there and smiled because she actually pulled off the theft of Mr. Steele's vehicle and fucked his fake boss' wife. *Winning*, she thought. Her phone vibrated. It was Symone again. This time, Donnie felt the need to reply.

If I can't have you...nobody will! Donnie meant every word. There was something about Symone that she could not shake.

Avery GOODE

Chapter Ten
· · · · · · · · · · · · · · · ·
This Christmas

Hang all the mistletoe, I'm gonna get to know you better, this Christmas. Chris Brown's voice traveled upstairs, accompanied by the smell of maple flavored bacon, cooking. Holiday tunes, music, and good food. It was finally Christmas time and the Christmas spirit was running all throughout the house. Keyon rolled over to pull Domynique's small frame into his body but she wasn't there. His eyes popped open and he rolled over to see if she was in the room. He heard the sound of running water in the bathroom and got up to surprise her. When he opened the door, he was the one who got the surprise. On her knees, in front of the toilet, was Domynique making the most gruesome sound and flushing down its contents. It looked as if she was praying to a porcelain god.

"Are you okay, baby?" Keyon asked, holding her hair out of the way.

"I'm fine. Just something I ate, I think," she lied.

"I came in here to wish you a Merry Christmas but it doesn't seem that merry now."

"It is a Merry Christmas, babe," Domynique said, flushing the toilet. "This is going to be the best day ever!" She squealed just like a child. Keyon loved that about her.

The couple brushed their teeth and washed their face, chatting away while doing so. Domynique was very excited, as this was her first Christmas with her new family, friends and the man she was so in love with. She knew that he bought her something for Christmas but what she had for him was going to knock his socks off. They went downstairs and joined the rest of the family. Keyon's mother and aunts were in the kitchen finishing up brunch for everyone, including Keyon's ridiculous number of cousins. His dad and a few of his uncles set up extra tables for the group to dine and everyone else pitched in where ever they were needed. Once all of the food was finished cooking, it was set up in a buffet style so the family could walk around and help themselves.

"This bacon looks ravishing," Domynique said, piling it high on her plate that was already heavily laden with food.

Keyon scratched his head in wonder. How could she be eating like a small horse and just few minutes ago, vomiting something that she ate? He didn't stand there trying to figure things out because the longer he stood there, the more people came in and piled up their plates. The doorbell rang so as soon as Keyon finished fixing his plate, he went to answer it. It was Shymon along with his friends and fellow group members of SKY-Hi, Khalif and Yancey, Keyon's most successful group on the label.

"Thanks, big bro," Shymon said, taking Keyon's plate. "You didn't have to fix me breakfast."

"I didn't," Keyon replied, trying to get his plate back to no avail. He fixed himself another plate and sat and talked with Shymon, wondering why he wasn't spending Christmas with his sister, Symone.

"I went over there already. Me and the fellas, didn't we, y'all?" He looked to his friends who all nodded in agreement. "No one answered the door. I sent her a text and she said that her and Donnie were away for the holiday. I was like 'fuck it' and came here. I didn't wanna be over there, anyway. I wanna have a merry Christmas, not a scary Christmas."

"Your ass is wild, Mon. But you're always welcome here." *Everyone was welcome at my home, everyone but Symone. Domynique's friends, Cha-Cha, Jynx and Devine, even stopped through to enjoy the celebrations*, Keyon thought as he admired the room.

Keyon was sure to introduce the fellas to all of the family

members and friends, including Domynique. Of course, everyone moved on to eating and drinking up the entire house, leaving only empty plates and cups behind.

After brunch, the family sang while cleaning up. SKY-Hi sang the Boyz II Men song, *Let It Snow* and the all of the young girls burned off their plate of food from dancing all over the house. Once the house was clean, everyone began to exchange gifts in no particular order. Keyon wanted to save his gift for last. Unbeknownst to him, so did Domynique. The cell phone in Keyon's pocket vibrated and against his mom's ' no cell-phone on Christmas' rule, he pulled it out. It was a text message he had been waiting for.

"May I have everyone's attention?" The entire house quieted. "Grab your coats and let's head outside."

The family didn't question Keyon. Adults and children alike grabbed their jackets and went outside. They all expected something great but were surprised to see that there was nothing outside.

"As you all know, some genius stole my car the other day. Well, the police found my Jag but the insurance company ruled it a total loss. The cops are going to get the surveillance tapes from Houston's to see if they can find who stole it in the first place. Until then, I decided buy something a little more low-key and safe.. Tah dah," Keyon said, waving his arm.

"Boy, have you been messing with my weed?" His grandmother asked him loudly. "Ain't nothing out here but the shit that's been out here."

"Gran, please stop talking about weed so loudly. What if my neighbors hear you?" Keyon admonished.

"Who you think I get it from, Grandson? Chill out. I got this."

"Whoa," one of Keyon's little cousins said as a black, 2015 Mercedes Benz GLK SUV pulled up.

"It's beautiful, babe," Domynique said. "You deserve this." She walked over to him and kissed him on the lips.

"Get a room," someone yelled out, causing Domynique to blush.

"Son, this is very nice. Sleek," Keyon's mother said.

"It's cool," Shymon said. "I can't see you in it, though. This looks like a chick's SUV," he finished honestly.

"Funny you should say that Shymon, because this is actually yours, babe," Keyon said, turning to Domynique, handing her the keys.

"What? Y-y-you got this for me?" She stumbled over her words.

"Yes, ma'am. It's all yours."

Domynique turned slowly to look at the expensive car and before she could say 'thank you', she fainted. Keyon caught her before she hit the grass and rushed her inside the house. His grandmother lingered in the yard, lighting a blunt before she went back inside.

"This is cause for celebration," the matriarch said to herself.

Inside the house, Keyon panicked. There was something wrong with his woman.

"Mom, is she okay?" He asked nervously.

"Yes, baby," his mom answered as Domynique was coming to. "She just got too excited, that's all."

"Humph, that ain't all," Keyon's grandmother mumbled.

Keyon gave his grandmother the side eye but didn't say anything to her. His main concern was Domynique.

"Are you all right, babe? I was so worried."

"I'm fine, Keyon. I was just overwhelmed by your generosity," she lied again.

"Humph," his grandmother snorted.

"I'm not used to anyone buying me anything for Christmas, let alone a car. I don't know what to say."

"Say yes, Chile'," Devine said.

"Wow. Thank you, Keyon. I promise I'll take care of it."

"No doubt," he said.

"What'chu get for Keyon?" Cha-Cha asked.

"Oh, um. It's that big blue box right there," Domynique pointed near the Christmas tree. "I hope you like it," she looked up to Keyon nervously.

"I love everything you give me, babe."

"Ugh, subliminal messages being passed," Jynx laughed.

Keyon unwrapped the box with the excitement of a child. He loved getting gifts. The wrapping paper was scattered all around him when he pulled the black box out. It was a pair of basketball shoes.

"What! How did you get these?" Keyon jumped up and down like a little boy. Inside was a pair of retro Jordan shoes that were a very limited edition. Only five pairs were made and sold, so to a sneaker head like Keyon, this meant the world.

"I knew someone who knew someone. I told them how much you loved your J's and they suggested this as a gift for you. You like 'em?"

"I love 'em, babe. You're the fucking best!" Keyon's aunts and uncles told the little ones to cover their ears.

"Damn, how can I get a pair?" Shymon asked enviously.

"What else is in the box?" One of Keyon's little cousin's asked.

Keyon peered inside the large box and noticed a smaller box inside.

"Another gift, Dom?" Keyon asked. Domynique nodded coyly.

"What's this about, babe?" Keyon asked, holding the tiny shoes in his large palm. "Are these for us?" Tears began to fill his eyes.

"I knew it!" His grandmother yelled out but Keyon just sat there, confused.

Keyon's mother looked at Domynique anxiously, waiting for her answer. It was so quiet in the house, all that could be heard was the clock on the mantel.

"Domynique, what's going on? Are you...are we going to have a baby?" Keyon asked softly. He really was that stupid. He acquired all the book smarts needed to get by in the business world, but held on to no common sense, whatsoever.

"Yes. In about six months," Domynique cried.

The whole family erupted in cheer, even Shymon who was genuinely happy for Keyon, whom he thought of as his big brother, for real. Everyone offered their congratulations to the couple. Carolyn looked down at Domynique, then sat on the sofa next to her.

"I am so excited for both of you. You're going to make an excellent mother. I love you, Domynique."

"I love you, too, Mama Carolyn." Domynique said.

"Oh my God! I'm gonna be a father!" Keyon shouted, picking Domynique up and spinning her around. "I was going to do this anyway," he said, putting her down slowly. "But now, the timing is perfect."

Keyon got down on one knee and held Domynique's hand in his. "I haven't picked out a ring yet, but I'll buy you whatever you want as long as you say 'yes' to being my wife. I love you, Domynique and I want to spend my life with you. Will you marry me?"

"Yes, baby. I will."

• • • • • • • • • • • • • • • • •

"So, are you gon' marry me, or what?" Donnie asked.

Symone hadn't given an answer yet. She was speechless. Donnie was just threatening to kill her two days prior and now here she was asking for her hand in marriage. This was some bullshit.

"Are you going to answer me anytime this century?" Donnie asked, getting annoyed.

"Are you ready for marriage, Donita? I mean, you're still sowing your royal oats," Symone replied sarcastically.

Donnie gritted her teeth and exhaled slowly in an effort to remain calm.

"Symone," Donnie began calmly. "I know I've said and done some foul shit these last few months and I know I have a fucked up way of showing it, but I love you, girl. I love you more than anyone I've ever been with. You've changed my life for the better and I wanna spend my days making you happy."

Symone didn't say anything. She was still staring at the ring that Donnie slid on her finger. Could it really be called a ring, though? It was a small circular band but it was only ten karat gold. The diamond, which may or may not be real, was a sixteenth of a carat. Symone didn't even know they came that small. It was a

poor excuse for a ring; a disgrace for an engagement ring.
Symone's displeasure of the small token must have shown on her
face.

"Oh, so my ring ain't good enough for you? While you
turning your nose up at it and shit, keep in mind I'm the only muhfucker proposing to you. That nigga, Keyon, sho' in da hell ain't."

"I didn't say there was anything wrong with your ring,
Donnie. "I was just thinking."

"Yeah, 'bout dat nigga, I'm sure. And you ain't had to say
shit was wrong with it, your facial expressions are a dead give-
away. But I tell you what, if you want a bigger ring, how 'bout I
take this Rolex back and get you the ring your ass think you deserve!" Donnie was heated because she knew Symone spent a grip
on that watch, all for Keyon.

"The ring is beautiful," Symone lied. "I was just thinking
about my brother and how I wanted him present at my proposal."

"Mmmm, hmmm. I was born at night, but not last night.
So, what's it gonna be, Symone?" Donnie pressured. Symone knew
Donnie was full of shit.

"Baby, I love you. But marriage is a big step. I think that
you and I should attend marriage counseling. We have a lot we
need to work on." She knew that being patient and calm was the
only way to be with Donnie or she could fly off the handle at any
minute.

"Yeah, I guess you're right, but just so you know, I gave up
the drinking and popping pills just for you," Donnie conceded.

"That's great, baby. It's going to make us better, baby.
Watch." Symone was not so sure and had a strong feeling that
Donnie had not stopped taking the Oxy's.

"I hear you. But I wasn't playing with you the other day, if
I can't have you, nobody will."

Pillow PRINCESS- Part 2

Chapter Eleven

The Truth Shall Set You Free

There were two things in life that Miracha Rodriguez was scared of; polyester and spiders. That is, until Cleo came back into her life. Now she was scared of him. Ever since Cha-Cha's ex-boyfriend came over to her apartment, he made it a point call or text her daily. Their conversations would always end with him threatening her or Cha-Cha's new man, Michael, in some way. Threats that intensified with each call and scared Cha-Cha to her core. Cha-Cha was learning the hard way. There were different sides to Cleo and one of them was a dark, evil side.

Cleo was a very powerful man. Cha-Cha knew that from the first time she laid eyes on him. That was one of the things that had initially attracted her to him. He was kind to Cha-Cha and respected her best friend, Devine. Cleo was generous to a fault and loved spending time and money on Cha-Cha. It was Cleo who offered to cover the remaining medical costs associated with Cha-Cha's surgery. She loved him for that, and so much more. He seemed to love her in return, or so she thought.

It wasn't until after Cha-Cha felt like she couldn't breathe without Cleo, that she found out he was married. By then, it was too late, she had fallen hard. Cleo explained to her that he and his wife lived separate lives and were married in name only. He lived in Sandy Springs and his wife lived in Alpharetta. For appearance sake, he would spend time with his family when the occasion called for it. Birthdays, holidays, and public events. With him, Cha-Cha knew that she was first. They had a pretty steady rhythm going and continued to enjoy each other's company. Until the day she caught him in bed with two young men and that's when everything changed between them.

That day, Cha-Cha had just closed on the building that now housed her boutique and a couple of other upscale shops. She wanted to share the news with Cleo but when she called his office, his secretary told her that he had taken the rest of the day off. Cha-Cha drove to his house and saw that his car was in the driveway.

Using the key that he had given her, Cha-Cha walked in the home in search of her man. There were noises coming from his bedroom and she stopped to listen for a bit. She turned the doorknob slowly and walked in on what she already knew was taking place. Cha-Cha didn't scream or make a scene. At first, she just stood there and watched Cleo. While he pounded a thin black guy from behind, he kissed a young white boy who was holding a dildo in Cleo's asshole. It was quite a scene.

Cha-Cha walked around the bed, unnoticed, towards the closet to grab her suitcase. That was when Cleo saw her. He jumped up so fast, he forgot he was cumming in the other man and jizz flew everywhere. The young guys scattered and Cleo just stood there, naked and embarrassed. Nothing he could say or do made Cha-Cha want to stay. Cleo begged her not to leave and told he her was just into men at times, but would stop just for her. Cha-Cha now knew why his wife left him, not because of the men, but because he was a cheater.

After the pain and hurt caused by Cleo, she didn't think that she would find someone to truly love her until Michael came along. Now, as she sat the desk in her office, she couldn't help but think about how her past could upset her future. Cleo had stopped calling long ago, so him popping up now meant something else. There had to be a way for Cha-Cha to talk some sense into Cleo. Cha-Cha didn't think that he really wanted to be with her. He just didn't want anyone else to be with her. The office phone on her desk buzzed. It was the receptionist.

"Hey Cha-Cha, Cleo is here to see you," the young lady

said.

Damn, I must have thought him up. Cha-Cha rolled her eyes and shook her head.

"Send him in, Bubbles."

Cha-Cha stood up and smoothed out the wrinkles in her black pencil skirt. She walked around the desk when he came in and stood in front of him. His arms were loaded down with packages.

"What is it, Cleo?" Cha-Cha asked, not really caring what his answer was.

"Is that any way to greet your man, babe? I come bearing gifts," he said, placing the gift wrapped boxes on the leather sofa in her office.

"You're not my man, Cleo and Christmas is over. You're a few days late."

"You know holidays are spent with the wife and kids. Why are you being so disagreeable, baby?" He asked, caressing Cha-Cha's cheek and wrapping his arms around her. She stepped out of his embrace quickly and flinched like his touched burned her.

"Cleophus, you could've kept your gifts. I don't want anything from you. We've been through this already. Let bygones, be bygones and move on, once and for all.

"But I want something from you. You're mine, Miracha, and I will have you again."

"Look, if you don't leave me alone I'm going to call the police."

Cleo doubled over in laughter. "And tell them what? That the man who took care of your ass after your family threw you out on the street paid mega bucks to make you look like the woman you've always desired? Or that he came to your office bearing gifts? But go right ahead," he said handing her his cell phone. "Tell the chief Cleo said hello and that we're still on for golf this Saturday."

Cha-Cha knew that Cleo's influenced reached far and wide here in Atlanta. She exhaled and spoke softly.

"We were no good together, Cleo," Cha-Cha reasoned. "It's bad enough that I was fucking you and you're married, but then you went and added a harem of dudes and other bitches to the

Avery GOODE

equation. I had to share you with your wife, I wasn't about to share you with all of Atlanta."

"Cha-Cha, you know how they say; you never miss your water til your well runs dry? Girl, I'm over hear dying of thirst without you. I need you, baby."

"You didn't want me a month ago, Cleo so why now?"

"Things were different then."

"How? The only thing that was different was that I was single."

"You need to leave that man alone. Now, Cha-Cha or else!"

"Or else what, Cleo? If I leave Michael alone, will that make you happy? Even if I do, I guarantee I won't be single for long. Look at me. I'm beautiful," Cha-Cha said, antagonizing him.

"And you have me to thank for that."

"Like hell! I was beautiful when I was born. Yeah, you helped me complete my gender transition, but that's it. Female parts don't make you a real woman any more than sitting in a church makes you holy. I was a woman true and through, even before they added the pussy."

"A pussy that belongs to me. I paid for that, remember?"

"Is that what this is about, Cleo? Money? You want the money back you spent on my surgery? If so, I can write you check right now and be done with you so I can get on with my life."

Cha-Cha walked briskly over to her desk but Cleo was fast on her heels. He swung her around to face him. They were so close, his nose grazed hers.

"Don't you ever downplay anything that I have ever done for you by assigning a dollar amount to it! I love you and I will have you again. This has never been about money. It's about me owning these two things right here." Cleo pointed to Cha-Cha's heart and rubbed his hand over her womanhood. He leaned into her and sniffed her neck, then licked it. "Mmmm, you smell so good. I bet you taste even better."

Cleo ran his hand up Cha-Cha's thigh until it touched her panties. He massaged her nether lips in a circular motion.

"It feels so real, baby. I can't wait to sink this fat dick inside you and hear you scream my name like you used to

100

when I would take your ass. You liked me fucking you doggy style, didn't you Miracha? My nasty bitch in heat."

Cha-Cha didn't move. She barely breathed as he molested her. All she could do was stare at the wall ahead and will her body to remain as still as possible. There was no way she wanted to respond to him in any way. Cleo stuck his thick, onion tasting tongue into Cha-Cha's mouth and palmed her ass, drawing her closer to him. Not able to take it anymore, Cha-Cha bit down on Cleo's tongue. He reached back and hit her so hard, she flew over the desk and hit the floor.

"You stupid bitch!" He began. "Clearly, you need to be retrained. I have my work cut out for me. That nigga you fuck may let you run over him but that shit won't fly with me. My wife and I are going to her parents for New Years. I'll be gone a few days. When I get back, you need to be prepared to tell me that you've ended things with that tall bastard. If not…well, you know how much I like choices, so I'll let you choose the color you'd like."

"A color for what?" Cha-Cha cried.

"Michael's casket."

• • • • • • • • • • • • • • • •

Donnie had no clue why an Atlanta Police detective wanted to talk to her. But he did. So here she was, sitting in an interrogation room, scared shitless because she's done so many fucked up things in her life, any of them could be coming back to haunt her. Donnie wasn't going to let this place get to her.

It couldn't be anything too bad or else they would have come to pick her up instead of allowing Donnie to drive down by herself. Well, she didn't exactly come alone. Symone drove her and sat in the waiting area until everything was over. Donnie's knee bounced angrily as she thought about Symone, who still hadn't given an answer to the proposal. Shit, if Symone fucked around and waited too long, Donnie planned on moving on. The pretty officer who escorted her to the interview room would make a lovely choice. *It ain't like Symone gon' be my only bitch. She'll just be my main one. Shit, I got bitches all over the A-T-L thinking that I wanna be with them. Dumb ho's for believing that shit.*

"If you'll wait here for a moment, Ms. Stone, I'll go get Detective Blair. May I get you something to drink? We have coffee, water and a few soft drinks," Kimmy asked.

"Water'll be good. Thanks."

Five minutes later, Kimmy came back with a chilled bottle of water and a tall man who looked like Blair Underwood. He was six feet tall with a milk chocolate complexion, hazel brown eyes and a perfectly trimmed goatee. The detective wore a black skull cap and black leather jacket. Donnie snickered because she felt like he was trying to portray a hard role.

"Find something funny, Ms. Stone?" The detective asked.

"Nah, nah. I was just thinking 'bout something. You the cop who wanted to see me?"

"Yes, I am. I am Detective Blair and this is my junior detective, Officer Bradshaw."

"Why you wanna talk to me?"

"We'll get to that momentarily. Did you have a hard time finding the office?"

Donnie told the detective that she and Symone didn't have any issues. He made small talk with Donnie trying to feel her out while Kimmy took notes. Once he felt that Donnie had let a little of her guard down, he got to the point of why he brought her in.

"I wanna talk to you about Morgan Calloway."

"What about her?"

"When was the last time you saw her?"

"I'on know. August, September. Why?"

"Are you aware that she's missing? No one in her family has heard from her in months."

"What that got to do with me?" Donnie answered smartly.

"You tell me, Ms. Stone," the detective emphasized 'Ms'. He wanted to let her know she wasn't the man she thought she was.

"We used to fuck around."

"How did the two of you meet?"

The detective allowed Donnie to talk without interruption. She was very detailed with how she first met Morgan and how they made out in the dressing room in Saks. Kimmy was still taking notes, looking for inconsistencies with anything that Donnie said. After Donnie finished speaking, another detective entered the room and whispered something in Detective Blair's ear, who then gave Donnie the side eye.

"If you'll excuse me, Ms. Stone, I need to speak with my captain. Kimmy come with me, please."

Donnie was freaked out. She didn't know what the other officer said that made the detective leave so suddenly. A nervous Donnie drummed her fingers on the wooden table and tapped her foot. *What's going on with Morgan? How is this the reason they questioning me?* Donnie could not figure it out. Twenty minutes later, Donnie got her answer when the detective came back in. This time, he was alone. He didn't say anything immediately. For a minute or two, he looked over some notes and shuffled some papers around. Finally, he looked up at Donnie and spoke sternly.

"Are you aware that Morgan Calloway is missing and you're the last person who spoke with her?"

"Look, I told you I ain't seen Morgan in some months when you asked me the first time."

"Indeed, you did. Yet, according to your Facebook page, you posted pictures of the two of you at party a few weeks ago."

"Man, those were some old pictures. I was just flossing for social media. You know how it is."

"No, I don't. Why don't you tell me?"

"Dude, I just be posting shit on that page. People in the community look up to me and shit. They know I fucks with bad bitches and from time to time, I show 'em."

"Hmm. Does your girlfriend, Ms. Morrow, know about Ms. Morgan and the other quote unquote 'bad bitches you fuck with'?"

"Symone knows I love her, man."

"In other words, that's a 'no'?"

"She knows I been doing a lil something here and there, but that shit don't mean nothing. She know she got my heart."

"Does she, now? When was the last time you held down a job for longer than six months?"

"What does one thing have to do with another?" Donnie was getting upset. The detective must have had something on his mind causing him to ask her that.

"Both Ms. Morrow and Ms. Calloway are women of substantial means, wouldn't you agree?"

"If you saying that they both got gwap, then yeah."

"Tell me why educated women with the world at their fingertips choose to fuck with a no job, no money having, fake dick wearing bitch like you? You must have a golden tongue."

His antagonistic questions sent Donnie over the edge.

"Da fuck you talkin' about, son? Bitches love me and the way I handle business in the bedroom. I can't help it that they wanna take care of a nigga's needs and shit. I'on force nobody to do shit for me. I been getting money even before I knew those two."

"According to a bit of information that I received, Morgan had stopped paying your car note, is that true?"

"Honestly, it is. But so what? Where she left off, Symone picked up. No biggie."

"Were you angry at Ms. Calloway for cutting you off financially?"

"Frankly, I wasn't. Morgan is grown and can do whatever she wants."

"I see." Detective Blair took note of Donnie's constant use of honestly and frankly. That meant she was lying about something. He decided to test her.

"Do you live with Ms. Morrow, Donita?"

"Nope. Me and my brother got a spot over in Mosley Park." Sometimes Donnie still took girls over to the crib in Mosley, just for somewhere to fuck their brains out.

Detective Blair had already spoken to Stephanie, Donnie's brother's wife, who told him that Donnie moved in with Symone Morrow in late September. Even her mail was forwarded to the new address. Although the detective knew Donnie was lying, he didn't have anything to hold her on. Morgan was missing but there were no clues yet that pointed to foul play. The tip Kimmy had received said that Donita Stone knew where Morgan was. Since Morgan was the ex-wife of Detective Blair's cousin, Randall Calloway, he wanted to find out what had happened to her.

Kimmy, on the other hand, was now Randall's fiancé and she wanted to find out where Morgan was so that she and Randall could move on with their lives. Detective Blair stood up and tapped on the door, signaling for Kimmy to come back into the room. When she entered, she handed the detective a file. He opened it, scanned the contents and closed it.

"Ms. Stone, we'd like to thank you for your time and patience. At this time, you're free to go."

"Uh, ok. Will you all lemme know if you find out anything about Morgan."

"Absolutely."

Kimmy and Detective Blair walked Donnie out. "Ms. Stone, I hope to never see you again but I have a feeling that won't happen," Detective Blair said through a fake smile.

"So, what do you think?" Kimmy asked her boss.

"I think she knows more than she's saying. Soon we will know the truth and the truth will set her free."

Chapter Twelve
Friends, How Many of Us Have Them?

Symone didn't want to go into the New Year with unresolved issues with her friends. Jynx had sent her a text after the mall incident telling Symone that it was unreasonable of her to expect them not to have other friends. It was a bitter pill to swallow but Symone knew Jynx was telling the truth. It didn't make sense to ruin five years of friendship over something as petty as that. At the moment, Symone felt like all she had was her brother and her friends. Donnie was still talking marriage but the jury was still out on that. She didn't want to alienate the only people who had stood by her and being with Donnie pushed her to that. So Symone sent the friends a text and asked them out to dinner. Her treat. They all accepted.

Now, here she stood outside of the Justin's on Peachtree, nervous, for no real reason. The paranoia was all in her head and she just needed to get back in the groove of things after being stuck up Donnie's ass, or rather Donnie was stuck up her, literally. It had been a minute since she had seen her friends and Symone was not sure how she would be received. The hostess asked Symone if she had a reservation and Symone told her 'yes' and gave the pretty young lady her name.

"Your party has already arrived, Ms. Morrow. Follow me, please." Symone could not believe they beat her there.

The hostess escorted Symone to a table on the far left side

of the restaurant that overlooked the patio. Symone looked around and noticed that the restaurant was packed for a Wednesday night. When Symone got to the table, each of her friends stood to greet her and hugged Symone so tightly she got tears in her eyes. The love was still there even though Symone had acted like a moron.

"Honey Chile', you're working those Alexander Mc-Queens. Lemme see those heels," Cha-Cha gushed over the expensive, black snake skin shoes that adorned Symone's feet. They complimented the leopard print pencil skirt and red-silk, droopblouse. Cha-Cha nodded her approval. This was the Symone she was used to seeing. Not the one who was garbed in oversized, dirty looking sweatpants and uncombed hair. It was nice to see her friend getting back to the person she once was. Symone knew what Cha-Cha was thinking and was just thankful her friends had not written her off.

"Yes, you are looking fierce," Devine agreed.

A waiter came up and took their drink and appetizer orders and the friends chatted away like they had never been apart.

"So, what's been going on with you guys?" Symone inquired.

"Girl, we have all been so busy trying to plan my wedding," Jynx answered. Devine rolled his eyes. He was beyond tired of hearing about the planning.

"She's been busy planning her wedding," Devine pointed to Jynx. "We've been going along for the ride." Cha-Cha just listened in. She had no part in the planning since she was focused on Michael Steele

"Whatever, Devine. Y'all know we've been having a good time."

"You're right. I can't lie."

"This must be an exciting time for you," Symone said, dipping a raw carrot into the ranch dip and biting it.

"It is. That's why I'm, we're, so glad you called, Symone. Good things are happening in all of our lives and we want our bestie to be included in that," Jynx said, squeezing Symone's hand.

"Thanks, girl." Symone knew that Jynx meant every word she said.

"Have you seen the ring that Jonathan bought her?" Cha-Cha asked, holding Jynx's hand up so Symone could see the five carat solitaire diamond.

Devine looked away, "Hell yeah, she saw the ring. Who didn't? The motherfucker is big enough for a person in the next county to see."

"Uh, no. I haven't. This isn't the same one you had before, is it?" Symone commented, noticing a huge difference in rings. The one Jonathan had given Jynx initially was beautiful but smaller than the one Symone was looking at now.

"No, this one is better. He told me he wanted me to have the kind of ring a woman of my stature should have. It was a total shock to me because I loved the ring he gave me at first. Luckily, he let me keep 'em both."

Symone wanted to tell her friends that Donnie had proposed but she just knew they would ask her to see the ring and Symone was not about to pull out that piece of scrap gold. It would be too embarrassing.

"Wow," Symone said, hoping there was no envy detected in her throat.

"How are things between you and your girlfriend?" Devine asked, changing the subject.

"They couldn't be better," Symone lied. "Donnie has been really stepping her game up with me. Since the accident, she has been more attentive and we've been a lot more physical, too." Symone didn't need to tell them by physical, she meant that she and Donnie had been fighting more. It was none of their business.

"That's great. You know, Symone, we all really want you to be happy and if Donnie is what makes you, happy then go for it!" Jynx said, sort of wishing that Symone and Keyon were still together.

"Yeah, she's right, Symone. We don't have to like Donnie in order to love you but it sure would make things a whole lot easier for all of us if we did."

"Thanks for saying that, Cha-Cha. I love you guys very much," Symone choked.

"We love you, too, girl. Let's not allow anything or anyone

to come between us," Devine added.

Just then, the waiter carrying their entrée's came over and began setting their food before them. As he moved to the side, Symone spotted Keyon across the restaurant. He was with the same chick that she had seen her friends with at the mall. *Was this a set-up*, she thought. *They had to of known that girl was here with Keyon if they were friends with her. Besides, his own cousin was sitting here at the table. Did she not know? This shit is making me sick*, Simone said, all in her head. The same chick that was at Keyon's house on Thanksgiving. Symone always had a way of knowing.

Humph, this must be the bitch he was telling me about, she thought inwardly.

"Is that Keyon over there?" Symone asked.

The friends turned around and looked across the restaurant. Sure enough, it was Keyon and he was not alone.

"Who's that with him? I've seen her face before?" Symone squinted, trying to zoom in on the woman's face.

"You've seen more of that," Devine mumbled under his breath.

"What did you say?" Symone's neck snapped in Devine's direction.

"My steak is juicy," Cha-Cha marveled, trying to change the subject. Everyone knew Symone was pissed and this little situation could go either way.

Keyon was helping the woman into her coat and the two of them walked out of the restaurant arm in arm.

"It's nothing, Symone. Let's just enjoy our evening," Jynx said, trying to make light of things.

"Naw, it's something, all right. Who the fuck is she? Is that the same broad that was over Keyon's for Thanksgiving and with y'all at the mall?"

"How did you know? Never mind," Jynx began. "Um, the reason you recognize Domynique is because…well, she's um…"

"She's the girl from the sex tape, Symone," Cha-Cha finished.

"What? Keyon told me that he didn't know who she was.

That he was set up."

"He didn't, Symone. Not at first, but he hired an investigator to find her so he could prove to you that he was innocent," Jynx said, defending her cousin.

"That's bullshit!" Symone said. Her heart was beginning to beat faster and her legs began to shake. This was not happening. "If that's the case, why didn't he come to me?"

"Well, you left him so fast that he really didn't have a chance. After Watson found Domynique, she and Keyon just hit it off and he ended up falling in love with her." Jynx knew that was a lie but she was trying to spare Symone's feelings. Truth is, Keyon felt an instant connection to Domynique the moment he laid eyes on her in the video.

Symone looked around the table at her so-called friends. They managed to do it again. Stab her in the back. So much for loyalty.

"Damn, y'all sure are good about keeping secrets and shit. Might as well tell me everything before Devine dies over here," Symone pointed to her gay friend. "With your guilty looking ass."

Devine did look like the cat who swallowed the canary. He tried his best to look around the restaurant or pretend that he was focused on the food on his plate but it didn't work. Everyone knew that if you wanted to keep something a secret, do not tell Devine. He could not hold water. But he was doing well keeping one secret.

"Keyon and Domynique are getting married, Symone, and they are going to have…" Jynx began.

"What the fuck?" Symone interrupted angrily. She shook the table with such force that Cha-Cha's margarita tipped over. "Y'all bitches ain't true friends. You're shady and you betray me every chance ya' get. Each of you can lick my bloody pussy and kiss my shitty ass. We ain't friends no more! All of y'all are dead to me!" Symone didn't care that her friends were only trying to protect her. They figured she had moved on and there was no sense in opening old wounds.

Symone was screaming so loud, the patrons in the restaurant stopped what they were doing so that they could watch the scene unfold. The manager was walking over to the friends' table hurriedly so that he could diffuse the situation. By the time he made it to them, Symone had hastily exited the restaurant.

"Is everything all right over here?" He asked concerned.

"Yes, we apologize for the scene," Jynx said.

The manager walked off and the friends just sat there quietly, staring at one another in disbelief.

"Damn, if she acted like after finding out Keyon was engaged, how do you think she would have acted knowing Domynique was pregnant?"

• • • • • • • • • • • • • • • • •

If Symone didn't know, she did now, and she was all alone. Hot tears streamed down her face as she drove. Symone gripped the steering wheel so tight her knuckles were white. Not only had her friends befriended the bitch that was responsible for ruining Symone and Keyon's relationship, they tried to hide the fact that Keyon was marrying her. Things were all fucked up. Symone had planned to get Keyon back. Keyon told Symone he was seeing someone but that didn't matter. She knew he was still in love with her and was just using the other woman to pass the time. But now, things were different. He was engaged.

"I can't believe this shit!" She yelled and pounded the steering wheel at the red light.

A few blocks later, Symone was pulling into her assigned parking spot in front of her condo.

"Fuck!" She exclaimed.

Donnie was home. Symone didn't want to deal with her bullshit tonight either. She looked into the mirror on the visor and fixed her make-up. The last thing she needed was Donnie questioning her about why she was crying. It didn't take long to grab her handbag and make it upstairs.

"Fuck. Now I gotta deal with this shit!" Symone turned the key in the lock and braced the knob before she turned it. The door began to open slowly without any help from Symone.

"Welcome home, my love," Donnie said, ushering Symone inside.

There were no lights on in the house. It was ablaze with

Lavender and Chamomile scented candles of different heights, at least twenty scattered all over the condo. Symone had dreaded coming home and was still a bit angry, but the scene before her was serene and peaceful, so it helped calmed her down.

"Wow, Donnie. What is this?"

"I wanted to do something special for you this evening. It's time for all this fussing and fighting to stop."

"I hear you, Donnie. I wanna believe you, but..." Symone was caught off by her lover.

"Don't say another word. I know I gotta regain your trust. I haven't had one drink today and I flushed my pain pills down the toilet. You're all I want. Everything I need. I love you, Symone," Donnie got down on one knee. "I'm serious about spending my life with you. Will you please, please marry me, baby?"

Donnie opened the lid on the small velvet box and a sparkling three carat, pear shaped diamond ring glistened in the candlelight. Symone coughed.

"This is breathtaking," she stammered. "When did you get this? How?"

"I sold that Rolex. You're more important to me than any expensive watch. Will you, baby?"

Clearly you forgot the watch wasn't for you, Symone thought. She didn't wanna spoil the mood and Donnie was trying. *Shit, I ain't got nobody else. Might as well stay with her.*

"Yes, Donnie. I'll marry you and I love you, too."

Donnie picked Symone up and carried her to their bedroom. There were candles lit and rose petals on the bed and on the floor. She lay Symone softly down on the bed.

"I see you were prepared. You must have known I was going to say yes."

"No, I didn't, honestly. But I was hoping."

Donnie dipped her low and kissed Symone deeply in the mouth. She touched Symone's breasts and Symone instantly got a sensation between her thighs. Kisses trailed from Symone's lips down to her neck. Donnie sucked on it for a minute, putting a hickey on the right side. The wet saliva tickled Symone. Nimble fingers began to massage Symone's breasts.

"Take that blouse off," Donnie said.

Her voice was deep, sultry and turned Symone on. The top slid off with ease. Symone wasn't wearing a bra.

"Damn."

Donnie's hot mouth covered one of Symone's nipples. Now Symone felt a different kind of wetness. Both nipples were hard and Donnie alternated sucking on each of them. The breasts kept Donnie's mouth busy but her hands were free to push the pencil skirt up Symone's thighs.

"I love it when you don't wear panties."

Symone pulled Donnie's face to hers and began kissing her hard on the mouth. She sucked on Donnie's tongue like it was a small dick. Twirling her own tongue around it, wrestling. Moisture gathered at the entrance of Symone's lips. Two of Donnie's fingers gracefully entered Symone and began to dance around in the wetness. Symone's hard nub was nestled between Donnie's index and middle fingers. Each time she thrust in and out, the nub was stimulated on each side. Juices began to drip into Donnie's hands. Symone's legs began to shake.

The more Symone sucked Donnie's tongue and kissed her, the more aggressively Donnie finger fucked her. Their movements were synchronized; suck, thrust, suck, thrust. Symone's heart was beating like bass in a car. Sticky juices began to flow down Symone's thighs on each outward thrust. Donnie could feel Symone's pussy begin to contract. The orgasm was on its way. Symone wasn't sure when Donnie undressed. All she knew was that Donnie's hard, naked body was now pressed against hers. Donnie rubbed the head of her strap-on, up and down, at the opening of Symone's lava box. Once it was wet, she slid in to the wet hole, hitting a few of Symone's spots on the way in. Symone's legs flew in the air as she took Donnie completely inside.

"Fuck me, baby." Symone panted in ecstasy. As Donnie pumped her man-made dick, Symone imagined that it was Keyon inside of her with his heaven sent, nine-inch, hard dick.

"Oh yes, that's it, baby. Keep it coming."

Donnie did as her woman asked. She pulled her dick out and slid her middle finger inside of Symone, wetting it. With ease, she slid the wet finger into Symone's ass and put the dick back in her pussy.

"Your ass is tight, baby. I love this shit." Donnie bit her lower lip as she looked down on Symone and reveled at the fuck faces she brought out in her lover. Long strokes filled Symone up. Symone writhed in pleasure as she grabbed both of her breasts and kneaded them like dough.

Fuck me Keyon, her mind whispered.

Tiny pulses of electricity coursed through Symone's body as she began to orgasm. All she could see was Keyon's face, feel his touch, smell his essence. This moment was theirs. Keyon's and Symone's.

"Ah, baby. It feels so good." Symone was cumming harder than she had in a long time.

Heavy breathing filled the room as the lovers came off cloud nine. Donnie laid behind Symone in the spoon position. Feeling the always hard dick at her ass, Symone began pressing into Donnie, grinding into her lover once more. Donnie got the hint.

Symone, lying on her side, rubbed her clit. She was turning up the heat again. Donnie rolled on her back and reached inside the nightstand and grabbed a tube of lubricant.

"Mother, may I?" She asked Symone, lubing her asshole.

"Yes, you may."

Donnie spread Symone's ass cheeks and eased the thick dick into Symone's anus.

"Ah, shit. Easy, baby. Ooo, wee. Yeah, like that."

The dick slid in and out so freely. With each stroke, Donnie went further in until she couldn't go any further. A frown spread across Symone's face as she thought about Keyon. *He must really be into this bitch,* she thought angrily. Sweaty skin slapped against Symone's.

"Take this dick, you nasty bitch," Donnie growled. "I'm killing this ass." Donnie kissed and sucked on Symone's back and rammed the dick in and out, round and round. Symone was going to cum again. Donnie was killing her ass and she was loving every minute of it.

"Kill this ass, baby. Take it!"

Suction noises came from Symone's pussy and a big smile began to form.

"I love you, baby!" Symone yelled out to the face in her head. "Yes. Yes! Harder baby, I'm gonna cum." Symone had an idea. She was going to get Keyon back. All she had to do was get rid of Domynique.

Chapter Thirteen
An Unlikely Ally

Charmaine popped the cork on the bottle of wine and grinned. She was going to send Donnie and Symone the bottle as an engagement gift. She poured some wine out of bottle to make room for her addition.

"It's times like these I wish I had a dick because it's hard as hell peeing in a cup," she said out loud.

She pulled her pants down, squatted over the toilet, and began to collect her specimen. Holding a 16 ounce Styrofoam cup under her vagina, she loosened her muscles. All morning she had been drinking water so that she would have enough pee to add to the wine. Charmaine's bladder was full and once the urine started to flow, it couldn't be stopped. She peed so much, it ended up running over the rim of the cup and streaming down her hand.

Damn. It's mine at least, she thought.

She opened the bathroom cabinet and reached beneath the sink to grab a small baby food jar. It was half full with blood from her last menstrual cycle. Charmaine removed the lid and turned her nose up at the smell. Fish and ass. Period blood was disgusting. She poured pee from the cup into the jar, replaced the lid and shook it up. Seeing it was still thick, she added more urine and repeated the steps until the urine thinned out the blood. Using a funnel, Charmaine poured the mixture into the bottle and put the cork back on.

"Congratulations, bitches," Charmaine snarled, washing her

hands.

It only took a brief moment to place the bottle in the fancy box and attach the card that the clerk filled out for her. Once that was done, Charmaine grabbed her purple Burberry tote, the keys to the new car her father had surprised her with and stepped out the door of her Atlantic Station townhome. The light breeze kissed her cheeks. Today, she did not have any prosthetics or \pancake make-up on her face. She was fresh out of the beauty salon with a natural look. Nails done, hair done, everything did. Armed with a new do, she was preparing to put an end to her lying, cheating ex, once and for all. For this plan, she was going to have to be herself. Literally. Not Charmaine Franklin, but Zabria Moreland.

The silver 2010 BMW 328i Coupe glistened in the winter sun. *Thanks, daddy.* Because of her lineage, Zabria was able to live a life that Charmaine never could. Even though Zabria used a portion of the allowance, that her father sent her, to fund a few 'projects' for Charmaine, the small sum didn't put a dent in her bank account. Zabria sat in the car for awhile before pulling off. It was funny that Donnie wanted someone who was pretty and had money to be with. A woman willing to take care of her. Donnie didn't think that Charmaine had the means to do that so she kept looking. *If only Donnie had just been faithful to me, I would've told her the truth about me and we would be rich and happy together right now.* But Donnie already burned the bridge to Charmaine's heart and it could never be repaired. Their final meeting placed Donnie on Charmaine's hit list and she was going to make her pay.

The engine whispered, as Charmaine pulled carefully out of the driveway and onto the prestigious street. A UPS office was a few blocks away so Charmaine stopped there to send the happy couple's gift off and then she headed to Midtown. There was a sports bar there, Logan's, that many of the Atlanta Police officers and detectives frequented.

She was only interested in one particular man, though. Detective Blair. The man who paid Donnie a visit. Charmaine called the anonymous tip line and said that Donnie was the last person to see Morgan Calloway alive. Charmaine had done her research. She knew that the detective was the first cousin of the Oscar winning actor, Randall Calloway, the ex-husband of Morgan. She also knew that Morgan was an attention seeking, gold-digger, who loved to sit on Donnie's face. The latter being the reason why Charmaine had to take her out.

There were stories all over the internet about Morgan and how she was trying to milk her rich husband for every dime she could. It was pretty safe guess that Morgan's husband would think something was up when she just all of a sudden stopped hitting him up for money. Sure enough, Charmaine found out that he suspected something was awry because Morgan hadn't cashed any of the alimony checks that were mailed to for the past few months.

There was a parking spot at the front door and Charmaine pulled into it. A few men, who she pegged right off as cops, offered to help her out of the car. She declined their attempts in hopes of spotting Detective Blair. For the past couple of days, she staked this place out to see how often he came. Unlike the other cops, he only showed up on Mondays and Thursdays. Well, today was Thursday and she was expecting him to show up. V-103 was playing the latest Kanye track that featured Rihanna and Charmaine started singing along.

Turn up the lights in here, baby,
Extra bright, I want y'all to see this
Turn up the lights in here, baby
You know what I need
Want you to see everything
Want you to see all of the lights

Charmaine was so into the song, she didn't see the man come up to her car and tap the window.

"Excuse me, Ma'am. I'm going to need you to turn that music down." It was him. Detective Blair.

Charmaine let the window down. "I'm sorry, Sir. I didn't realize I had it up that loud."
Damn. He looks even better up close. "It won't happen again. Scouts honor."

"May I ask why a beautiful lady such as yourself is sitting in her car, in front of a sports bar, instead of being inside, where men can lavish you with compliments and drinks?"

119

Charmaine looked at her watch. "Well, I was waiting on some friends but I didn't even realize it was so late. They must not be coming. Wish they would've called to let me know something." She started her car. "You have a good evening."

"Wait. Don't go. Stay. Have drinks with me," the detective asked.

"Well," she spit out. "I guess it won't hurt."

"My name is Keenan. Keenan Blair," he extended his hand to her after she got out of the car.

"Like Keenan and Kel?"

"I see you got jokes. But yes. And yours?"

"Zabria Moreland. Nice to meet you."

"Anybody ever tell you that you look like Rihanna with your hair red like that?"

"Not yet, since this is the first day I'm sporting this look. But, thank you. I'll have to tell stylist. That's the look he was going for."

"A man did this? He must be uh, gay, huh?"

"Yes, he is, but I don't judge him. He has a kind heart and blessed hands."

"I see. Let's go inside, shall we?"

The couple found a booth in the back away from the bar and the large plasma televisions where most of the noise was. It was peaceful and cozy so they could talk. Charmaine enjoyed the conversation with him. He was witty, charming, very intelligent and sexy as a mofo. He told her that he was a police detective and she truthfully admitted that she was a medical student. They instantly hit it off. There was a real sexual energy between the two, and at the moment, it was unbearable. Slight touches on the hands, the hungry looks they exchanged. It was all there. Charmaine almost came unraveled when Keenan whispered in her ear. His soft lips grazed her lobe and his cool breath caressed her neck. She was horny as hell.

Donnie had been the only person she had slept with in almost four years but it had been about six years since Charmaine had been with a man. Her pussy was probably virgin tight. She wasn't sure. But one thing she did know was that she wanted this man to run up in her. Now.

Without a doubt…she was going to have him tonight!

"I know you probably came here to watch the game, just like me. Me and my friends always end up eating and talking like you and I just did." They both laughed. "I figured I'd miss it, so before I left my house, I set my DVR to record it. You wanna come over and watch it?" *Please say yes! Please say yes!* She begged inwardly.

"Are you sure you don't mind? I wouldn't want to impose," he said, trying not to appear too excited. He was hoping that their evening would continue. Zabria Moreland was sexy and beautiful and she had her own. Independence in a woman was an aphrodisiac to Keenan. They had just met and he didn't know too much about her, but he liked what he saw so far and was interested in learning more. Much more.

Charmaine told him that it would be her pleasure to watch the game with him and the two of them left Logan's. *I see he's not in his cop car today*, Charmaine thought, watching him climb into a burgundy Nissan Armada. The truck looked good on him. He followed Charmaine the three short miles to her condo and was impressed when he pulled in behind her.

"Wow. Nice place," he said.

"Thanks. Come on in."

She took his coat and offered him a drink after she gave him instructions on how to find the game she recorded. A few commercials had taped and he was watching those when she sat his drink in front of him.

"You can fast forward through commercials. That's why I tape 'em. I don't want nothing coming between me and my Falcons."

"I feel the same. Thanks for the drink."

"You're welcome. I'll be right back, I'm going to jump in the shower if you don't mind. I was at the hospital before I went to the bar and I need to wash that place off of me," she said.

"Go ahead. I'll watch something else until you get back."

Charmaine ran excitedly to her bathroom and turned on the water. She pulled out a $350 perfume and bath set she bought at

Bloomingdale's, called Creed. The perfume was off the chain and the bath gel wasn't too far behind. Careful not to take too long, Charmaine hit all of the essential spots and shaved the excess hairs off her mound.

"Just in case, I don't want him to get any hair in his teeth." she snickered. Ten minutes later she was clean and smelling very good. Charmaine put on a long silk Kimono with nothing else on underneath. She secured the belt and went into the living room.

"Whew, I feel so much better. Ready to watch the game?" She asked.

"Uh, yeah. Sure."

Charmaine sat on the opposite side of the sofa and pulled her feet under her. The kimono opened in a split, all the way up to the top of Charmaine's thigh. Keenan looked at the creamy thigh and licked his lips. He took his hand and adjusted his collar trying to let some cool air in. It was getting hot in there.

"Is there something wrong, 'Bria?" Keenan asked, comfortable enough to assign her a nickname.

"Actually, there is. I think I just got bit by something on my thigh. It's stinging. Can you see a bite?" She asked, presenting her thigh to him as she stood up.

Keenan leaned in close. Charmaine could feel his cool breath on her thigh. It traveled up to her womanhood, warming her center. Before Keenan could answer, Charmaine asked him to kiss her thigh.

"What?"

She repeated herself. "Kiss it. Make it all better, baby."

Softly, Keenan kissed Charmaine's thigh. He rolled his tongue in circles over the spot she pointed him to. He kissed her inner thigh sensuously, then, in an impetuous move, he began kissing further up her thigh. Heat permeated between her nether lips. Moisture formed and began to drip from her sweet center. A little ran down her thigh and Keenan lapped it up with his tongue.

"Damn. Is that peaches I taste?" He asked. "That's my favorite fruit."

Smiling down at him, Charmaine didn't say a word. Donnie used to tell her she tasted like peaches all the time. That was because she made an all natural douche using nothing but peach juice and water. Donnie's loss was Keenan's gain. The sexy detective put his hands on Charmaine's ass and pulled her into his mouth while he sat on the sofa.

"Oh, my." Charmaine moaned. His thick tongue was long and hard and curled when it entered her. Donnie had never done it like that.

Keenan leaned back on the sofa. "Sit right here," he commanded her, pointing to his face. Charmaine waited until he slid down enough for her to climb on. Her round ass cheeks fit perfectly in his hands as he squeezed and kneaded them in circular motions while he ate her out.

"Ooh, Keenan. Yes, baby, yes!"

He inserted two fingers inside her wet snatch and moved them back and forth. She pressed down and gyrated on his mouth. Charmaine was on the verge of popping. Keenan removed his two fingers and replaced it with his thumb. He massaged her hard nub and inserted his middle finger into her ass. His dick was rock hard and straining to burst out of his jeans. Using his free hand, Keenan unfastened his belt buckle and unbuttoned his Levi's.

"Hmmph," he grunted as his member popped out.

Charmaine turned around to see the impressive, thick, ten inch dick.

"All that's you?" She panted in pleasure. It had been a minute since she beheld a real penis.

"Yeah and it's all yours," he mumbled. Keenan sucked loudly on Charmaine's clit. The delicious sound of sex sent Charmaine over the edge and she came in Keenan's mouth. Slowly, she descended from Heaven back to Earth.

"Are you ready for yours now, babe?" She asked Keenan. Not waiting for his answer, she got down on her knees and took his stiff meat into her mouth. Charmaine spit on his dick and got it soaking wet. She knew she was going hard because his legs began to shake and he couldn't form any words, only inaudible noises.

"I-I-I'm close baby. I'on wanna come like that. Come here," he said, pulling her mouth away from him.

"Before I board the train, lemme do this." Charmaine took

the condom wrapper out of Keenan's hand and opened it. She took the tip that was sticking out and sucked on it and put the rim of it under her lip. Looking devilishly into Keenan's eyes, Charmaine put the rubber in her mouth, leaned over and rolled it down the length of his shaft.

"I've never seen anything like that before in my life," he admitted.

"Stick with me, baby and I'll teach you a few things,"

Charmaine climbed on top of Keenan and positioned his hardness at her entrance. Sensing her apprehension, Keenan, pulled her down to his mouth and kissed her deeply.

"I'll go slow. You told me it's been a while."

Reassured, Charmaine began to relax. She took off her camisole and let the fullness of her breasts spill out. It had been years since a man caressed her the way Keenan was. He entered her gently and began a slow dance with their bodies. As much as she used to love Donnie, Charmaine knew that she could easily get used to this. This man was a very skilled lover and unlike Donnie, he took his time. Only when Charmaine increased her pace, did he speed up.

"Zabria, your pussy is too tight. I'm finna cum," he growled.

"So am I," she panted as she threw her pussy to meet the thrusts of his dick. In sync, the two lovers came. Juices flowed from Charmaine like a river. The strangers just laid in bed, staring at one another, amazed at the magic they just made.

"That was amazing. But uh, was it a one-time deal?"

"That really depends on you," Charmaine said honestly and also putting her guard up. "This isn't typical of me. I mean, I felt an instant connection with you at the sports bar, like I'd known you forever, but I don't wanna read anything into it."

"What if I told you that I felt the same way and that I don't want this to end, Zabria? I'd like to see where it could go."

"I'd say, let me show you to the bedroom,"

A few hours later, Charmaine lay in Keenan's arms, spent. He worked her body like a real man. She really did like him and was excited about dating a man again. The fact that he was head of the Bizarre Crimes Division, which was investigating all of her, or rather, Charmaine's criminal acts, was just icing on the cake. She planned on seducing him but liking him was a bonus. Now with him on her side, Donnie's days were numbered. Before she nodded off, a tune popped in her head *"I'm on some new shit, chucking my deuces up to her, I'm moving on to something better, better, better, and now it's Donnie's turn to hurt. Symone is going to say, bye-bye, say bye- bye, say bye- bye to her."*

AveryGOODE

Chapter Fourteen

Slipper's Count

Charmaine was still high from her night with Keenan. That man learned what turned her on very quickly. She hated to compare him to Donnie but the only thing that Donnie had on him was the fact that Donnie's dick stayed harder longer. And that's only because it was fake. No, there really was no comparison. One thing that Charmaine loved was that she could be completely transparent with Keenan. She loved the fact that he knew her real name and what she really looked liked. This morning, she hated putting her disguise back on.

I'm going to do away with Charmaine Franklin very soon. Everything is almost over.

There was a lot of trash littering the street, Charmaine noticed, driving down the block of her other house. That was one of the woes of having a house in a mixed income neighborhood. Not everyone cared about how they lived. Some of the yards were unkempt and it seemed every other house had a broken down car in the driveway or in front of the house. Charmaine's next door neighbor's yard was pristine. Ms. Tucker, who was about 85 years old, was in the yard, daily. Pulling weeds, planting or pruning flowers, edging her grass. You name it, she did it. She was a nice old lady but she was nosey as hell. Charmaine had to be very careful around her because the woman was always looking.

Charmaine pulled the 1997 Chrysler Cirrus into the driveway and went to check the mail after she got out. She got to the front door and lifted up her welcome mat. All of the little baggies she had in place were still intact.

"Hmm, no one's been over. That's always good," she said, picking up each piece off the ground.

"Hey Charmin," the elderly lady said from her yard. "If you having a party tonight to bring in the New Year, tell your company not to walk across my yard. I just planted some new flowers."

"Yes, Ms. Tucker. I'm going out with a few friends, I'm not having company." Charmaine didn't bother correcting the name mistake. Inside the house, she heard a soft chirp that came every few seconds. The smoke alarm needed a new battery. Charmaine made quick work of tidying the house and cooking a meal for herself and her houseguest. In order for her plan to work, she was going to need a lot of the video footage she had made. Although the film was labeled, it was going to take too long to go through it, so she gathered it all up and packed it in a large duffle bag. There were a few new pairs of shoes and outfits that Charmaine forgot to take to her other place, so she loaded those up as well. It took a couple of trips but everything that she wanted from the house was safe in the trunk.

There was a bag sitting by the door that Charmaine brought in from the car. There was a bag sitting by the door that Charmaine brought in from the car that contained groceries.

Charmaine put the food away and began preparing dinner which consisted of oven grilled ribs, store bought potato salad and homemade baked beans. While the food cooked, Charmaine sat at her computer and edited the video footage she had been taping. Carefully, she spliced some of the short clips and combined them, making them one long video. She altered a few of the digital still images and made it appear that Donnie was in a few places where a few heinous crimes occurred. When the time was right, Charmaine was going to make sure the videos ended up in the right hands

"Shit! I forgot about dinner." Charmaine went back into the kitchen and checked the meal. The ribs were perfect but the beans were lightly scorched. If the temperature hadn't been on low, they would have burned.

Feeling benevolent, Charmaine fixed Angela a generously portioned plate with a dessert and a coke. It was New Years Eve so she might as well bring the New Year in with a good meal. Thankfully, Charmaine, or rather Zabria, had a date and wouldn't have to sit at home when the peach dropped. It was quiet in the basement. The only light that was on came from a night light that was in the hall. Angela was lying in bed. It looked like she was asleep but she was staring at the ceiling.

"Angela, I have dinner for you," Charmaine said.

"I'm not hungry."

Charmaine flipped the light on. "Wow, you don't look too good," she said. Angela's complexion was sallow and her lips were darker than normal.

"You need to eat," Charmaine insisted.

"No, I need to go home," Angela yelled.

"Who the fuck are you yelling at?"

Angela tried to sit up but she was weak. She did need to eat. "I'm sorry. I'm just hungry and I've been cramping. I'd like to eat now, please."

"Now, that's more like it. Look what we have here. A rib-eye steak, tossed salad, and a baked potato. After that, you have a hefty slice of chocolate crunch cake and an ice cold cola. Not bad, huh?"

To tired to speak, Angela just nodded her head. Charmaine took the cuffs off of her guest's hands and cuffed her feet instead. Angela was hungry. With each bite she ate, the more strength she gained. After she was finished, she asked Charmaine why she was holding her there.

"I told you, because you fucked Donnie and tried to play house with her. I had been watching you like I do all my prey. I used the information that you gave Donnie against you."

"What do you mean?"

"Well, you told Donnie you needed to gain clients for your decorating and design business. You left cards at her house and I helped myself to one. I knew you'd jump at the chance to come and give me an estimate on a design job."

"Is your name really Jasmine?" Angela asked.

"Nah. There's not too much about me right now that is real."

"How can you do something like this and think you'll get away with it?"

"It's as easy as taking candy from a baby. You find out your opponents weakness and then you capitalize off it."

Tears ran down Angela's face. "Please let me go. I have family who depends on me and wants me back."

"Damn! I forgot to check in with them for the past two weeks. You right, they may be worried now. Shit!"

"How long have I been down here?" Angela asked. The days and nights just melted together when you were imprisoned.

"Since before Thanksgiving."

"How long do you plan on keeping me here? What are you going to do with me?"

"I don't know to both questions. I was going to kill you."

"Kill me? Please don't. If you let me go, I promise I won't tell anyone anything. I just wanna go home. I'm begging you. I'll do…"

Charmaine interrupted her. "Blah, blah, blah, blah, blah, ooh ooh, wee wee," Charmaine mumbled, plugging her ears. "I don't wanna hear this," she said and got up and walked out.

"Come back here and listen to me!" Angela screamed. This was the first time she had displayed an act of bravado. She shook her feet vigorously, rattling the cuffs against the brass bed. "Let me go! Let me go!" She yelled.

"This bitch don' lost her mind," Charmaine said of the noise that filled the house. She was about to go back downstairs when someone knocked on the front door.

"Who is it?" She yelled.

"It's Mrs. Tucker, dear."

Fuck! What does her nosey ass want?

"Yes, Mrs. Tucker? How may I help you?"

"Well, I was in my backyard garden and I heard a bunch of yelling and banging. I came over to see if you were okay." The old lady peaked around Charmaine, trying to look into the house. "You

130

are okay, aren't you?"

"Yes, Mrs. Tucker, I'm fine. It's just me and a few friends having band rehearsal."

"That's funny, I didn't see anyone come over and I didn't know you were in a band. Where did they park?"

"They came over when you went in for your nap. Yes, we've had a band for a year now and they took the metro. Anything else?"

Knowing that she was pushing it, the old lady said there was nothing else and went home. Charmaine slammed the door, angry that Angela had brought attention to her house.

"I'll show this bitch who's boss!" Charmaine grabbed a tube of KY Jelly, a metal vibrator and a small whip. "She's gonna pay for this."

Charmaine stomped angrily downstairs.

"What the fuck do you think you're doing?" Charmaine yelled.

"Let me go!" Angela yelled, flailing her arms because they were free. Charmaine hadn't put the cuffs back on.

Angela was wilding out and Charmaine needed to control the situation. Charmaine leaned back with the small whip in her hand and brought it down hard on Angela's legs. Angela squealed like a pig as Charmaine continued to whip her.

"Be still, heifer, before I really give you something to cry about."

Angela immediately stilled. Charmaine took one cuff off Angela's foot and put it on her hand. Angela's fist was balled up and squeezed tightly so when Charmaine put the cuff on it was not as tight as she thought it was. Then she put the next cuff on.

"You've been a naughty girl, Angela, and you're going to get punished."

Charmaine hiked her skirt up, showing Angela her ass.

"You like that?" She asked, making her ass cheeks clap. "You didn't think I could twerk, did you?" Charmaine leaned over and bounced her ass and rolled it around, before she climbed in bed with Angela.

"You know what time it is, bitch," she said, pushing Angela

on her back and sitting on her face. "Eat!"

Angela sucked and nibbled on Charmaine like she had in times past. Only this time, Charmaine wasn't getting turned on, at all.

"STOP!" She yelled. Her body wasn't responding to anything Angela did. Normally, she was so wet, it felt like she was peeing on herself, but today, nothing.

Could her body be desensitized to a woman's touch after only one night with a man? *Nah,* she shook it off. But something was going on.

"Your ass better thank God, I have a date tonight. That was some slick shit you did," Charmaine said pulling her skirt down. I'll deal with you next year," she laughed.

"N-n-next year?" Angela stammered.

"Yeah, tomorrow. It's New Years Eve, stupid. I told you that. Now, I'm going to leave you here. But if I come back and Mrs. Tucker is at my door, I will bury you in my backyard. Alive."

Charmaine ran upstairs, jumped in the shower and prepared to leave. She was excited about seeing Keenan again. They had been texting all day. Smiling, Charmaine laid her liquid filled a variety of baggies on the porch, covered them with the welcome mat, locked the door and left. She drove the older car four blocks from her Atlantic Station home and walked the rest of the way. She had a feeling that tonight was going to be a good, good night.

In the basement of Charmaine's home, Angela shook with fear. She didn't make one sound until she was sure the house was empty. In her haste to leave, Charmaine had left the tube of KY Jelly lying next to Angela on the bed. The hand cuff on the right hand was not as tight as normal but it was still a bit snug. Determined to get out, Angela folded her thumb into the other fingers and pulled with all her might. There was a distinctive sound of a bone breaking but Angela didn't care. Her hand was free. Crying silent tears, she picked up the lubricant and greased her other hand. It slid out with less resistance.

"I'm free," she whispered.

Angela tried to stand up out of the bed but collapsed. She had been lying down for so long her legs were weak. The cigarette burns and smalls cuts that were all over her body made it hard to walk.

"I've got to get out of here, before she comes back."

Since she was already on the floor, Angela stayed there. She crawled out of the room that had been her home for months. It must have been some date, because Angela knew that the door was usually locked. *God has made a way to escape for me*, she thought. It was dark in the basement with the exception of the light that was coming from the room she had been locked in.

Sore, but trying to move as fast as she could, Angela saw a utility room. There were clothes in the dryer and a muddy pair of tennis shoes on the floor. She found some clothes to put on and slid her feet into the sneakers that were half size too big but she didn't care. All she needed was something cover her body so she could leave. There was a door in the basement that had a regular lock on it. Wasting no time, Angela opened the door and got out of there.

Fresh, night air slapped her in the face and almost took her breath away.

"Thank you, God!" She cried.

There was no one outside. She limped towards a neighbor's house but decided against stopping. She'd been locked up too long to stay near that house of horror. Mustering up all the strength she could, Angela took off running down the street. All she could hear was the beat of her heart and the sound of her feet hitting the pavement. Angela was running away from pain and agony and running towards a life of freedom.

I'll never mess with another bitch again, she thought as she rounded yet another corner. Angela wasn't even in to chicks. Donnie was just so charming and sexy that she ended up giving in to the persuasive stud. Before they ever made love, Donnie had asked her if she ever licked pussy before. Angela had told her no and that's when Donnie had called her a pillow princess.

"What's that?" She remembered asking.

"A pillow princess is a lesbian or bisexual chick who just likes to receive and not give," Donnie answered.

No, Angela wasn't going to put her mouth on another woman's pussy. She had no idea that a few weeks after that conversation she would end up being a sex slave and forced to eat pussy just about every day. It was going to take some time for Angela to heal; physically and mentally. What was important was that she was alive. The lights of Interstate 75 were ahead. *I'm almost to safety*, Angela thought. She was panting, out of breath and thirsty. She hadn't drunk anything in a couple of days. But that wasn't important right now. The familiar sign of a Chevron gas station loomed ahead. She was almost there.

Angela's legs were beginning to feel like jelly and she was beginning to feel nauseous. Her legs were so heavy she tripped over a rock because she couldn't lift her feet. *Now I know why girls always fall in scary movies and end up dead.* Angela was living her own real life scary movie. A few cars were coming down the street and Angela ducked behind a dumpster in case it was her kidnapper looking for her. The cars whizzed by and took off running again. There were a lot of people at the gas station when she got there.

"Help me," she said but she was too hoarse. No one heard her.

She took a few more steps, grabbed the door handle, and passed out inside the store.

Chapter Fifteen

Before The Peach Drops

Never in a million years did Domynique Segar imagine that she would be living the life that she was now. Living in the lap of luxury in a Buckhead mansion, shopping at all of the finest stores, engaged to one of Atlanta's most eligible bachelors, all while carrying his child. This was a very good life. And it was all a lie. Domynique stood in front of the full-length mirror in her black, silk Versace dress that had a thigh-high split and diamond shaped cut-outs in the front and back. The black and gold triple platform Versace heels that she wore accentuated her thick legs and gave them definition. The couture outfit that she wore cost more than she used to earn in six months. As happy as she should have been, she wasn't.

Domynique felt like all this came about as a result of her deception. The love she had for Keyon was real but was the love he had for her? Had it not been for Domynique, she was sure that Keyon and Symone would be headed to the altar. That it would be Symone standing here, rubbing her abdomen that carried the life inside, instead of Domynique. With her conscience getting the best of her, Domynique knew she could not go into the New Year with the secret of knowing why Keyon was set up and how. Even if it meant losing him, she had to tell him. And there was no time like the present because Keyon had just walked into the room.

"You are so beautiful. I'm going to be the envy of all the

men tonight," he said, coming up behind her. His long arms draped around Domynique's shoulders and he kissed the top of her head. "I love you so much, Dom. You and this little one right here," he ended, rubbing her stomach.

"I love you too, Keyon. Um, baby can we talk?" Domynique asked and dipped out of Keyon's grasp.

"Sure, what's up?"

"I need to tell you about what I've been holding on to, so that I know if all of this is real," Domynique's hand flourished.

"What do you mean if all of this is real?" Keyon didn't understand.

"All of this baby. This new life I have, your love for me, us! Is all of this real or did I win your love by default? Since you can't be with the one you love, you might as well love the one you're with?" Keyon was really confused now. "I can't go into the New Year wondering and I really need to get this of my chest."

"Domynique, where is all of this coming from? You know I love you. I don't know how many times I can tell you that. Fuck, or even show you!"

"Baby, I know you love me. God knows I do. But I've got to tell you what happened because, maybe, if I hadn't done what I did, you'd be doing all of this with Symone and it would be her who was having your baby and not me, " Domynique finished in a whisper. "I can't go into the New Year feeling like I'm living a stolen life. Please, just sit down and listen to me," she cried.

Keyon sat down and said, "Go ahead. But before you begin, please know that there is nothing that you can tell me that is going to stop me from loving you."

I hope so, Domynique thought before speaking. "I was hired by a lesbian stud named Donita Stone to sleep with you. It's not something that I wanted to do but I didn't want to go to jail."

Keyon looked as if he was getting ready to speak but Domynique put her hand up to stop him.

"I didn't know this at first, but Stone was obsessed with Symone and she would have done anything to have her. Stone knows a lot of women and has a way of getting people to do what she wants. Including me. You know how I used to work at Saks in

Phipps Plaza? Well, so did Stone, in loss prevention." Keyon was starting to catch on as he listened intently.

Domynique continued, "After Britain died, I lost my mind and started skimming money from the register so that I could bury her. Stone had been watching me all along and instead of taking me in to the office, she blackmailed me."

"And that was setting me up?" His clipped words let Domynique know he was pissed off.

"Not at first. At first she just wanted to…" Domynique's voice trailed off.

"Wanted to what, Dom?"

Domynique was embarrassed but said quietly, "She wanted to eat my pussy and tape it."

"The fuck?"

She put her hands up to still him. "My job at Saks was seasonal. After that, I got laid off but Stone didn't let me off the hook. She tracked me down somehow, reminding me that she was still watching me and gave me a prepaid cell phone. Told me to keep it in case she needed me, and so I did, still scared she would report me. Months went by before I heard from Stone again and then out of the blue, she called with this plan."

"Did she tell you I was engaged?"

Domynique detected hurt in his voice and it made her cry harder.

"No. I didn't know anything about you. Not your name, what you did, nothing. She said that you owed her money and refused to pay. Blackmailing you was the only way to get it."

"And how much were you offered?"

"Five grand. I know it wasn't a lot but I was sharing a tent with another lady. We slept under I-85 at the Grady Curve. I was going to rent me a cheap apartment and try to put my life back together with it."

"You were going to put your life back together by ruining mine?" Keyon barked angrily. He got up out of the chair and started pacing back and forth.

"Yes. I mean no. Jesus! I'm so sorry, baby. I never meant to hurt you. Stone never told me that this was about breaking you and

Symone up. I only figured it out after the fact. My back was against the wall. I didn't want to do it. But after I saw you lying in the bed, I did want to make love to you. You were so handsome. I'd never seen a man like you before and with the way things had been going for me, I didn't think I would. There was something about you, baby, that drew me to you." Symone was sincere.

Domynique caressed Keyon's cheek when she said that. He understood because he felt the same way. Even through video, Domynique's magnetism drew him to her. But he didn't tell her that.

"I don't understand how Stone set all this up, though."

"Stone had a girlfriend whose mom owned the staffing agency the hotel used that night to cater your party. That's how she was able to get close to you. She was a bartender that night. Another chick she messed with was a pharmacist and that's where she got the drugs from. Apparently, Stone made a signature drink for you and spiked it."

"I remember that. That was a woman bartender? I could have sworn that was a man."

"She works very hard to appear as such. Anyway, after you were drugged, Angel, who had been attending your party, escorted you upstairs."

"Hey, I remember that," Keyon snapped his fingers. "A pretty Latina chick?"

"Yes, that's her."

"What did they give me? I can remember some things but not others."

"Rohypnol and Lithium. They call that a Mindless Mickey. Out of it enough not to know what you're doing but lucid enough to enjoy it. That's why you were able to perform so well. It's like an Ecstasy pill with memory loss."

Keyon was breathing loudly. "But you were a virgin. Why would you do this? Why me?"

"I told you, I didn't wanna go to jail. Stone painted a horrible picture of what would happen to me if I didn't cooperate and when she offered the money, I couldn't refuse, Keyon. And you were in the way of Stone getting what she wanted. Symone."

"Hmmph, and now you're pregnant," he stated emphatically. "Awfully convenient."

"What! Are you implying that I got pregnant on purpose?" Domynique was devastated by his assumption. But she wanted to get the truth out. Good, bad or ugly, here it was.

"Shit, I don't know, did you? I don't know what to think right now. This shit is confusing."

By this time, Keyon was crying. He was shocked and confused. He did love Domynique with all of his heart. The words she just spoke pierced his soul so he could only imagine how she was feeling. He looked at Domynique doubled over in tears. Yes, he hurt her badly.

"After it was all over, I wanted to kiss you. Believe it or not, I fell in love with you. But Stone got angry with me and beat me up before we left the room. I never saw her again after that. She never paid me. I floated from shelter to shelter and then one day, Watson found me and brought me to you."

Keyon exhaled. "I fell in love with you, too. Watson found you because I needed to know what I was feeling while I watched that video and if it was real or because of the drugs. I need to know if…FUCK! FUCK! FUCK!"

"I love you, Keyon. Baby, please believe me."

"Save it, Domynique. This is bullshit!"

Keyon walked to the bedroom door and stopped when Domynique called his name. He didn't turn around while she spoke.

"Baby, please. Let's talk this out. I love you."

Keyon didn't respond with words. A low growl began in the pit of his stomach until it burst forth from his mouth. "Arghh!" He yelled and punched the wall, putting a hole in it.

"Please, baby, forgive me. I'm so sorry. Keyon don't go. Please don't go!" Domynique wailed, but Keyon didn't stop walking.

Just like all the other New Year's Eve's, Domynique would be bringing it in alone.

*Avery*GOODE

Chapter Sixteen

∙ ∙ ∙ ∙ ∙ ∙ ∙ ∙ ∙ ∙ ∙ ∙ ∙ ∙ ∙ ∙ ∙ ∙

New Year's Revolution

The mansion at Chateau Elan was elegantly decorated. Man of Steele Records was holding its annual New Year's Eve celebration and everybody who was anybody showed up. Jynx was very excited to be bringing in the New Year with the love of her life and soon-to-be-husband. Jonathan was behaving like his old self again and Jynx was happy. He came home the other day and apologized to her for being short and not giving Jynx the love and attention she deserved. Jonathan asked for Jynx's forgiveness and of course she forgave him. Afterwards, he made love to her in a manner that let Jynx know he was very sorry. Now here they were in one of the most beautiful places in Georgia, about to bring in the New Year.

Couples made their way to the dance floor as the band played smooth grooves. There were a lot of people there but not many who Jynx knew personally. Jynx and Jonathan swayed slowly to the music. Jonathan lovingly caressed Jynx's back.

"You are breathtaking this evening, babe."

"You're looking mighty dapper yourself, honey."

"Jynx, I'm ready to tie the knot. I don't want us to keep living apart. I'm ready to see this six pack of yours swollen with my seed." Jynx was elated to hear his true feelings since she was feeling confused lately, about everything.

"Seriously, Jonathan?"

"Yes. I've never been more serious about anything in my

life. There's a few loose ends I need to tie up real soon, but I'm ready." Jynx was elated and planted a wet kiss on his cheek. He looked down into her eyes and kissed her passionately as they writhed seductively on the dance floor. He spun her around and Jynx came face to face with Cha-Cha.

"Hey beautiful, don't you look gorgeous? I see you got your J-Lo going on tonight," Jynx told Cha-Cha.

"Yes, Lovely. And this *is* Versace. Who is this you're wearing? Alexander McQueen?"

"Girl you know your designers, don't you?"

"A queen has to," Cha-Cha laughed.

" Is Devine here, too?" Jynx asked, looking around for her friend.

"Yeah, he's here. He's supposed to be meeting his lover here."

"Really? Have you met him yet?" Jynx asked Cha-Cha. Devine had been elusive regarding his new man. Usually, he was quick to introduce his two best friends to the guy but this time, he had been keeping things under wraps.

"Nope. Devine has been very sneaky with this one. The other day though, the guy called the house phone and I answered it. He sounds a little like Jonathan on the phone but his voice is just a tad bit deeper. Devine almost chewed my head off when he realized that I was on the phone."

"You mean, you didn't hang up after Devine picked up? Nosey ass."

"I sure didn't. You know me, Jynx. I'm not nosey but I do have an inquiring mind and I wanted to know."

Cha-Cha laughed, playfully poking Jynx in her side as the slow jam ended. Jynx and Jonathan parted and she and Cha-Cha went to the ladies room while the men headed towards the bar. When the two ladies were on their way back to the bar, they spotted Michael, who looked preoccupied, but Jonathan was nowhere in sight, as usual.

"Where's Jonathan, Mike?" His cousin Jynx, asked.

"Last time I saw him he was headed to the john."

"Humph. Me and 'Cha-Cha just came from that direction

and I didn't see him." Jynx became suspicious.

"Well, this house *does* come with eight bathrooms, cuz."

"Right. I'm trying to find him before we are seated for dinner."

"You have plenty of time for that. Uh, babe, we got some things to handle," Michael said rushing off with Cha-Cha, leaving Jynx alone. Jynx spotted a girl from the gym where she and Devine worked out, so she walked over to speak.

"Hey, girl, how are you?" Jynx said.

"Oh, hey lady. What's up? I didn't know you'd be here."

"Yeah. My fiancé works at M.O.S. By any chance, have you seen Devine's ass running around here?" Jynx questioned.

"Yep, about ten minutes ago. He met up with a fine ass man. They are probably getting acquainted in one of the rooms," she winked. "If I wasn't married, and in love with my husband, I would give Devine a run for his money," she added. Jynx didn't say a word as a lump formed in her throat.

"You and Devine know how much I love Boris Kodjoe and that's what Devine's new friend looked like."

"B-b-bor...Are you sure?" Jynx said, trying to fight the wave of nausea that overtook her suddenly. Jonathan looked like Boris Kodjoe.

"Now, when have you ever known me to lie about a sexy ass man? Girl, what's wrong with you? You just turned four shades of green and ain't none of them cute. You might wanna go to the ladies room. I'll see you later. I need to go find my man." And so did Jynx.

She heard a bunch of hustling and bustling coming from the Grand Ballroom and assumed it was everyone getting ready to go into the dining room for dinner. Eating was the last thing on her mind. Since she didn't see Devine enter the ballroom, he must have entered another door. She was on a mission.

With every door she opened, her heart beat faster and harder. Her mind was racing and she felt like she was on a soap opera. This was not how her New Year's eve was supposed to go down. Hot tears ran down her face and her jaw was beginning to hurt because she was gritting her teeth so hard. From the throbbing vein in her neck to the heavy breathing, it was obvious that Jynx was angry. When she got to the last door at the end of the hallway, she held onto the doorknob tightly before opening it. She heard muffled, indescribable noises coming from inside. *This is the room*, she thought. Jynx hesitated.

Slowly, she twisted the knob and crept inside the room with the finesse of a cat burglar. It was dark with the exception of the light coming from under what she believed to be the bathroom door. Jynx removed her heels and carried them in her hand as she crept closer to the door. Bile rose to her throat and burned her esophagus in disgust at what she heard.

"Mmm, yes. You know how much I missed this big dick, daddy. Give it to me, baby," she heard Devine moan in pleasure and that was all it took to send her over the edge. With one quick twist of the knob, she pushed the bathroom door open and the knob punctured a hole in the wall when it slammed into it.

"Oh shit!" Devine said as he stood to right himself and pull his pants up.

"You could have knocked, shit!" Devine's partner said, reluctantly putting his still hard dick away. Jynx could not get over the audacity this man had. The same big dick that less than six hours ago, Jynx was riding. The same dick that she sucked on and drained dry, swallowing every ounce of cum, just as he liked. A dick that had been in a man's ass and in her mouth. Jynx snapped at the realization and started swinging wildly at both men with her six inch spiked Louboutins. She was flailing her arms like a windmill, her anger giving her strength to land hard hits on both of the men.

"What the fuck are you doing, Jynx? Stop this crazy shit." Devine yelled. "I was just having a moment with my man, damn."

"Your man? Your man! This is the hunk you been telling us about?" She yelled, still swinging. "Well, guess what? This bastard is my fiancé." Jynx started spitting on Devine's friend.

"Your what?" Both men yelled.

"No, Jynx, you got it all wrong. You're going crazy. This is *not* your man" Devine screamed.

The security guard who was making his rounds, heard the

commotion and radioed for back up because there was a distur-
bance in the west wing.

"Bitch! I ain't your man!"

"Oh, so I'm a bitch now?" She cried as she started pounding him in his chest with her small fist. He grabbed her hands and
squeezed her wrists tightly to end her assault on him. Hurt and pain
replaced her anger and soon her energy was zapped. All she could
do was lay her head on his chest and cry.

"How could you do this to me? I loved you so much. You
lied to me. All those suspicious calls and late nights at work. This
is what you were doing." Tears poured from Jynx as pain made its
way through her body. "Devine, you were supposed to be my
friend. My brother. I trusted you."

Devine was crying, too. "Sweet Tart, I swear, it's not what
it looks like. Please listen to me."

He and Jynx walked out of the disheveled bathroom and
sat on the bed just as Michael, Cha-Cha and security walked into
the room. No one paid attention to the man who entered quietly behind them.

"What in the hell is going on here?" Michael wanted to
know.

"You tell me and we'll both know," the man in question
said, coming out of the bathroom. He had small drops of blood on
his white tuxedo shirt from the scratches caused by Jynx's spiked
heel.

Michael recognized his good friend and walked over to him
and gave him some dap, followed by a long hug.

"Man, it's been too long. Thanks for showing up this time.
But do you have to cause a scene everywhere you go?" They both
laughed.

"I don't see shit funny! This muthafucka..." Jynx immediately started going off, she felt her life was ruined.

"Jynx, watch your mouth?" Jonathan said angrily, remaining calm but walking towards the man.

"Jonathan?" Jynx said confused.

"Again, what's going on in here?" Michael questioned.

Jynx rose up from the bed, looked in the man's direction

then towards Jonathan and back to the mystery man. Back and forth like a tennis spectator. She went to take a step, but passed out, landing comfortably on the bed behind her. It all happened so fast.

When she came to, it took a minute for her to get her bearings. Jynx was just about to ask what was going on but Jonathan beat her to the punch.

"What the fuck are you doing here?" Jonathan spewed with venom. Jynx knew he was angry because the vein in the side of his neck was throbbing and his voice was low and deathly calm.

"Surely, you didn't think I would stay away, did you? You didn't pay me *that* much money."

"Jonathan, what's going on here?" Jynx finally asked.

"Nothing. Let me handle this."

"Afraid she'll find out the truth about you?"

"Fuck you, man. I ain't scared of shit," Jonathan said.

"What is he talking about, Jonathan? What truth? Who are you?" Jynx was getting more upset by the minute.

"Isn't it obvious?" The man said.

"Get the fuck out of here!" Jonathan demanded. "Don't say shit. Just leave!"

"Nah. I'm happy and I ain't going nowhere."

"He sure isn't!" Devine added. "This is my man!"

"Devine, stay outta this. This doesn't concern you!"

"Anything that has to do with this man has to do with me. Believe that, boo!" Devine snapped.

Cha-Cha came into the room at that moment.

"What the fuck is this?" She asked Michael, looking incredulously at the scene unfolding before her.

The mystery man was about to open his mouth, but before he could, Jonathan charged him and punched him in the face. The two men landed hard blows on one another, hitting each other in the head, face and stomachs. The security guard ran into the room and joined Michael and Devine in their efforts to break up the fight.

"Stop this now!" Jynx cried, pulling Jonathan around to face her. "Tell me what the hell is going on? You've been acting fucked up for the past couple of months and I wanna know why? Is

146

he the reason?" She said, pointing to the other man. "Who are you?"

"Do you wanna tell her or do I have to?" The man said.

"I gotta make my rounds," the security guard said. "You got this?" He asked Michael who nodded 'yes'. "All right then, come on folks, shows over," he said, escorting the nosey party guests out of the hall way back to the ballroom.

"Jonathan," Jynx pleaded. "Please tell me the truth. Wait, is there someone else? You've been acting strangely. Hanging up the phone when I come into the room. Lying about where you've been. Staying out late. Are you seeing another woman? Or...man? Who the fuck is this look alike man?" She was talking so fast but the last word she spoke was barely audible.

"No. It's complicated," Jonathan began.

"This shit ain't complicated," the man began. "My name is Charles. Julian Charles Brandon and I'm your fiancé's brother. Five years ago, when your perfect man first came to Man of Steele Records, he got himself a girlfriend. 'Girl' being the operative word." Jonathan was with M.O.S. from the beginning gas Chief Financial Operator. He never thought, in a million years, his own twin brother would reappear to spill the beans. At least, not through a relationship with Devine.

"Shut up, man!" Jonathan screamed. Julian ignored him.

"His girlfriend happened to be the now Platinum artist, Destinie Shontay."

"What?" Jynx began. "Five years ago. But she just turned 21 two weeks ago," Jynx whispered as realization dawned on her.

Julian knew she was getting the picture but kept on talking so she would hear the truth in its entirety.

"Yeah," Julian said, nodding his head. "Your man had a little ass girl for a woman. They were fucking like rabbits and she ended up pregnant. When Keyon found out she was pregnant, he threatened to drop her from the label and she'd lose millions. Her money hungry aunt wasn't happy about that."

"Keyon? You mean he knew about this?" Jynx's heart was breaking that her cousin would withhold this kind of information about her fiancé from her.

"No. He didn't know. And this is where it get's interesting. The aunt took the girl to have an abortion but wanted hush money. Jonathan wouldn't give it to her. The woman said if he didn't, she would go public with a video tape of him and her niece fucking. It would ruin him."

Jynx looked over to Jonathan who had sat down and put his head in his hands. Hot tears streamed down her face. Cha-Cha and Devine came over to her and sat her down on the bed to console her.

"What happened?" Jynx asked.

"I didn't pay her," Jonathan cried. Jynx's heart melted, seeing her man in tears. " She sent the video to Fox Three News and then filed a ten million dollar civil suit against me. Authorities got hold of the tape and I was arrested. When I got out on bail, the aunt began texting me telling me how she was going to make millions off the tape and the scandal. She said that she was even going to write a book about it. My lawyer got the texts and was able to prove that she was attempting to extort money from me. He threatened her with criminal charges if she didn't drop the charges."

Cha-Cha and Devine listened and was dumbfounded. Michael, who knew the story, waited to see how it would play out.

"But what does this have to do with Julian?" Jynx asked quietly.

Jonathan exhaled before continuing. "When the criminal charges were filed against me, I told the authorities that it wasn't me who was in the video but my brother. He was arrested. I bailed him out and asked him to take the case for me. Keyon had worked so hard to get Man of Steele going and I didn't want to ruin his company before it took off."

He continued, trying to get through to Jynx, "Babe, I hired the best lawyer for my brother. I didn't think that they would find him guilty since Destinie told them it was consensual but…"

"But, his ass thought wrong. I fought the case for two years but was convicted of statutory rape and sentenced to three years in prison. In Georgia, anyone who engages in sexual intercourse with a person under the age of sixteen can face charges for statutory rape, even if the other person consents to the act. The only way I would've beat the case would have been to marry her. And of course I wasn't going to do that because I'm gay," Julian finished. "Is this why you've been acting funny?" Jynx asked her fiancé.

"Yes. When Julian came back to town, he wanted to meet you. I told him that I hadn't told you about him yet and to give me time. It fucked me up when he started dating Devine, of all people, because that's your best friend. I just knew he was going to tell him and then Devine tell you."

"But, why didn't you tell me, Jonathan? That's the question."

"I didn't know how. Every time we were alone I wanted to tell you, but I didn't want to lose you," he answered honestly.

"Devine, did you know?" Jynx asked her best friend.

Julian saw how much this hurt Jynx and didn't want to cause her anymore pain.

"No, he didn't know. I didn't tell him."

Cha-Cha looked at Devine and knew instantly that Julian was lying. Devine had been acting out of sorts like he always did when he was holding something inside. But Cha-Cha knew they were all trying to spare Jynx so she didn't say anything either.

"The phone calls, crazy hours and all that espionage was me trying to get my brother to keep this quiet," Jonathan admitted.

"Were you ever going to tell me the truth?"

"Yes. After you were Mrs. Jonathan Brandon. I've been riddled with guilt for what I allowed to happen to my brother." Julian looked at his brother and shook his head.

"Hmm, interesting. So lemme get this straight, I'm engaged to a man who had sex with a sixteen year old artist, lied about having an identical twin brother and paid said brother to stay away from him? Wow."

"Baby, I know it sounds bad but please believe me, I love you. Destinie and her aunt planned the whole thing. They lied to me about her age. I thought she was eighteen all that time. I didn't find out the truth until the A & R department began to market her. I told her I was ending things and that's when it turned ugly. I'm not a pedophile, babe. I swear."

"He's telling the truth about that, Jynx," Michael vouched for him. "I was there through it all. And before you ask, the reason I kept it to myself is because whatever you two have going on is none of my business."

"It's okay, Michael. Can you all please give me and my fiancé some privacy? We need to talk."

Cha-Cha, Devine and their mates left out of the room, leaving the couple to talk. Jynx's mind was swirling. She felt drunk. When she woke up the following morning, this was not the way she envisioned her New Years to turn out.

• • • • • • • • • • • • • • • • •

"Don't be in that bathroom all night, babe," Donnie yelled to Symone.

"I won't. Pinky swear."

"Mmm, hmmm. That's what you always say."

Donnie was pleased with the way things were going the past few days. Since Symone had said 'yes' to her proposal, things between the couple had improved 100 %. Symone was the attentive, caring and more importantly, giving woman she had been before and Donnie was elated. There hadn't been anymore issues from Symone's ex either. Just then, Symone's cell phone vibrated.

I just thought this muhfucker up; Donnie thought when she saw that the text was from Keyon.

"What this nigga want now?" She said, picking up the phone.

Symone, ur GF is the reason
we not 2gether anymore.
I got proof. Call me asap! Key

"Sonofabitch! This nigga ain't about to ruin shit now. We just got things back on track."

Donnie deleted the text message but was curious to know how Keyon found out. Symone did tell Donnie that Keyon was with someone else but she never said who. Donnie was interested in finding out.

"Babe, didn't you tell me your ex was with someone?"

Donnie asked, walking into the bathroom.

Symone knew better than to ask how Donnie knew so she just went along, "Yes. Oh, damn. I forgot to tell you that he's with that chick he cheated on me with in the video. Ain't that some shit? You were right. No one makes a sex tape with someone he doesn't know. Set-up, my ass. He knew that bitch all along," Symone ended bitterly.

Keyon was dating Domynique? Damn. No wonder he ain't tripping about Symone. Darling Nikki's pussy tastes like apple pie. I shoulda fucked her when I had the chance, Donnie thought. *But if she told this nigga about what went down, I'm gonna have to teach her ass a lesson.*

"Don't worry 'bout that nigga. I got you, babe."

"What are you doing?" Symone giggled as Donnie climbed into the shower with her.

"I know we have all night, but ain't nothing more important than this moment right here. Right now."

Donnie no longer had her arm in a cast. It was removed the day before and she was happy as hell and ready to fuck. Horny as hell, Donnie pressed Symone's body up against the ceramic tile wall and kissed her hard on the mouth. Symone's body was already moist from the water but her womanhood began to drip as well. Two of Donnie's thick fingers slid inside her and just rested.

"I can feel your pussy contracting on my fingers. That shit turns me on." Donnie removed her fingers from the heat and licked them. "Shit taste good, babe."

Donnie took the adjustable shower sprayer off the hook and trained it on Symone's clit. The pressure of the water caused tiny pulsating shocks to travel through Symone's body.

"Oh yes, Papi. Mmm, ahh."

Symone's ass gyrated under the water. With one hand, Donnie caressed Symone's breasts and flicked her nipples.

"Lemme get in that pussy," Donnie said, kneeling in front of her girlfriend. She dropped the shower sprayer and used both of her hands to part Symone's nether lips. At first, Donnie licked it like an ice cream cone. Then she sucked it like a lollipop. Donnie pushed three thick fingers inside of Symone and moved in and out in perfect rhythm. Symone threw her head back and enjoyed all that Donnie was doing to her. Keyon was still on her mind but for right now, it was all about her and Donnie. She'd bring the New Year in with her girlfriend but when the date changed, so would everything else. Symone was determined to get Keyon back by any means necessary.

"Oh, yes, Donnie. Nobody sucks it like you, baby. Mmm, yes."

Donnie loved the way Symone called her name when she was eating Symone's pussy. There was a slight vibrato in Symone's voice. Kinda like she was calling Donnie's name while standing in front of a blowing fan. It turned Donnie on every time. Donnie lifted Symone's leg and let it rest on her shoulder. She stuck her tongue inside of Symone's pussy and then concentrated on sucking the hard nub. When Symone's legs began to vibrate, Donnie she was on the verge of cumming. One hard suck later and Donnie was being showered with Symone's liquid heat. Not satisfied, Donnie picked Symone up and carried her to the bed. She put her strap-on in place and went to town in Symone's pussy. By the time they made it to the Midtown club where they had New Years Eve plans, it was ten minutes until the New Year.

Symone held on to Donnie's hand while they stood outside on the rooftop bar and watched the peach sway back and forth in the December wind. It was almost time. Everyone partied in Atlanta without a care in the world, but when the peach dropped, so would everything else.

Chapter Seventeen

My Boyfriend's Return

No one had to tell Cha-Cha that her ex-boyfriend was in her office, she could sense his presence. When Cleo stepped into the room, everything changed. It was as if a dark cloud settled over the place. Exhaling, Cha-Cha got up from her desk and went to meet him. He was famous for causing scenes and she didn't want him to bring that drama to her office even though she was the only one there.

"You're looking well, my love. Still working on New Year's Day, I see," Cleo said, kissing Cha-Cha on the shoulder.

"Don't do that, Cleo," Cha-Cha said, dipping her shoulder. "And not too much has changed about me." After everything that happened last night, this was the last person she wanted to see.

"Ah, I beg to differ. Quite a bit has changed. This time last year you had a dick. A big one, too. One that I loved yanking while I fucked that pretty round ass of yours."

Cha-Cha cringed at the visual that ran through her mind. Cleo saw the look on her face and knew that she was thinking of their lovemaking as well.

"Turns you on, doesn't it, my little Latin lover?"

"No. That was then. This is now."

"You know you miss this dick," Cleo said, rubbing Cha-Cha's nipple through her blouse.

"Will you stop that?"

"I see you're still playing hard to get."

"I'm not playing. I am hard to get. We're done."

"It ain't over until I say it's over. You are mine."

Cha-Cha rolled her eyes. "Cleophus, I'm with someone else and you're married with mistresses. I don't wanna be an option for you when I'm already someone else's priority."

"Cute. Been watching Ayanla again, I see. And I don't have mistresses, I just have…friends."

"Friends. Right. Cleo, I have work to do. What do you want?"

Cha-Cha knew why he was there. He wanted an answer. One she was not prepared to give.

"I still love you, Miracha. Where did we go wrong?"

"*We* didn't. *You* did," Cha-Cha pointed at her ex. "If you loved me so much you wouldn't have cheated. I knew you were married and I understood the arrangement you and your wife had, but all of the others, I couldn't take it."

"I'm sorry. This is why I'm asking you for another chance. This time I'll be better."

"Heard it all before," Cha-Cha sang. "And plus, it's too late."

Without warning, Cleo walked up behind Cha-Cha and put his arm around her neck. He squeezed lightly. It wasn't hard enough to make her lose her breath but it was tight enough for her to know that he meant business. Cha-Cha really never thought of fighting back simply because Cleo could take her down, easily.

"It's never too, late. And as long you have that pretty pussy between your legs, you will always be mine. Always, Miracha!"

"My heart and my body belong to someone else."

"Hmm, interesting. Did you leave him?"

"Leave who?"

"Don't play with me, Miracha!"

"No, Cleo, I didn't leave Michael. I love him. Why are you doing this?"

"Because you're mine and because I can."

There was no reasoning with Cleo. The more Cha-Cha tried to talk with him, the more frustrated she became.

"You're starting to piss me off."

"Better pissed off than pissed on," she retorted.

"Now look here, Miracha," Cleo said, jacking her up by the lapels. "I love you, but don't take my kindness for weakness."

"Kindness? You call forcing me to leave the man I love, who loves me back, kindness? Get the fuck out of here. This is unreal."

"I gave you a deadline. One that you obviously didn't take seriously."

"Cleo, I'm begging you."

"Oh, I want you to beg. But I want you naked on all fours with my dick in your pussy while you're doing it."

Slow tears streamed down Cha-Cha's face. Cleo wasn't trying to hear anything she had to say. "I can't do that," she whispered.

"Well, then you leave me no choice." Cleo pulled his cell phone out of his coat pocket and pushed one digit. Cha-Cha could hear the phone dialing as she stood there shaking. He pressed the speaker button and a man answered the phone.

"Yes, Boss?"

"Do it," Cleo said calmly.

"Done," the man replied and Cleo pushed the end button.

"Do what?" Cha-Cha asked, frantically searching for her cell phone.

Cleo didn't answer. Instead, he turned on his heels and laughed as he walked out of Cha-Cha's office.

"Cleo! Cleo!" She yelled.

Cha-Cha chased him to the main office, nearly slipping in her Manolos. He didn't stop or turn back around. As soon as he got to the elevators, one opened and he stepped inside. Before the doors closed, he blew a kiss at Cha-Cha. Cha-Cha ran back inside her office to the desk. She needed to call Michael and make sure that he was okay. Whatever Cleo was planning, it involved Michael and Cha-Cha needed to warn him. She picked up the phone and called Michael's office. His voice mail picked up and Cha-Cha heard a message saying Man of Steele Records was closed for the holidays.

"Fuck! I forgot it was New Year's Day. I'm the only idiot at work." Cha-Cha hung up and quickly dialed his cell phone. There was no answer but she left a voice message.

"Baby, it's me. Please call me when you get this message. My ex-boyfriend's back and he's starting trouble. Please call me, baby. It's urgent!" Reluctantly, Cha-Cha ended the call. Panic filled her as she paced back and forth trying to figure out what to do. She considered calling the cops but quickly dismissed the notion.

An uneasiness formed in her stomach so she dialed him again. Still no answer. Although she didn't leave a message this time, she waited for his answering machine to come on. Cha-Cha needed to hear his voice even if it was a recording. Something inside told her that she may never hear Michael's live voice again. She called him 14 times in a row and failed to get an answer either time.

Unable to concentrate, Cha-Cha decided to leave her office to go find Michael. She called his cousin Keyon to see if he'd heard from him. He hadn't. From the tone of Keyon's voice, she could tell he was going through something of his own. She didn't want to bother him with the details of her own mess. Shit was fucked up for Cha-Cha. *How could I have involved Michael in this foolery? I should've told Cleo that I left Michael just so I could take the heat off. Damn*!

For it to be a holiday, the traffic on Atlanta streets was almost as bad as it was on regular work days. Cha-Cha bobbed and weaved on Piedmont Road headed towards Michael's condo in Brookhaven, a small Atlanta suburb just outside of Buckhead. There were voices in Cha-Cha's head telling her that Michael was in big trouble. Thoughts of him lying somewhere bleeding to death made Cha-Cha scream out. She had to get to him and fast. She was so frazzled that she almost tuned out the song that began to play in her handbag. Cha-Cha pulled her cell phone out and shouted with joy! It was Michael.

"Hey babe, what's up? I have a ton of missed calls from you. Is everything all right?" Michael asked breathing heavily.

"Oh my gosh, Papi, I've been so worried about you. Where

are you? I need to see you now!"

"I just finished playing racquetball with my homie, Jules. Come up to the club and we'll talk. I'm gonna hit the showers."

"Okay, baby. See ya' soon." Telling Michael about Cleo was not something she ever wanted to do but she knew she had no choice.

Cha-Cha breathed a deep sigh of relief. He was just fine. A smile spread across her face as she drove the short distance to the racquetball club. Luckily, she was already headed in that general direction and wasn't far from him. Once she got there, she parked and went inside. The receptionist told her that Michael left a message for Cha-Cha to wait inside the café. Cha-Cha ordered a cup of coffee to help settle her nerves while she waited for her boyfriend to come out.

"What's good, babe?" Michael asked, kissing Cha-Cha on the top of her head before sitting down.

"Michael, I'm so glad that you're okay. I've fucked up," Cha-Cha admitted guiltily.

"What? Tell me what's going on." Michael's forehead scrunched up.

Cha-Cha explained Cleo's ultimatum to Michael and how her ex had been stalking her. She told Michael about Cleo coming over one morning after Michael left and threatened her.

"That fool put hands on you?" Michael questioned, angrily.

"Yes, but that's not important. I just needed to make sure that you were all right. If anything happened to you, Michael, I'd die. Especially, if it was my fault. How would I be able to live without you?"

"Baby Girl, don't worry so much. Nothing's going to happen to me. I promise. Now let's eat something."

Cha-Cha wished that she was as assured as Michael was. It was easy for him to be confident. He hadn't seen the look of pure evil in Cleo's eyes. Michael hadn't felt the touch of hatred. No, only Cha-Cha had and she was scared. To death. Careful not to let her fear show, Cha-Cha plastered a beauty pageant smile on her face and went along with the easy conversation. Michael looked at his woman and knew that she was more afraid than she let on. He wasn't a fool. He had done a little research on Cleophus Abignol and knew that the man was unscrupulous in his business dealings. The streets talked and everyone knew Cleo. Michael had also learned that Cleo had a fetish for young men.

Cha-Cha spent the next few minutes filling him in on the real Cleo. Apparently, Cleo belonged to a lifestyle group that supplied high class business men who catered to 'tops'. Michael didn't even know what a top was. It was Cha-Cha's best friend, Devine, who enlightened him. A 'top' was a man who gave sex. A 'bottom' was a man who received it. In the black community of Atlanta, some men didn't think they were gay if they were the one giving. Their reasoning was that gay men were the ones who were fucked in the ass. This is why the A-T-L had so many down low brothers. Their minds were all fucked up.

Michael also knew that Cleo was infatuated with Cha-Cha. Before her gender reassignment surgery, Cha-Cha was a very beautiful man. She had soft feminine features. Tiny hands, a small waist, high, naturally blushed cheekbones and big pouty lips. The stretch from male to female was not a long one for his new girlfriend. Michael didn't consider himself gay. He loved women. Cha-Cha had a pussy and that made her a woman. The doctors had even formed a clitoris in her vagina and Michael could make her juices flow like a river. Just thinking about her in that way, made his dick hard.

"What are you thinking about?" Cha-Cha asked her man. He had a strange look on his face.

"Honestly, diving my hard dick deep into your pussy."

"Funny. I was thinking the same thing."

"Well, let's go handle our business then."

"Where? Here? We can't do it here, babe."

"Shit. Watch us."

Michael escorted Cha-Cha to a private sauna. Before they went inside, he turned the temperature down. They'd make enough body heat on their own. Cha-Cha had never seen Michael's dick so hard. It was curled up tightly in his sweats and she couldn't wait to free it. Michael locked the door and pulled his sweats down. His hard dick sprang out like a jack-in-the-box.

"I'm glad I have on a skirt," Cha-Cha said.

She removed the flats she was wearing and pulled her skirt up just enough to climb aboard Michael's love train. She never wore any panties. Michael loved that about her. Cha-Cha was the perfect woman for him. She had all of the parts but no period. They could fuck everyday if they wanted to.

"Shit, I love how tight your pussy stays. It's like elastic. It just snaps back into place."

"Ah yes. It was made for your big dick, Papi. Only yours."

Cha-Cha wrapped her arms around Michael's neck and kissed him deeply on the mouth. This was exactly what she needed to take her mind off of Cleo. Michael knew that too, which is why he suggested this. Well, it was one of the reasons he did anyway. Cha-Cha's natural juices lubricated Michael's dick, making it easier for her to glide up and down. He could feel everything as she alternated between gripping and releasing his manhood with her vagina. It felt like a suction device was on his dick.

"Damn, girl, this shit feels good. Your pussy is hot!"

"Mmm hmm," Cha-Cha moaned. She couldn't form words at the moment. The friction of his log in her fire pit was sending her over the edge. The sauna was getting hotter with each stroke. Tiny beads of sweat dripped down both Michael and Cha-Cha's face. His large hands gripped her from behind and guided her up and down on his member. With each downward stroke, Cha-Cha's thighs slapped Michael's. All one could hear was slapping skin, moans and the suction noises from her wet box.

"Baby, I'm 'bout to bust!" Michael growled through gritted teeth as his nut sack got ready to explode.

"Cumming, too, baby," Cha-Cha panted.

The lovers came in sync with one another. Michael's head collapsed on Cha-Cha's breast and he rested there.

"That was amazing," Cha-Cha said.

"Wasn't it? We've got to come here more often. That's what I call a workout."

Cha-Cha giggled, got up and fixed her clothes. Juices were running down her legs. "I need to shower, my love."

"You can do that at home. I'm ready to go. We've got a few

more rounds to go. But come here, though."

Michael got up, pulled up his pants and sat Cha-Cha down. He got down on his knees and licked the juices off her legs. His tongue traveled up her thighs and rested on her nether lips. Michael sniffed her pussy and went in for the kill. He licked and sucked until he pulled Cha-Cha's juices out of her. She came so hard it made her legs wobbly when she tried to stand.

"Yeah, we gotta get home quick." she said.

As they exited the gym, a homeless man approached Michael and asked him for change. *It was odd, seeing a beggar this far north*, Cha-Cha thought but homelessness was an epidemic in Atlanta so she really wasn't that surprised. Michael told Cha-Cha he'd meet her at home as they walked to their cars. She heard a scuffle behind her and turned just in time to see the homeless man pulling the long blade out of Michael's stomach. The homeless man took off when Michael hit the ground and Cha-Cha ran over to him.

"Michael!" She screamed. "Somebody help me! Please!"

Blood seeped through Michael's fingers as he tried to press down on the hole in his stomach. His eyes pleaded with Cha-Cha to do something. A man came out of the gym and called 9-1-1.

"I love you," Michael stammered.

"Don't talk baby, save your breath. Help is on the way."

Small droplets of blood came out of Michael's mouth. Cha-Cha screamed in agony. If Michael died, she was going to die as well. But not before she killed Cleo.

Chapter Eighteen

Love Should Have Brought You Home

"Did you fuck her?"

"No."

"Are you back with her?"

"No."

"Do you want to be back with her?"

"No."

"Where've you been?"

"A hotel."

Unable to talk any more, Domynique broke down in tears. Keyon didn't even know she was awake when he walked into the room. She was curled up in a ball, wearing the clothes she was in last night. Sobs shook Domynique's body. Seeing her cry uncontrollably, hurt Keyon. Especially knowing he was the reason behind some of it. Regardless of how angry he was, he shouldn't have stayed out all night, he reasoned. All Domynique wanted to do was clear the air between the two of them so that they could start their New Year off fresh. But Keyon made this about him and the crazy thing was, he didn't even know why.

He had a pretty good idea that the video was a set-up even if he never knew the truth from Domynique, but he never expected this. Breaking him and Symone up just so Donnie could get with his ex was the last thing on his mind. But apparently, Donnie knew his ex better than he did, because it worked. Symone's leaving really was a blessing in disguise. If Keyon hadn't learned anything in the past 24 hours, he learned that.

"Baby, please don't cry. Look at me, Domynique," Keyon held her face between his large hands. "I love you. I am in love with you and regardless how you came to be a part of my life, I am so glad that you're here and I wouldn't change a thing."

"Are you sure?" She sniffled.

"I'm positive."

"Then why did you leave me? I thought you were going back to Symone."

"You don't ever have to worry about me going back to her. My relationship with Symone was over before you even came into the picture. I was just too stupid to let go."

"I love you, Keyon and never thought that I would have a man like you. Believe me, hurting you was the last thing on my mind when all that went down. It was about self preservation. Unfortunately for me, it was all for naught."

"Not really. You got me now and I ain't going to let anything happen to you or our baby."

Keyon walked over to Domynique, kissed her hard on the mouth and hugged her tightly. As dastardly as the deed was that brought Domynique to him, he was not inclined to lose her. The few short months with her have been better so far than the five years he had spent with Symone. Domynique was a beautiful sexy nymph who only had the hots for him. She was an impeccable cook and homemaker and he loved coming home to her. The other day, she came to the door with a French maid outfit on and greeted him with a kiss. Symone wouldn't have ever done that because she thought being a homemaker was belittling and repulsive. Domynique was a gem and everyone in his family loved her. Especially him. It made Keyon hard knowing that he was the first and only man who'd tasted her nectar. Domynique had made him happier than he'd been in ages and now she was about to make him a father.

"Sorry I ruined your New Year's Eve. You didn't even get to wear your beautiful dress out."

"Baby, I'm about to be your wife. That's the only beautiful

dress I'm going to need."

"You got that right," Keyon said, leaning down for another kiss. He began to caress Domynique's breasts through her dress and her nipples responded by getting hard like raisins.

"Mmmm," she moaned in his mouth.

Keyon's large hands caressed Domynique's thighs, raising her dress in the process. He used his thumbs to slide her panties down over her hips. When they were down, his right hand found the warmth of her center and his fingers began to play in the short curly tendrils of her pubic hairs. His long middle finger began to rub on her clit and Domynique's legs got weak. Walking her back towards the bed, Keyon laid his woman down after removing her dress, stroking her with purpose. Domynique responded by opening her legs. Her panties dangled from her foot and she kicked them off.

Slowly, Keyon trailed kisses over her body. He sucked on her neck firmly, leaving a hickey on her fair skin. Then he kissed and sucked her breasts, her stomach and finally his lips found the sweet cream they sought. Just as Keyon's nose rubbed Domynique's hard nub and his tongue flicked her lips, the couple heard a hard, police like knock at the door. Keyon kept going.

"Babe, it could be your parents. You should get it."

"They have a key," he said between licks.

"Keyon," Domynique said, scooting back. "We can pick up where we left off. Come on, babe," she said, grabbing her robe off the side of the bed.

Reluctantly, Keyon stopped and got up.

"I'on know why you wanna go downstairs. My parents have a key. It's probably one of my neighbors or a Jehovah's Witness."

"On January 1st? I don't think so."

By the time Keyon and Domynique got downstairs, there was no one at the door.

"See, I told you," Keyon said, puffing his chest out, believing he was right.

Domynique playfully punched him in the arm and said, "It's probably, Shymon or one of the guys playing. Watch."

Domynique yanked the door open, expecting someone to come from around the corner. Instead of finding a person, there was a beautifully wrapped gift sitting on the porch.

"Look babe, someone left a gift."

Keyon looked around the neighborhood and didn't see anyone outside. Other than a few neighbors' cars that were parked in their driveways, there were no other cars on the street.

"Let's open it, babe," Domynique said excitedly. She didn't wait for Keyon to make it to the family room before she started tearing the paper off and then the lid. Just as he walked up on her, she froze. There was an ashen look on her face as Domynique looked inside the box and then up at Keyon.

"What is it, Dom?" Keyon took the box from Domynique and looked inside. There was a clock inside the box that was connected to a small hour glass tube containing a pinkish-red liquid. The timer, which was attached, was counting down. The time began ticking the moment Domynique took the lid off.

"What have I done, Keyon?" Domynique was hysterical and crying.

"It's not you, babe. This is from Big."

"Look, we only have 45 seconds left! Let's go, babe!"

Keyon grabbed Domynique, who was still in her bath robe and the two hurried to the garage. Keyon's hands were shaking so hard he couldn't get the key in the ignition.

"Fuck!"

"Just breathe baby and calm down. You can do this. Now put the key in the ignition and let's go!" Domynique was trying to be the voice of reason.

Domynique looked at the time on her cell phone. Time was almost up.

"Dammit, Dom! These are your fucking keys!" Keyon yelled, realizing his fatal mistake.

Tears streamed down Domynique's face. It was about to be over for her and Keyon. But if she had to go, at least it was with the man she loved.

"I'm sorry, babe," Keyon cried. He pulled Domynique into him and covered her head. Neither was sure what the timer read, as they left the bomb in the house, but Dom knew they had seconds.

"I love you, Keyon."

"I love you, too."

They held on to one another and braced themselves for an explosion. Keyon didn't know how long he held onto Domynique but it was at least ten minutes. He didn't let her go until his cell phone began to vibrate. It was his mother so he answered it.

"Ma, what's up?" He clicked the speakerphone button, breathing heavily

"Baby," she said, obviously crying, "me and your dad just got this package. Son, we thought that we were goners."

"What? Was it a silver gift wrapped box?"

"Yeah, son, it was. Lawd, Jesus, we were so scared." Carolyn was sobbing on the other end.

"Mama, me and Domynique got one, too. We were trying to get in the car and leave the house but I grabbed the wrong damned keys. We're here in the garage holding onto each other for dear life. We thought that we were goners, too."

"Go inside, Son. There's a message inside the box."

"Okay. I'll call you all in a few. And Mom?"

"Yeah, Baby?"

"I thank God you all are okay."

"Same here, baby. Is Domynique all right?"

"Yes, Ma'am," Domynique said in the background.

"All right. Y'all go in and pray these demons away. Cover that house from top to bottom with Jesus' blood. Our New Year is going to be blessed. We're coming out of this nonsense."

Keyon was stunned. Exhaling loudly, he got out of the car and helped Domynique out. The box was on the floor by the family room where he dropped it. On the side of the clock was a little scroll that wasn't there before. It must have popped out when the time ran out.

Your time is almost up. Kaboom!

Hurt and anger overtook Keyon and he started punching the air. Big was not only fucking with him, he was messing with his family. When Keyon first borrowed money from Big, things were cool. It wasn't a very large sum but it was enough to get Keyon off the ground. Big was cool and seemed like a legitimate business man. After Keyon paid him back for the first loan, the seedy loan shark told him that he could always come back for more.

"You paid your loan off ahead of schedule, with interest. Keyon, my boy, your credit is good with me. Call again if you need to."

Only when he got bigger ideas for Man of Steele Records did he take Big up on his offer. An offer, in hindsight, he should have refused. But it was too late now. In less than four days, he was going to have to hand over two million dollars or he was going to lose everything that he worked hard for. Domynique didn't know what to say. She saw the hurt and anguish in his eyes. She walked over to him and placed her small hand on his back to still him. Keyon froze in place.

"Baby. We're going to be okay. Don't let this get to you. God will make a way for you. For us. We just have to trust him."

Keyon, knowing that she was right, dropped to his knees and sobbed. Domynique cradled his head in her arms and said a silent prayer for her fiancé. When he hurt, she hurt. Domynique didn't know she could love anyone the way that she did Keyon and she wanted to do everything in her power to help him.

"Do you have all the money to pay him back, babe?"

Keyon wiped his eyes with the back of his hand before responding. "No. And that's why this is all so fucked up, Dom. This man is out for blood and he doesn't want to hear any excuses."

"Do you think that he'd give you an extension?" The question seemed stupid, but Domynique was serious.

"I doubt it. This man wants to use my label as a front for other things that he has going on. It's all in our contract. He changed the timeline on me. He wants it now and he knows I don't have it. He's all but admitted that much to me. He wants the company too bad and he ain't fucked up about killing me to get it."

"How much do you need?"

"A million and some change."

"Damn. Well, you can take my car back. That'll give you some more money."

Keyon looked up at Domynique lovingly. He couldn't believe that she was willing to part with something that she so obviously loved just to help him. That was another huge difference between Domynique and Symone. One was selfless while the other was selfish.

"I'm not taking your truck, babe. I've got a few irons in the fire and we should be good. I'm just praying that this time when I pay him that it's all over. The last time I gave Big some money, he handed me some bullshit ass line saying 'it ain't over until he said it was over'. I haven't regretted much in my life. But this shit here. This has been the worst mistake of my life."

"Keyon, I love you and I have faith that God is going to provide a ram in the bush. That's something I just feel in the pit of my stomach." Domynique was growing with maturity by the minute.

"That's my son you feelin', girl," he said, rubbing Domynique's small pooch.

"Naw, that's your daughter, Sir.

"Son, daughter. It's my seed, woman."

"Indeed it is, man. Your family is hungry. You wanna grab something to eat?"

"Yeah. Lemme call and check on Mom and Pops. Then we can go. Any place in particular you wanna go?"

"No. As long as I'm with you, I'll go anywhere."

"How did I get so lucky," Keyon said, standing and hugging Domynique.

"I was just about to say the same thing myself."

Fifteen minutes later, Keyon and Domynique pulled out of the garage. His hand covered hers and he gave it a gentle squeeze.

"I don't care what I have to do; I'm going to protect you and our baby. Believe me."

"I do."

They drove down the street, passing a black Porsche Cayenne. The person in the front seat watched and waited. Keyon and Domynique had no clue that another threat loomed on the horizon.

Chapter Nineteen

Runaway Love

They say the best way to get over an old love is to get up under a new one. And Charmaine did just that. Ever since she, or rather Zabria, met Keenan, the two spent every free moment together. Keenan's conversation was great and the sex was even better. Charmaine felt like she was in a dream. But now, it was time to come back to reality. It had been a couple of days since she had checked on Angela and she knew it was time that she made her way over there. Before she left, Charmaine made sure to fill the hamster water dispenser that was attached to the brass bed and put some granola in the matching food dispenser next to it. Angela was able to reach the nozzles by tilting her head back and sucking on it. *That's the only way to feed a rat* Charmaine thought. Now that Charmaine was happy with Keenan, she thought about letting the hostage go. It didn't make sense for her to keep Angela cuffed in the basement all because of a fling with Donnie. Clearly Donnie had moved on with Symone and Angela wasn't even an afterthought in Donnie's mind. But as much as she wanted to let the woman go, she couldn't. There was a deep seeded need for revenge that flowed through Charmaine's veins. No, Angela was going to get hers. Just like Donnie.

Thinking of Donnie, Charmaine wondered how long it was going to take the Atlanta Police Department to act on the tips she had supplied them. Her anonymous calls about Morgan's disappearance piqued their interest and upon further investigation, the tips panned out. The police would be foolish not to believe anything else that came from 'a concerned citizen.' On behalf of all the lesbians and bi-curious females of Atlanta, Charmaine mailed in an envelope containing pictures and letters from women who had suffered some misdeed at the hand of Charmaine. But thanks to technology and ingenuity, Charmaine made it look like Donnie was the one who performed all of the acts of mischief. From the Nair in Sasha's hair conditioner to the destruction of property and acid burns that Lynn Shaw received, Donnie was going down.

And it will be my pleasure to help her, Charmaine said out loud.

"It'll be your pleasure to help who, babe?" Keenan said, fresh out of the shower.

"My neighbor. She just sent me a text asking if I would help her clean out her shoe closet. She said if I do, I can have my pick of any pair of shoes she has. Even her Louboutins."

"Cool. Listen, I know we were supposed to have lunch today but I gotta head to the station. Chief just called and told me to come in ASAP. He said some more evidence arrived from some random witness and he needs me to check it out. There may be something that can help me solve a few cases. I sure hope so because I need to lighten my case load."

"I hope so too, babe. I'll be praying for you," Charmaine said, rubbing Keenan's naked chest slowly.

"Stop that before Mr. Officer breaks out of jail and I lose my job."

"Lose your job? How?"

"If you keep messing with me, I'm going to call off of work and stay knee deep in your pussy forever."

"Okay, boy. Get dressed and get out of here before I lose control and help you stay in this pussy, 'cause that's what I like."

"Damn, that made my dick jump."

"Silly goose. I'm going to run a few errands. Will you be here for dinner?"

"No doubt. I'll pick up some wine."

"Cool beans. See ya' later, Boo."

• • • • • • • • • • • • • • • • •

Charmaine jumped in her car and made her way to the southeast side. The closer she got to her old house, the more she dreaded going.

I hate coming over here, she thought.

She pulled up in the driveway a few minutes later and turned the car off. Here I go again.

The mailbox had a few pieces of junk mail in it and she looked through it. The trash can was still at the curb from the other day and she pulled it back up to the house. Charmaine noticed that her neighbor was peeking out the door as usual.

"Good afternoon, Mrs. Tucker. How are you?"

"I'm just fine, Charmin. How are you? Haven't seen you for a few days."

"I know. I went to visit some friends in Florida," Charmaine lied.

Charmaine knew that the old lady knew how to say her name correctly but mispronounced it to get under Charmaine's skin. It worked. The two exchanged pleasantries for a few more minutes and then Charmaine made her way to the house. She stepped up on the porch and looked down at the welcome mat. It had gone undisturbed. Charmaine leaned down and picked up the miniature zip lock baggies that were filled with food coloring. She always left them at the door as a way to tell if anyone came up on her porch. In addition to the hidden security cameras she had placed around the house, this added an extra layer of security.

It was quiet inside the house when Charmaine crossed the threshold. Everything was just as she had left it. The clock in the dining room had stopped ticking because the battery had died but other than that it was all good. Charmaine sat her purse down on the sofa table in the foyer entry and made her way to the kitchen. She was pretty sure that Angela would be hungry so she prepared lunch. Since it had been a few days, Charmaine decided to make a hot meal instead of the cold sandwich that she was planned initially.

Charmaine pulled out the deli sliced turkey, some Italian

171

bread, olive oil and provolone cheese. She was going to make Angela a grilled Panini sandwich with creamy tomato basil soup.
After the soup and sandwich were done, Charmaine placed them
on the tray along with a bottle of apple juice and two sugar cookies.

"My ass can cook," Charmaine said out loud.

On her way out of the kitchen, Charmaine grabbed the key
to the basement door and went to unlock it. Careful not to drop the
tray, she balanced it as she walked down the stairs one step at a
time. There was an end table by the heavy steel basement door so
Charmaine sat the tray down and fished for the key in her pocket.
It was gone.

"Damn, it must have fallen off the ring."

She ran upstairs and found the key on the floor and ran
back down just as quickly. Charmaine put the key in the door and
turned it but the door was not locked.

"Hmm, that's strange," she mumbled.

Charmaine picked up the tray and pushed the door open
with her back.

"Look what I have for you, roommate," Charmaine sang
out, walking into the room. When she turned around and looked at
the bed, it was empty. Angela was gone. Horrified, Charmaine
dropped the tray. The ceramic dishes hit the concrete floor, shattering in tiny pieces.

"Oh my God! Angela! Angela!" Charmaine screamed out.

She ran over to the bed and looked underneath it. Nothing.
Then she ran through the basement checking each closet. Dread
filled her as she walked over to the back door. It was ajar.. Charmaine opened the door all the way to find that all of the baggies
had popped. There were dried up spots of purple under the welcome mat that she had placed under it. Bile rose up in Charmaine's
throat as she walked through the backyard. There was no sign of
Angela anywhere.

"How did she escape? Fuck!"

Charmaine ran around the house and up the small hill to the
front yard. Her neighbor, Mrs. Tucker, was sitting on the porch,
watching her as usual. By it being January, Charmaine would think

that the little old lady would be too cold to be nosey but she wasn't. Mrs. Tucker sat in her rocking chair with a coat on and small blanket across her lap.

"Mrs. Tucker, have you seen anything out of the ordinary the past few days?"

"Naw. Can't say as I have."

"What about any new people in the neighborhood? Have you seen anyone you didn't know lurking around?"

"Hmm, well now that you mention it, I did see a strange woman the other day."

Nervous, Charmaine asked, "Really? What did she look like?"

"Chile' it was a white woman. Looks like Cordell Moss a few houses down done went and snagged himself a honky girlfriend. I told you to get with him a long time ago. He's a good man. Good job and er'thing. But naw, you had to lolly gag around and now we done lost another strong black man to the other side."

"You're right, Mrs. Tucker; I should have made my move long ago. That's my loss. Other than that, though, have you seen anything else? Has anyone been around my house maybe?"

"Nope. Ain't seen nobody at your house other than the mailman. Did someone break into your house? I can call the cops. You know I got 'em on speed dial."

"Nothing is missing. I was just asking. Thank you so much, Mrs. Tucker. Have a great day."

"You too, Charmin."

Charmaine ran back down the hill to the basement and locked the door. She didn't know exactly when Angela had escaped but she did know that she didn't have much time to remove her presence from that house. Quickly, Charmaine grabbed a pair of thick black rubber gloves and a spray bottle filled with pure bleach. She sprayed each door knob and surface and wiped everything down. She didn't want to take any chances with leaving fingerprints or identifying marks around the house.

The other day when she left, Charmaine had packed her video footage and what few valuables she had over there so there wasn't much for her to take. As she walked through the house spraying and wiping, Charmaine thought about all the times she had made love to Donnie in that house. From the bedroom to the kitchen, there wasn't any place that the two of them didn't fuck.

It was fun while it lasted.

Charmaine went to the kitchen, carefully picked up the lamp that she left on the kitchen table and brought it back into the living area, placing it on the sofa table. Gently, she plugged it into the wall and backed away slowly. Next, she went to window and pulled the room darkening shades down and made sure the blinds were closed. In the distance, Charmaine heard the distinct sound of sirens and got spooked. She didn't know if they were police sirens or those from an ambulance but it was time for her to go. Charmaine left the house without another thought. Looking back for the last time, Charmaine said goodbye to a piece of her that had been a part of her life for almost three years.

Chapter Twenty
Twenty Questions

Detective Blair was pleased with the information that the Chief presented him. He knew that Donita Stone was a menace to society and he wanted her dyke ass off the street bad. The information the department obtained may not have been enough for a warrant but it was enough for Detective Blair to keep Donita Stone coming back for questioning. Earlier that day, a package came in with an old cell phone that used to belong to Donnie. It linked her to Morgan Calloway and a few others who had filed complaints with the Atlanta Police Department. The phone was a link but there was nothing incriminating in the phone that the D.A. could use for a warrant. Not yet.

Keenan went through the phone after it came back from processing. The only set of prints that were on the phone belonged to Donnie, leaving the police with no inclination of who was sending them the tips. There were a lot of pictures in the phone of naked women and even a few videos of women masturbating. One of the videos had been of Morgan, his cousin's ex-wife. She was sucking the strap-on dick of Donita's who was the one taping the whole thing. Watching that sickened Keenan. His cousin, Randall, had told him that Morgan was into some strange things but Keenan never imagined that. The detective was absentmindedly strumming his fingers on the box that the cell phone came in when his chief walked into his office.

"It's crazy how evidence seems to drop out of the sky into our laps," the Chief said. "It's like every time we hit a brick wall, something comes along to help us."

"I can't explain it either, Chief. But I was taught to never look a gift horse in its mouth. This woman, if that's what you wanna call her, is going down."

"Are you all picking her up or is she coming in voluntarily?"

"I thought it would be more fun bringing her in. Spook her a little. Make her think I know more than I do."

"Good idea, Keenan. Let me know what you find out after questioning."

"Will do, Chief."

Keenan got up and strapped his weapon to his hip. He and Kimmy were heading to Donnie's current resident to escort her in for questioning.

"Ready, Keenan?" Kimmy asked.

He nodded his head yes and the two of them headed to the Atlanta area of Vinings, where Symone lived. Twenty minutes the later, the two officers ascended the stairs to Symone's condo. Keenan was about to knock when Kimmy noticed that the door was ajar.

"Someone was in a hurry to get inside," Kimmy said.

"I see. Shall we?"

They walked quietly inside, careful not to alert anyone in case something was amiss. Sounds of lovemaking were coming from the bedroom and the two of them turned to face one another.

"Well, let's go see the master at work," Keenan said sarcastically. He knew that Donnie was in a serious relationship with Atlanta radio host, Symone Morrow, and he was expecting to see her in a compromising position. He stood in the threshold, watching Donnie eat pussy like it was a delicacy.

"Mmm, that's it baby. Lick it good. I'm getting ready to cum," the woman screamed.

Without saying a word, Keenan walked over to the side of the bed and the woman, who chose that moment to open her eyes, stared straight into his eyes. She got scared.

"Oh, baby. Stop!" She pleaded, trying to push Donnie out of her pussy but Donnie kept on licking. Scared or not, with the police standing right there, the woman came down Donnie's throat.

"Are you finished, Ms. Stone?" Detective Blair asked Donnie.

"Man, what the fuck are you doing in my house?" Donnie was pissed off.

"Correction, this is Ms. Morrow's house. And the last time I checked, this woman right here is not her," Keenan said, busting Donnie. "Aren't the two of you engaged? Hmm, you all must have an open relationship."

"Fuck you, man and mind your business," Donnie shot back.

The woman who Donnie had just fucked glared angrily at Donnie and shifted to cover her naked body.

"Ma'am, you're free to dress and leave. Our issue is with Ms. Stone."

The young lady hurriedly dressed and got out of there.

"Put some clothes on, Ms. Stone. We need to ask you a few questions down at the station."

Not wanting to cause a scene, Donnie dressed and left with the officers. Once they were back at the station, Donnie was shown to an interrogation room where she was told to wait. Donnie was angry that the police kept fucking with her. She had been sitting in the room for almost fifteen minutes and no one came in to question her. Glancing down at her watch, she exhaled loudly.

"This some bullshit," she said out loud.

"Thank you so much for your patience, Ms. Stone," Detective Blair said. "May I offer you something to drink?"

"Nope. You can tell me what you wanna talk to me about and let me go. That's what you can do for me."

"In due time. Do you smoke? Want a cigarette?" Keenan asked.

"Nah. Let's just get this over wit," Donnie said cockily, holding her strap-on. Keenan saw her caressing her 'manhood' and laughed. "Whatchu want wit me now, dude? I told you, I ain't seen

Morgan."

"So, I remember. But I don't wanna talk about Morgan. Not today anyway. Tell me what you know about Kelly Vanderbilt."

"She's one of my ex-girlfriends. When she comes to town we kick it. Otherwise, our contact is limited to texts, Skype and email."

"When was the last time you saw her?" The detective asked.

"Shit, I'on know. This summer, maybe? Why?" Donnie was agitated. Kimmy, who stood on the other side of the glass, took note. The lesbian's body language told them a lot more than her mouth did.

"Were you aware that Ms. Vanderbilt died? Actually, she was murdered."

"What the fuck! Kelly's dead? Fuck! When? How?"

"She died September 29, 2010."

"B-b-but, I was just with her the day before. I don't under-stand."

"Actually, you were with her that morning. Once she left your house, she returned to her hotel. There, she was poisoned and later died at the hospital. Wanna tell me what you know about that?" The detective propped his leg up on a chair and rested his chin in his hand.

"Dude. You got it all wrong. I loved Kelly. She was my ace. I'd never hurt her."

"Did you love her the same way you love Symone Mor-row?"

"Yeah. No. I loved Kelly. She got me in a way that no one else did. But Symone, she got my heart. I'm in love with Symone. She's going to be my wife."

"Hmm, you're in love with one woman but was fucking an-other when we got to your house? Interesting. But back to Kelly. Tell me what you know about methyl salicylate more commonly known as wintergreen oil."

"Da fuck? I'on know shit about nothing that I can't pro-nounce. You trying to say I killed Kelly?"

"Did you?"

"Hell naw. Man, get me a lawyer. Y'all trying to pin some shit on me. Tryna frame a nigga like me."

"You're more than welcome to have an attorney present. We're just asking a few questions."

"Well, unless you're charging me with something, I'm out."

"You're free to go, Ms. Stone. But don't leave town. I'm sure we will be in touch. Very soon."

"Man, fuck y'all. I'm out."

Detective Blair smiled as Donnie walked out of the interrogation room. He could have held her longer because he had more questions for her but he let her go. His plan was to keep fucking with her until she broke down. The whole time he questioned her, Donnie fidgeted in the seat. He knew she was hiding something and he was going to get to the bottom of it. Donita Stone was a lying, cheating dyke and Keenan believed she was a murderer. He wasn't going to rest until he proved it.

Chapter Twenty-One
The Discovery Channel

Charmaine didn't come out to play much these days. Now that Angela was Lord knows where, telling people Lord knows what, Charmaine was done. Living life as someone else for so long had taken its toll on Zabria. Every morning that she woke up, she had to look in the mirror and reaffirm who she was.

"I am Zabria Moreland, *NOT* Charmaine Franklin."

On the outside, she could see that she was different. It was great for Zabria to get up, wash her face and go without having to add the prosthetics and heavy pancake makeup. No, she was fine on the outside; it was inside where the struggle lay. It was inconceivable at first that Zabria would battle with any sort of identity crisis but in truth she had been living a double life since she was fourteen. There was always a battle within her soul for good and evil.

As a teenager, she did shit that would have doctors questioning if she was a sociopath. A few months before her fifteenth birthday, Zabria hit a kid with Down's Syndrome in the head with a rock. She thought he was stupid and wanted to knock some sense into him. She was mean and just pure evil at times. Zabria's mother, Melissa, would try to tell her father, Zachary, about his daughter but he didn't believe her. Zachary would accuse Melissa of lying and claim that she was jealous of her little girl.

"Really, Melissa? I can't believe that you would go to such

lengths to undermine the relationship I have with another woman by constantly calling me with lies about our daughter. Julie thinks it's a ploy to get me back. Even if half of the bull you tell me is true, there's no need to call me at one or two in the morning."

"This isn't about you and some bitch, Zach. This is about *our* daughter. I call you when there are things going on that need immediate attention. And if that's during the time that you're fucking some bitch then that's too damned bad."

And so it went. Zabria may not have been the reason her parents separated but she was definitely the reason that they stayed that way. Zabria exhaled and walked into her home office. *My crazy mixed up life. I am about to be 25 years old in two months. It's time for a change.*

She sat down at her desk and logged into her computer. She had a paper due in her psychology class and she hadn't even started it. To the right of her, Zabria saw movement on her 'Pad monitor. It was from the camera she had set up at Donnie and Symone's house. "Hmm, it's lunch time in the Morrow-Stone household. "Ooh, look," Zabria pointed to the screen, "They got the engagement present I sent them. Let's watch, shall we?" Zabria turned up the volume on the device and sat back to watch the show.

"Hey love," Donnie said to Symone. "I made us a special lunch. Hungry?"

"Starving. What do we have here?"

"I made a grilled chicken salad with arugula, topped with a raspberry vinaigrette dressing and whole grain bread sticks, accompanied by a bottle of cabernet sauvignon and chocolate covered strawberries."

"Wow, Donnie. Sounds delish. What's the occasion?" Symone asked. Donnie wasn't just being a good Samaritan.

"Do I have to have a reason to treat my lady good? I love you. After we're married, you can expect things like this to happen often."

Donnie did feel guilty about being caught by the cops fucking that other broad. She was just happy that it wasn't Symone who walked in because if it had been, it would have been all over for Donnie. The last thing she wanted to do was return to her brother's house. Without Symone, Donnie would be broke with no way to pay for her car and it would get repossessed.

"Whatever the reason babe, I love it. You're very sweet," Symone gushed.

"You're very sweet, babe," Zabria mocked. She put two fingers in her mouth and pretended like she was gagging herself. *"I think I'm going to be sick,"* Zabria said. She turned her attention back to the screen in time to see Donnie pouring the red wine that she had put the period blood and pee in.

Donnie and Symone sat at the table and talked about their pending nuptials.

"When you wanna set the date?" Donnie asked.

"I don't know yet. Let me talk to my brother about his schedule because you know I want him there."

"Gotcha! I wanna make sure my peeps are there, too. This is the only ceremony we're having so I wanna make sure it's special."

"Yes, babe. Let's toast. To us," Symone lifted her glass.

"To us, love and happiness," Donnie said, raising her glass.

The glasses made a clinking sound when they touched. Donnie tilted her glass and swallowed it in one gulp. Symone savored hers and allowed it to caress her pallet.

"This is some good ass wine," Donnie said, refilling her glass.

"Indeed. It has a very distinctive taste," Symone agreed.

On the other side of town, Zabria was cracking up. She knew what the ingredients were and it was funny as hell to her that the two people she hated the most were drinking something other than the grapes the vintner originally used. Donnie excused herself to the restroom at the same time Symone's cell phone vibrated. It was a text from Keyon.

Symone, I need 2 c u. Been texting u 4 a while now. We need 2 meet. Urgent!

Symone wasn't surprised that Keyon had texted her and she hadn't received it. Donnie was still checking Symone's phone and deleting messages that she didn't want Symone to see. Shaking her head, Symone hurried up and sent Keyon a reply text.

Meet me at the radio station at 3pm.

When Donnie came back to the room, Symone told her that she needed to run to the office for a short meeting. Donnie was fine with that because she had a few errands that she wanted to run herself. An hour later, Symone strolled into the office like she owned the place. Her head was held high and she was very happy to be meeting Keyon there. The last time he stopped by her office, they ended up having some of the best sex ever. If she was lucky, maybe she could duplicate that scene. The secretary buzzed Symone's office to let her know Keyon had arrived.

"Hey, Symone. How are you?" Keyon opened.

"I'm fine, babe. How are you?" Symone went over to Keyon and wrapped her arms around him, hugging him. Keyon quickly peeled her hands off of him.

"We need to talk," Keyon began.

"I know. But first. I have something to show you. Tah dah," Symone said, wiggling her fingers in front of Keyon so he could see her engagement ring. "Donnie and I are engaged."

"Are you serious, Symone? You'd actually consider marrying *that* woman? I thought you wanted to have children?"

"I can do artificial insemination. People do it all the time."

"Whatever," Keyon said disgustedly. "Before you go through with that, I think it's something you should know about your fiancé."

The word fiancé dripped off his lips like it was coated with vinegar.

"Your girlfriend is the reason that you and I are no longer together. She set the whole video shit up. With the help of a few chicks she used to mess with, Donnie was able to perform the ultimate divide and conquer."

"Was Domynique one of those women?"

Keyon dropped his head, confirming that she was.

"Yeah. Donnie used a lot of people and she hurt so many along the way. Don't marry her, Symone. She's bad news." Keyon pleaded.

"Wow. I'm so glad I found this out before I said 'I do'. This changes things significantly." Symone walked over to Keyon and wrapped her arms around him. "Baby, I am so glad that God blessed us to find all this out before we both ended up marrying the wrong people."

Symone stood on her tip toes trying to kiss Keyon. He leaned back as her face got closer to his and then he turned his head.

"Symone, I don't think I'm marrying the wrong person. Domynique is the one for me and she's pregnant with my baby."

Symone coughed, "Pregnant?" Bile rose in her throat, burning her esophagus.

"Yes. She's not showing much yet, though."

"How do you know it's even your baby?"

"Domynique was a virgin when I first made love to her," Keyon answered.

"Oh, so you made love to her, huh? When the video first came out, you said you didn't *fuck* her. Hmmph! Now it's 'making love.' Interesting. "

"You saw the tape. Clearly, I made love to her. My dick never left her tight pussy." Keyon only said that to get back at Symone for questioning his child's paternity. He *knew* Domynique's baby was his.

Furious, Symone started swinging like a windmill on Keyon. He was trying to grab her arms but wasn't able to catch them. Outside of Symone's office, Mona, her show's producer, and Juanita, one of Donnie's paramours, listened the entire time and giggled when Keyon shut Symone down.

"Will you calm down, Symone? You're acting stupid." Keyon was getting angrier by the minute. His breathing was heavy and the large vein in the side of his neck was throbbing. Every time he tried to get around Symone. she blocked his path. Mona chose that moment to enter the office, offering Keyon a way out.

"Mona, thank God you're here. Please call security to get this woman off of me."

"This woman. Motherfucker, I'm the same woman you were going to marry. The same one whose pussy you used to eat up like a fat kid does cake. Don't act brand new, Keyon."

"Symone, calm down and lower your voice. You're embarrassing yourself. Do you want the whole station in your business?" Mona admonished.

Symone stopped swinging and Keyon stepped around her.

"Goodbye, Symone. Have a nice life," Keyon said.

Juanita whistled as he walked past her and she shook her head. Symone was stupid for leaving Keyon. He was a great catch. Tall, handsome, wealthy and by the way he walked, Juanita assumed he had a very big dick. Some women were very stupid. Symone just happened to be one of them.

"Symone, clearly you need a little bit more time off work. This display of foolery could have cost you your job but I'm going to let you keep it. Your show is doing well and I'm not going to pull the plug on it. But you need to rest and relax."

Mona didn't give Symone the room for any rebuttal. After she said her piece, Mona walked off and left Symone to process the information Mona just laid on her.

Symone packed a few things from her desk so she could work from home and she left the building. Keyon was hers. There was no way Symone was going to let him go without a fight.

"This shit ain't over by a long shot!"

• • • • • • • • • • • • • • • • •

Donnie sat outside of Keyon and Domynique's Buckhead home, seething with anger. Domynique talked too fucking much and Donnie was going to make her pay for telling Keyon about the plot. While she sat, Donnie thought about Domynique and how good her pussy tasted. She was determined to feel those soft lips against her own once again. Donnie pounded her right hand into her left hand over and over until her left hand hurt.

Now that Donnie had Keyon's schedule down, she knew exactly what time to come over and visit Darling Nikki. Donnie stroked her dick through her pants just thinking about the beautiful woman that Keyon was now fucking. Donnie got out of her car and looked around before walking up to the front door. She knocked on the door and then turned her back. When the door opened, Donnie turned back around and stared Domynique straight in the face.

"I've been waiting on him to leave. Happy to see me?"

Chapter Twenty-Two
· ·
What's The Big Deal

It took every ounce of courage that Domynique had in order to walk into the bank. She was going to meet with Big and try to work something out so she could help Keyon. She wanted to get this thing with Big out of the way because now, she had Donnie to deal with.

"Hello, my name is Domynique Segar. Here to see Mr. Abignol," she spoke nervously to the secretary.

"One moment," his secretary mumbled under her breath, walking away. She came back with a sour look on her face like she had been sucking on a lemon. "He'll see you."

Fear took over and settled in her stomach like a ton of bricks. "I *can* do this," she encouraged herself.

"Come in and sit," a powerful voice commanded.

She didn't see the man at first because he was sitting in a large chair and his back was to her. "What can I help you with, Ms. Segar?" He asked, spinning around in his chair.

"I need to talk to you about Keyon Steele."

"What about him?"

"Well, uh, I was wondering if…I thought that maybe I could help him pay his debt to you."

"And how were you planning to do that?"

"Well, I'm very smart. I was thinking maybe I could work for you."

"Doing what?"

"I saw online that you needed tellers. I have two years of experience and I know I could do a good job here."

Domynique almost got up and ran out of the bank when he started laughing. A big, boisterous laugh.

Slightly offended, she asked, "What's so funny?"

"Oh my," he began, trying to catch his breath. "Do you really think that I'd allow the whore of a man who owes me almost a two million dollars, work in my bank so you can rob me blind? Come on now, I didn't get where I am today by being stupid."

"That's not my intention. I'm trying to help Keyon, not hurt him."

"You're serious about this, aren't you?"

"Yes."

"How much is clearing up his debt worth to you? What are you willing to do?"

"I'll do anything. Cook, clean, yard work. You name it."

"I have a housekeeper and a landscaper. I need something else."

"What is it? I know I can do it."

"I know you can, too. I have a client coming into town who needs some entertainment." He wrote down an address on a post-it note and handed it to her. "Come to this address tonight at eight. No need to dress up. I want to, uh, audition you myself before I turn you over to my client. Make sure your performance is up to par."

"Audition me for a client?"

"Indeed. If you do a good job and the client is satisfied, I will knock $50,000 off of your boyfriend's debt."

"Fi…fi, fifty thousand dollars? Doing what?" Her head began to spin thinking about all that money.

"Fucking."

"You want me to have sex with someone?" Domynique was dumbfounded.

"Yes. I'm in position to make millions if all goes well. The money Keyon owes me is pennies compared to what I'll gain by getting into bed with him. Or rather, by getting *you* into bed with him." He laughed cynically.

188

"I don't think I can do that. Keyon is the only man I've been with."

"You mean to tell me you were a virgin when you got with him?"

"Yes," she said hanging her head.

"Sonofabitch! Some guys have all the luck," he said, getting up and walking around his desk to her. He rubbed her hair slowly and let his hand trail down her face, caressing her skin with the back of it. His hand opened slowly as it neared her breasts and palmed the left one, gently kneading it, while rubbing his dick with his free hand. Domynique could not believe how crazy he really was.

"Damn, your pussy is probably still tighter than any other I have ever had. I really need to fuck you now."

Tears streamed down her face as he molested her. "Please don't do this. I love Keyon."

"Be at that address tonight or else! Now get the fuck out!"

She left immediately and drove back to Keyon's house in a blur, crying all the way there. In her effort to help Keyon, she may have just made matters worse. But there was no way that she could not meet Big that evening. Domynique had no choice.

Once she got home, she did busy work. *What am I going to tell Keyon?* The phone rang and she jumped, startled by the shrill noise.

"Hello?"

"Hey, Babe." It was Keyon. "I hate to do this at the last minute but I'm going to have to work late tonight. We have some execs from the Grammy nominating committee coming into town and we need to schmooze them. I may not be in until eleven or so. Please forgive me."

Thank you Jesus, she exhaled. "It's okay, Keyon. I hadn't cooked yet. Handle your business."

"You're the best, Dom. I'll talk to you later."

She got off the phone and went to fix a sandwich. There was no way she was going to let Big touch her on an empty stomach. The very thought of him repulsed her and made her stomach lurch. A small flutter vibrated in her lower abdomen.

"I know, baby. I'm scared, too." She spoke softly to her little bun in the oven.

Before she knew it, it was time for her to leave the house. When she was getting into her car in the garage, she spotted a small utility knife on the workbench that Keyon installed for his dad and she grabbed it. *Just in case,* she thought. She put the address in the GPS and twenty minutes later she stood in the foyer of a beautiful, Sandy Springs mansion that sat on a secluded three acre lot. Big saw the apprehension on her face.

"Don't be scared. I assure you, the butterflies will disappear once I wrap my lips around your clit." Bile rose to her throat when he said that. "Follow me." He walked to the other side of the house and opened French doors that led to the largest master bedroom she had ever seen.

"Wow," she whispered, noticing that the French doors were located all throughout the room, even opening to the outside. She could not believe she was in his home.

"Impressive, isn't it? This room is almost 2500 square feet. Some three bedroom houses aren't even this big. Look what else is impressive," he said behind her.

She turned around to see that he'd removed his pants and underwear; his small, limp dick in his hand. She vomited in her mouth and couldn't speak. Swallowing the bile, she asked if she could freshen up.

"Make it snappy. Mr. Big's hard and ready."

That's what your dick looks like hard? No wonder Cha-Cha left you.

Five minutes later she was back, sitting on the edge of the massive California king sized bed.

"Glad you wore sweat pants. Take 'em off. Your panties, too."

Tears sprang to the corners of her eyes, threatening to spill over but she held them at bay.

All she could think about was how she was doing this to help the man she loved. Big got on his knees and slithered, like the snake he was, to her womanhood. He flicked his tongue and it barely grazed her nether lips but she scooted back anyway.

"Not so fast. Bring that pussy back here," he said, grabbing her thighs, pulling her back to the edge.

He held her roughly and began to suck painfully hard on her clit, making loud, slurping noises.

"Ah, yes. This is good pussy," he confirmed through slurps. He inserted one sausage like finger inside of Domynique and started jabbing hard and biting her clit. Unable to hold them back any longer, she let the tears fall.

"I can't do this. Please stop," she said quietly through tears.

He continued. "Stop, please," she begged, a bit louder this time. His laughter vibrated on her clit. She tried to push him back but he clamped down on her clit with his teeth, pulling her with him. She cried out in pain. He went to lick her once more and she pushed him back with force, this time succeeding and he fell back on the floor.

"I said, stop! Please!"

He advanced towards her only to stop short when he saw the sharp blade of the knife. "Bitch, please. You couldn't bust a grape with that little ass knife."

Domynique grabbed her clothes and held them to her body. "Just stay away, please. I'll do anything to help Keyon but not this. I can't do this."

A sob tore through her body and when she wiped her eyes, Big charged towards her, knocking the knife from her hand. It landed on the bed. Domynique ran and pulled the door open, thinking it was the bedroom door, but it was the closet.

"Shit! Stupid! Stupid!" She berated herself but the hid in the closet anyway, just like a small child. At least for now, she was safe.

"So, you wanna play hide and seek, do you? Why didn't you tell me you're into games? I would've had you dress up."

" Please, can we come up with another way to pay?"

"You amuse me, little girl. If you wanna pay your boyfriends debt, you'll come out right now. Otherwise, it's curtains for him. I like choices, so I'll let you decide."

Domynique didn't respond.

"Come out; come out, wherever you are?" His voice was

getting closer. Domynique started praying when she saw the door knob on the closet slowly turn.

"One, two, Big is coming for you. Three, four should have locked this door." Big giggled but didn't hear his bedroom door open.

"Cleophus Robinson Abignol, who the hell are you talking to?" The woman asked him.

"How in the hell did you get in here?" He asked, dropping his hand from the door knob.

"I have a key, remember? Why does it matter? After all, this was supposed to be our house, you fucking asshole. Or have you forgotten?" Cha-Cha was hysterical and had no interest in being there. As a matter of fact, she was nauseous being in his presence but she had to let his ass know she wasn't playing.

"I haven't forgotten anything, Miracha."

Cha-Cha. Domynique recognized the voice.

"Who were you talking to just now? And why are you naked, you sick fuck?"

"As usual, your mind is playing tricks on you. I was headed to the shower for your information. What are you doing here?"

"Whatever. I know I heard a female voice. But I came here to ask you to please let me be happy. Michael is fighting for his life now because of you. I love him, Cleo. Don't you get it?"

"Oh, I get it. But do you think I'm going to sit idly by and watch you fuck another nigga with a pussy that I bought? Or did you forget that I paid for your gender reassignment surgery? Hell, I haven't even had a chance to fuck it yet and here you are giving it to someone else."

"How can I forget? You remind me every fucking chance you get!"

"Speaking of fucking, I'm ready to see what that new hole feels like," he said walking towards Cha-Cha.

"Go on, Cleo. I came here to talk."

"I bet it's tight," he salivated.

Cha-Cha didn't like the look in his eyes. "I'm not playing, Cleo. Stay the fuck away from me."

A very horny Cleo, charged Cha-Cha and punched her in

the head, causing her to fall on the bed when he got within arm's reach. The blow disoriented Cha-Cha long enough for Cleo to push up Cha-Cha's skirt and touch her womanhood. He kissed her sloppily with lips that tasted of another woman's pussy. The more Cha-Cha struggled, the harder Cleo's dick got. Using his considerable upper body strength, he held her down while using his strong legs to part Cha-Cha's thighs.

"Cleo, don't do this. I'm begging you." She could not believe this was happening when she came here to plead for Michael's life, and that only.

It was no use. Lustful rage had consumed him and he couldn't hear a thing she said. All he wanted was to feel her tightness wrapped around his hard dick. He literally had her right where he wanted her and she fell right in to the trap. With one powerful thrust, Big was inside of Cha-Cha. Domynique had never heard a scream like that in her life. Cha-Cha sounded like her insides were being ripped out with a pair of vice-grips. Domynique peeked through the door and saw Big pumping in and out of Cha-Cha.

I've got to do something. But what? Domynique panicked. She watched as sweat poured from his thick body onto her friend who begged and pleaded for him to stop. A few more hard pumps and Big let out a guttural howl, like a wounded animal and then he rolled over. Cha-Cha curled up in a ball away from him and prepared to get up when her hand hit something. Her fingers curled slowly around the handle and with lightning speed, she rolled over, plunging the knife in his belly and pulled it down, slicing him.

Next, Cha-Cha plunged it into his chest. His eyes held a look of surprise as the love of his life butchered his body. His final thought as life escaped him, was of his mother telling him how pussy was going to be the death of him. Oh, how right she was.

Domynique, who had dressed while she was in the closet ran out and hollered at her friend.

"Cha-Cha, stop! He's dead!"

With the knife in mid-air above her head, hands shaking, Cha-Cha turned around and looked at Domynique strangely.

"Domynique, what are you doing here?" Cha-Cha was caught off-guard. She knew they needed to get out of the mansion, and quickly. Cha-Cha put on her shoes and pulled Domynique behind her as they ran for the front door.

As they ran, Domynique filled in Cha-Cha with the reason she was there, "Keyon owed Big some money. I wanted to help him pay his debt off because Big kept threatening to kill us if we didn't get the money to him in three days. Well, I saw him today in his office and he told me he would wipe away a large portion of the debt if I slept with one of his clients. The catch was that he wanted me to do it with him first I wasn't trying to hurt Keyon, but I would do anything for him. I love him. I felt like I had no choice. Please don't tell him," she begged.

"It's okay, honey, but what did you just say? Cleo is Big? How'd you know?" Cha-Cha had no idea.

"I'd seen Big before, when I was with Keyon, but I made the connection when I saw your photo album of exes."

"Damn! This is the man Keyon owes money to?" Cha-Cha exclaimed.

"Yes. Well, he did before…" her voice trailed off.

Cha-Cha looked down on Big's lifeless body. "How could someone named after a preacher be so damned evil?"

"Wait! We can't leave him there like that? What are we going to do, Cha-Cha? I don't wanna have my baby in prison."

"Fuck that! Neither of us is going to jail. Help me clean this up!"

Domynique ran into the bathroom and gathered as many towels as she could find while a naked Cha-Cha went to the laundry room to get some bleach. There she took a towel and wiped her body down with pure bleach trying to erase the memory of what had just happened. Then she quickly dressed after she returned to the room, wiping it down with bleach as well.

"Wait here. I have an idea." Cha-Cha ran to the garage and got the gas can that Big kept in there for his riding lawnmower. She came back in the room and doused the Big and the bed with gas, making sure it was soaked and made a trail of gas towards the front door of the house.

"We need more accelerant. This house is going to burn faster than the Titanic sank."

The two friends found kerosene, rubbing alcohol, a small propane tank used for a gas grill and just about all of the liquor from Big's bar to help torch the house. Cha-Cha walked to the desk near the sitting room fireplace and got a long reach lighter to torch the place.

"One more thing before we go. Hurry up and follow me." Cha-Cha ran to a small room and moved an oil painting of herself to reveal a safe. Domynique scanned the room and noticed that all of the pictures in the room were of Cha-Cha.

"Is this some sort of shrine?"

"Girl, the man was obsessed with me."

"Creepy," Domynique said, shivering.

"Douse all of those pictures, Domynique. I don't want nobody connecting me with him."

Cha-Cha's nimble fingers punched in some numbers on the safe and soon all the lights changed from red to green.

"Voila," she said, opening it and showing displaying stacks of money. "This is probably all of the money that Cleo's been collecting from people and extorting from the bank."

"He stole from the bank?"

"Girl, you have so much to learn about people. But this man was as crooked as a pretzel. Shit! We need something to put it in. I'll be back."

"Wait, don't leave me." Domynique's plea's fell on deaf ears as Cha-Cha ran away.

Cha-Cha returned a few minutes later, rolling two large suitcases behind her, handing Domynique one as she came in.

"We gotta hurry. We've been here too long as it is. Grab the loot!" Cha-Cha barked.

Domynique took a stack of bills and placed them neatly in the suitcase. Cha-Cha looked at Domynique like she was crazy.

"What the fuck are you doing? Lemme show you how to do this." Cha-Cha squeezed her small arm in the safe and swept a large amount of cash into the suitcase. She repeated the action a few more times until the safe was empty. "We'll divvy it up later. 50-50. Let's bounce!"

Walking to their cars, Cha-Cha tried to comfort Domynique, "It doesn't matter if I get caught," Cha-Cha said, choked up. "But you have a baby on the way. I'll torch this place and if I make it out of here okay, I'll text you and we can meet up at your house later. I'm sorry all this happened. I love you, girl. You're a down ass, Mami."

"I love you, too," Domynique told her friend, crying as she hugged her friend for what could be the last time.

Cha-Cha placed the bag in her car, waved to Domynique and took the short stroll back to the house to set it ablaze. She was thankful this chapter of her life was closing. Getting back to Michael was all that was on her mind.

Chapter Twenty-Three
· · · · · · · · · · · · · · · · · · · ·
New Year, New Fear

Domynique sat on the porch trembling because of the cold weather and with fear so thick she could cut it with a knife. So much was coming at her she could barely get her bearings. Last night, she had witnessed her friend kill a man. A man who threatened her family. Now today, she was faced with another threat. Donnie was threatening to break up her happy home and she was scared shitless. The other day when Donnie popped up at the house, Domynique didn't know what to expect. Donnie came inside the house and didn't say one word for at least five minutes. She just walked around the house, scoping things out, purposely showing Domynique who was in control..

"I should fuck you up right now for running your mouth," Donnie finally said.

"I'm sorry, Stone. I just wanted to make sure Keyon and I didn't have any secrets between us going into the New Year."

"Awe, you love him, don't you?"

"Yes. I, do. We're going to have a baby."

"Hmm, is that right? That means you're set for life then, huh?" Donnie rubbed her hands together, licked her lips and shook her head. "Yeah, this is cool. I can use this to my advantage. Tell you what, darling Nikki, I'm going to head back to the Ponderosa and think of a master plan. I'll be back in a couple of days. Make sure that pussy is wet for me when I get here, too." With that, Donnie left. Now Domynique was on pins and needles because she knew Donnie was capable of ruining lives.

A chill ran through Domynique and she shivered like the chill was deep in her bones. Keyon was inside preparing to go into the office. She wanted so badly to beg him to stay with her but she didn't want to alarm him. Tomorrow was the day that his debt to Big was due and he was beyond stressed out. The last thing Domynique wanted to do was add to it. More than anything, Domynique wanted to tell him that Big was dead but she didn't want to have to tell him how she knew that. It was all a huge mess. She looked down the street to see if she could spot Donnie's car. Domynique didn't even know how Donnie found out where she and Keyon lived but since Donnie was fucking with Symone, it couldn't have been that hard.

Keyon told Domynique that Symone had been over a few times since she and Donnie had been together. It's highly likely that Donnie followed Symone over here. Regardless of how she found out, Donnie knew where Domynique was and that wasn't a good thing. When Domynique told Keyon about the whole setup, she didn't think that he would go and tell Symone. No, Domynique figured that he would just accept what she said and move on. But there was no way that a man could be with a woman, for as long as Keyon was with Symone, and not warn her about the type of person she was with.

Domynique exhaled and went inside. She walked into the family room and looked around. The Christmas tree was still up and the box of tiny Jordan's still sat on the table where Keyon had placed him. He was so excited when Domynique told him about the baby. They were going to be a family. *Were* being the operative word now. If Donnie had her way, Domynique was going to be out in the cold again. This time, with a baby in tow. Tears streamed down her face at the thought of losing the wonderful people she had grown to love and think of as family.

"Domynique!" Keyon yelled from upstairs. "Babe, come quick!"

Domynique wiped the tears from her eyes and went upstairs. Keyon was sitting on the bed in front of the television. His mouth was almost on the floor.

"What is it, honey?" She asked, genuinely concerned.

"Babe, Big is dead. It was breaking news early this morning. They said his wife came home and the house was on fire. After the fire was put out, they found his body."

"Oh my God. How do you know it was Big?"

"They said his name, Cleophus Robinson Abignol. Trust me, that's a name I'll never forget."

"What does this mean for us? Do you think he has someone else in line to collect his debts?" Domynique prayed that he didn't. That would be one less thing she had to worry about.

"I don't think so, Dom. I think all of that ended with his death."

"Thank you, Jesus!" She yelled.

"Whoo hoo!" Keyon exclaimed, picking Domynique up and twirling her in the air. "Baby, do you know this means? I'M FREE!!!!" Keyon cried tears of joy.

Domynique cried too, but for a different reason. Because of her, she and Keyon would never experience the life that he had planned for them. Donnie would see to that. Keyon mistook Domynique's tears for tears of joy.

"Babe, I know you're just as happy as I am. Thank you, Lord. I wish I could get all that money back that I paid him. But oh, well. It's worth it just having him out of our lives."

Domynique gave Keyon the side eye while he held her tight in his arms. There was the matter of that duffle bag that she had buried in the back of her shoe closet that Cha-Cha had given her. *Damn, some friend I am. I haven't even tried to call Cha-Cha since all of this went down. I don't even know if she's all right.*

"This is wonderful, babe. Since you got this great news, are you going to stay home today?" *Please say you will, please say you will.* Domynique pleaded silently.

"I wish I could. I have two big meetings today. Man of Steele has to prepare for the upcoming tours. The execs from IMG Touring will be there today. I'll try to sneak out early if I can, though. I'd like to celebrate with you tonight."

"Sounds great, babe. Looking forward to it." Domynique

hid her face, as not to show her true disappointment.

Keyon kissed her passionately on the lips and left.

Domynique locked all the doors behind her and peaked out of the blinds. Her first thought was to play like she wasn't home if Donnie came over, but that wouldn't deter the evil lesbian. She could also leave in her new whip but where would she go? That would just give her another reason to come by the next day. No, Domynique needed to face this fear head on. Domynique was staring so intently out the window that she didn't see Donnie walk up onto the porch. The knock on the door brought her back to reality. Domynique didn't hesitate to open the door.

"Darling Nikki. Can I sing you a song?" Donnie didn't wait for the answer, she just started singing in Domynique's ear, while caressing her back.

"I knew a girl named Nikki, I guess you could say she was a sex fiend. I met her in the hotel lobby masturbating to a magazine." Donnie ran her large hands over Domynique's sensitive breast.

"Don't do that, Stone. Please."

"Don't do what? Touch you? Bitch, please. Miss me with all that innocent shit. You and I both know how you like it. Don't we? Matter of fact, get naked. Now!"

Domynique stared at Donnie like she had grown two heads. Surely she must have been kidding. There was no way that Domynique was going to get naked.

"Bitch, do I look like I'm playing with your ass?" Donnie pulled a small caliber pistol out of her pocket and pointed it at Domynique who began undressing quickly.

"Yeah, that's what I'm talking about. Shit, your titties are bigger. Look at them nipples. All rosy and shit. My dick is hard. Come here, girl."

Reluctantly, Domynique walked over to Donnie. Hot tears ran down Domynique's face when Donnie wrapped her lips around her nipple. Donnie's tongue circled around the nipple. The pregnancy heightened the sensitivity of Domynique's body and her nipples hardened almost instantly.

"Please don't do this. I'll pay you. Please, Stone."

"You can pay me and fuck me. Simple as that. Sit yo' ass down and spread them legs."

Domynique hesitated a second too long and Donnie slapped her so hard she fell onto the sofa. A red print was left across Domynique's cheek. Since she was already down, Donnie went to the sofa and turned Domynique over. Donnie used her knee to part Domynique's legs, then she kneeled between them. To ensure that Domynique didn't try anything funny, Donnie pointed the gun at Domynique's stomach.

"Mmm, mmm, good," Donnie said as she sniffed Domynique's pussy. Her snake like tongue explored Domynique's caverns and tasted the sweet nectar that her body produced. Long, thick fingers slid inside of Domynique's pussy and she cried out in pain.

"Ahh, please stop, Stone!"

Undeterred, Donnie kept licking and fingering the pink flesh, roughly. Jagged fingernails scratched the sensitive skin as it went in and out. Donnie bit down on Domynique's pearl tongue with her teeth like it was a piece of meat. It didn't matter to Donnie if Domynique was pleased or not, this was all about Donnie and her pleasure. Unable to take the pain any longer, Domynique knocked the gun out of Donnie's hand and scooted out of her reach. Donnie punched Domynique in her leg and then grabbed her by the waist.

"The fuck you think you're doing? Get your ass back over here!" Donnie lunged towards Domynique who ran behind an end table and knocked a lamp over trying to reach her.

"Fuck!" Donnie yelled.

Domynique took off towards the stairs but Donnie caught her foot as Domynique tried to run up. Donnie was punching Domynique on her back as she pulled her back downstairs. Domynique was kicking and screaming as Donnie pummeled her fist into Domynique's body. In an effort to protect her baby, Domynique curled into a fetal position once she hit the floor and covered her belly. Donnie kicked her in the head and shoulders and then spat on her.

"I should kill your ass!" Donnie yelled. She ran into the

family room to grab her gun when she heard the motor of the automatic garage door opener begin to roar. "Damn!" Donnie tightened the belt around her jeans, picked up her ball cap, snatched her keys and headed towards the door. "I'll be back, bitch!"

Domynique picked herself up off the floor and went to the living room to put her gown and robe back on. She didn't know who was getting ready to come through the garage door but whoever it was, she didn't want them finding her naked. Her body was aching and a bit stiff. Domynique saw bruises on her legs and arms. There was no way she'd be able to hide any of them from Keyon. He liked her in the bed naked, at all times.

"What have I done?" Domynique cried out loud.

"I don't know? What did you do?" Keyon asked, walking up behind her. He touched her on the right arm and she jerked away in pain. "Are you okay, babe?"

Domynique turned around slowly and Keyon saw the red prints on her face and the bruising that was beginning to darken by her neck.

"What the fuck happened to you? Does Big have henchmen, after all?" Keyon scooped Domynique up and went to sit down on the sofa with her in his lap.

"No, baby. It wasn't that. It was...it was..."

"It was what?"

"Donnie. She got mad that I told you about the set up. She came over here, held a gun to my stomach and forced me to let her..."

Keyon's nostrils flared in anger. "To what, Dom?"

"She held me down and raped me. Her finger nails scratched me bad."

Keyon placed Domynique gently on the sofa and stood up to call the cops. He paced back and forth as anger coursed through his veins like hot lava. The vein in his neck was thick with tension, looking like an Earth worm. He let out a growl like a wolf. Keyon was going to kill Donnie.

Chapter Twenty-Four

In My Mind, I'll Always Be His Lady

Symone seethed with anger thinking about the phone conversation she and Keyon had just had. She was lying in bed. Donnie had just left the house, leaving Symone to bask in the aftermath of an Earth shattering orgasm. The entire time Donnie was licking and slurping, Symone was pretending that it was Keyon so she was excited to hear his voice on the end of her phone when he called. However, she was not prepared for what he had to say.

"I don't know what kind of game you and that dyke bitch are playing with me and mine, but y'all fucking with the right one. I'm going to kill that mutherfuckin' fiancé of yours and you gonna be a widow. Get your black dress ready!"

"Damn, I don't even get a 'hello' or nothing? What's got your panties all in a bunch?"

"Your fucking girlfriend, that's who! She came over here and put her nasty hands on Domynique. As soon as I see her, I'm going to fuck her up!"

"First off, Keyon, I spoke with Donnie and she said that she's never even heard of your chick and she wanted me to tell you that she's flattered that you think she's crafty enough to set up a plot like the one you told me about. And secondly, Donnie doesn't even know where you live and plus, she was with me so tell your video vixen to quit lying."

"Of course, she's going to deny having anything to do with

this. I keep telling you that. Your ass is acting real stupid, Symone."

"You calling me stupid? You're the one about to marry some chick who's carrying a baby that you don't even know is yours. How you know Big didn't do it? I know your broke ass probably still owes him money," Symone remarked snidely.

"Big is dead and if you pulled your head out of Donnie's pussy long enough, you'd know that."

"Keyon, I know you're still in love with me. Come home. I know the baby is the reason why you're still with her."

"Whatever. I'm not going to do this with you, Symone. Even if I wasn't in love with Domynique, my ass fo' sho' ain't in love with you. I was going to kick your lesbo's ass but instead I'm going to let the police handle this. See how Donnie likes being in jail with her other dyke sisters."

After he said that, Keyon hung up the phone in Symone's face. She sat up on the edge of her bed and looked down at the cell phone. Keyon was tripping. No matter how much he claimed not to be in love with Symone, she was convinced that Keyon was still as in love with her, as he was the moment they first met.

"You know I still love you, baby," she said to Keyon's picture in her phone. "And I know that you love me, too. Hell, the only reason you're with that trollop is because she's pregnant and you're doing the manly thing. But I'm going to take care of things so that you and I can be together once again."

Symone jumped up out of the bed, put her clothes on, and headed out. She wasn't expecting Donnie to come home for a few hours so she had the day to herself. With no job or friends to occupy her time, Symone drove to Lenox Mall and did some shopping. Bored with that, she left and drove the few short blocks to Keyon's house. She pulled in front of the neighbor's driveway, four houses down and cut her car off.

Keyon's garage door was open and his car was gone. There was a sleek gray Bentley Coupe in the driveway that belonged to Carolyn, Keyon's mother and a small black Mercedes SUV that Symone wasn't sure who it belonged to. She got her answer when she saw Domynique and Carolyn walk out to the car. Domynique hugged Carolyn and got in the truck and left. Symone slid down in her car when Domynique drove past to prevent being spotted. Symone waited for Carolyn to go back inside and close the garage before she pulled off.

"Fuck, I may have lost her," Symone mumbled angrily. But by the time she got to the entrance of the subdivision, Symone was only three cars behind Domynique. Careful not to get to close, Symone followed at a safe distance as Domynique maneuvered through the thick traffic. Fifteen minutes later, Symone was parking a few cars down from Domynique.

"Hmph, bitch must have a doctor's appointment," Symone observed saucily, reading the sign on the building indicating that it was a gynecology and obstetrics clinic. Bitterness overtook Symone as she thought about Domynique having everything that rightfully belonged to Symone. Keyon, the baby, the wealth and prestige that came along with being Keyon's woman. Domynique had stolen all of that, according to Symone. "I'm taking back everything that the enemy stole from me, though," Symone vowed. Even though passed the time away with Donnie, it was Keyon she would always fight for.

Domynique parked in the corner of the lot next to a big tree and a few bushes. Looking around to see if she was being watched, Symone took a tire iron from her trunk and began going through the motions to change a tire. Using all of the strength she could muster, Symone began loosening all of the lug nuts on the rear driver's side tire. The first one gave her a bit of trouble and Symone had to stand on the four way tire iron in order to get the lug nut to move. By the time she had managed to get it loose, she had worked up a small sweat. The second one was not that hard and neither was the third one.

"Shit!" Symone griped as female voices came her way. Symone stopped working on the tire and played it cool. She waited to see what was going to happen next. The voices got louder. Symone looked over and saw one of the lug nuts by the tire. She slowly reached under the truck to grab the lug nut without being caught. Two women were standing on the front passenger side near Symone. Symone didn't recognize either of the voices but hoped that one of them didn't belong to Domynique. The last thing Symone needed was Domynique calling Keyon, telling him that Symone was following her.

"Damn, they cackling like a pair of hens. Can they leave already?" Symone was getting antsy. It seemed like she was hiding forever. The women wrapped up their conversation and went their separate ways. Thankfully, neither of them were Domynique.

Symone quickly finished her task and got back in her car, out of sight. Not too long after, Symone saw Domynique come out and get into her SUV.

"Let the games begin," Symone said following Domynique out of the lot.

Inside the SUV, Domynique was very excited. The doctor had given her baby a clean bill of health and the ultrasound revealed a great surprise for Domynique. She was on the fence about whether or not to share the news with Keyon or keep him guessing. Domynique's cell phone rang and she switched the blue tooth on in her truck.

"Hello," Domynique said, stopping at the red light before she entered the interstate.

"Hey, Diva, we're just calling to make sure you're on your way to meet us at the bakery." It was Jynx.

"I wouldn't miss that for the world. I've never been to a wedding cake tasting before."

"You're going to love it. Plus, it'll give you some experience for when it's your turn," Jynx said.

It took some doing but Jynx and Jonathan were doing just fine. He convinced Jynx to go to marriage counseling and after only two sessions, Jynx was ready to forgive her man. She believed that Jonathan was set-up because her cousin Keyon had been. She had first hand experienced on how devious and conniving some chicks could be. Things between them couldn't have been better.

"That's right, Sweet Tart," Devine chimed in from the background. "You got next on this, honey."

Domynique laughed. "You sure are right, Devine. I'll see you all in a few."

PILLOW PRINCESS- Part 2

Domynique pressed end on her phone and merged onto the interstate. Symone, who had driven in the opposite direction, headed home. She didn't feel the need to follow Domynique any further. Whatever happened, happened. Symone had done her part. Traffic on the Georgia 400 was at a snail's pace during rush hour. Domynique looked at the clock on the dashboard. It was our o'clock. She had to meet the others at 5:30 and even though traffic was thick, she was confident that she would make it on time. The smooth sounds of Anita Baker made the journey peaceful for Domynique. A few miles up the road and the traffic thinned out enough so that driver's could drive the posted speed limit of 60 miles per hour.

"Oh wow, where has the time gone?" Domynique said, seeing that she had less than 30 minutes to get to Merci Beaucoup, one of Atlanta's most elegant bakeries. Putting the pedal to the metal, Domynique bobbed and weaved until she put some space between the lagging traffic and her exit four miles ahead.

"What's going on?" Domynique questioned as her steering wheel began to shake a little. Panic set in when the steering wheel was shaking so much that she could barely hold on to it. A man in the car next to hers began to wave at her trying to get her attention.

"Your tire," he was saying, but she couldn't make out the rest of it.

I must have a flat, she deduced. She put on her right blinker in an attempt to pull over onto the shoulder. Domynique was doing 65 miles per hour and decided to slow down. Wrong move. As soon as she decreased the speed, the back driver's side tire came off and the rear of the SUV collapsed. The metal and concrete scraped against one another and provided a loud screeching sound. Sparks flew as the small truck skidded along. Domynique fought hard for control. Honking horns, screeching tires and the sound of breaking glass was all that could be heard on the highway. The last thought Domynique had was that she was going to be late for Jynx's cake tasting. She never made it.

Symone sat on the chaise lounge in her room, sipping on her tea. She reached her hand inside her jacket pocket and pulled everything out. Laughing out loud, Symone kneaded the lug nuts

207

between her fingers like they were tension balls. "Bye, bye, bitch."

Chapter Twenty-Five
One For The Road

"I'on know why we always have to stop. It ain't like we taking a road trip or nothin'. Hell, we just going up the street."

"Devine, I swear that's all your ass does is complain," Jynx said. "I can't help it if I have to pee. Shit, it's five o'clock. I'll be damned if you catch me sitting on the highway having to piss and then can't. Fuck that. You can ruin your kidneys if you want to but I'm saving mine."

"You two argue like an old married couple. Must I always be the voice of reason?" Cha-Cha asked.

"Yep," Jynx and Devine said at the same time.

"Well, then let's go. Y'all were tripping about Domynique being on time and now we're gonna be the ones who are late."

"Right. Come on, y'all," Jynx said, exiting the Quick Trip where she stopped to pee and get a drink.

The trio jumped in Devine's new 2014 Mercedes- Benz CLS550 and headed down Sydney Marcus Boulevard towards the Georgia 400. Before they turned onto the on ramp, they saw that traffic was moving steadily.

"Thank God," Devine said. "The last thing we need is for the highway to be a parking lot. We've got places to go and people to see."

"Indeed. We'll make it on time," Jynx chimed in.

"Well, call Domynique and let her know we had to make a

pit stop and are running a bit behind," Cha-Cha said.

"Okay." Jynx called Domynique's phone but didn't get an answer so she left her a voice message. "She didn't answer. Should I text her?"

"Yep, tell her we're not too far away now," Devine said. "Damn, look at the traffic. I thought that we had gotten past all that."

"We did. It's a wreck and these people are too busy being nosey to drive."

Devine drove as fast as the slow traffic would allow him to. He didn't want to be late for the cake tasting because he was hungry and had been looking forward to this all day.

"It looks like they're cleaning up the wreckage now. See," Jynx said pointing to the wrecker who was loading the wrecked vehicle on the truck bed.

"Sonofabitch," Cha-Cha exclaimed. "Look at the tag on that truck. HZHEART. Y'all, that's Domynique's plate."

"Are you sure?" Jynx asked.

"I'm positive. Call Keyon and find out if Domynique is okay," Cha-Cha demanded.

Jynx's hand was shaking like a leaf and she couldn't even touch the numbers on her phone to call Keyon.

"I'll call him," Devine offered. He used the voice dial command in his car to dial his friend. The phone rang three times before Keyon picked it up.

"Oh my gosh, Keyon! We just saw a wreck and one of the cars looked just like Domynique's. Please tell us that she's okay?" Devine cried.

"It was her car. We're at the hospital now. The doctors are in with her now."

"Where are you? We're on our way."

"We're here at Northside, Devine. And thanks. I could really use the support right about now. "

With Devine behind the wheel, it didn't take the friend's long to make it to the hospital. Keyon's parents, Shymon and even Jynx's parents had made it to the hospital by the time they arrived.

"Any word yet, Key?" Jynx asked her cousin.

"Not yet. I just came out to check on Mama. She's really upset because she said that she had a funny feeling in her stomach when Domynique left earlier."

"I knew I should have gone to the doctor with her," Carolyn said.

"Mom, it's okay. This isn't your fault."

"I know Keyon, but I should've insisted. If something happens to her or that baby, I don't think I'll ever forgive myself."

"Nothing's going to happen. God's got this," Keyon said optimistically, praying his words were true.

"Let's pray, family," Keyon's father, Keith, suggested.

Family and friends grabbed hands and formed a circle while Keyon's father said a prayer for his soon to be daughter-in-law and unborn grandchild. No sooner than they had finished praying, the doctor come into the room to call Keyon out to speak with him privately. The room was so quiet you could hear a pin drop. Devine and Cha-Cha paced back and forth all most bumping into one another. Keyon came back in the room with a huge smile on his face.

"God heard our prayers. Domynique is perfect and so is the baby. Not a scratch on either one of them."

Cheers and praises rang out in the waiting room only to be interrupted by two Atlanta police who walked into the room.

"Mr. Steele, may we have a word with you? In private?" A detective said.

"Sure, what's this about?" Keyon asked, giving the men the side eye.

"We'd like to ask you a question?"

"What did you wanna know?"

"We have reason to believe that your wife's accident wasn't an accident at all. Do you know anyone who would want to hurt her?"

"As a matter of fact, I do."

• • • • • • • • • • • • • • • • •

Night sweats, insomnia, poor concentration, muscle tension and palpitations were just a few of the withdrawal symptoms that

Charmaine was experiencing. For the past few nights, she woke up trembling with anger. As much as she wanted to move on from Donnie and Symone, there was no way she could just let things go. Charmaine wouldn't rest until she gave them something to remember her by. It didn't have to be deadly. Honestly, she didn't want it to be. But it had to be something for the both of them. After that was, she would be done. Just one for the road.

What Charmaine had in mind was almost effortless. It would take a little time to put everything in place but it would be worth it. Charmaine threw on a baseball cap and went to the local hardware store to pick up a few things. Then she made a beeline to the dog park near Cobb Galleria Mall that wasn't too far from Symone's house. Because she never stopped watching Donnie and Symone, she knew that they would be out for the better part of the day but she had to work quickly. Using the key that she stole from Donnie's key ring a few months ago, Charmaine entered Symone's condo. She worked systematically, beginning in Symone's room and moving backwards until she was near the front the door. Once she was done in the house, she locked the door and sprinkled the ground in front of Symone's house with a special surprise. By the time Donnie and Symone came home, Charmaine would be long gone.

Later that evening, Donnie pulled Symone's new SUV into its assigned parking spot. The two of them had just come from dinner and Donnie was horny. All she could think about was getting Symone upstairs and tearing the clothes off of her.

"Come on, babe. Let's get upstairs so I can do what I been thinking about all day," Donnie told Symone.

"Make it do what it do, baby," Symone said and they both hopped out of the truck.

"What the fuck?" Symone yelled.

"Sonofabitch!" Donnie screamed at the same time. "These are brand new Air Force One's and these muhfuckas were white a minute ago! Fuck! Damn!"

"I think I got some inside my shoe. Ewww," Symone whined.

"Be careful stepping. When we get on the sidewalk we can

take our shoes off."

Donnie and Symone treaded lightly as they worked their way around the truck to cleaner ground.

"That is so damn nasty. After we're married, we're moving into a house. These bastards over here don't like cleaning up after their damned dogs."

Symone gave Donnie the side eye but didn't say anything about the 'moving into a house' comment. Donnie didn't have five on nothing. Broke ass. Careful not to say what she was thinking, Symone exhaled first, then replied to her girlfriend.

"My neighbors are usually good at pooper scooping after their pets. I don't know where all that shit came from. Look, we drove up in it. In the dark, it looks like mud. Someone's bag must have broken on their way to dispose of it."

"You always defending these peckerwoods. Take those shitty ass shoes off and get upstairs."

Symone could tell that Donnie was getting mad. Donnie didn't like Symone's white neighbors because they were always spying on her. Donnie called them the 'observe and report' team. But if she wasn't always doing shit, Symone surmised, they wouldn't have anything to report. Donnie came upstairs and unlocked the door. The two of them stepped inside the foyer and sat their shoes down.

"Didn't I tell yo' ass to leave the lamp on?" Donnie scolded. "I hate coming home to dark house. A nigga can't see shit."

"I did. The lamp is just on the other side of the room. Scary ass." Symone stepped off of the ceramic tile entry onto the carpet. She walked three steps onto the carpet and something snapped at her foot.

"What the fuck?" She yelled.

"What is it, babe?" Donnie asked, following Symone's voice which turned to screams.

"Ouch! Ah! Oh!" Symone yelled.

Snap! Plop!

"Shit! There's something in my foot. Glass I think."

"Hurry up and get those fucking lights on, Symone!"

"I'm trying, shit. I have to walk slowly. There's a bunch of these things on the floor. I'm already bleeding like hell."

"Something stuck me. I ain't moving until you have the lights on and I can see what I'm doing."

Symone rolled her eyes in the dark as she treaded lightly on the floor. No matter which way she stepped, she could not avoid stepping on glass or even what felt like stick pins. The blood on her feet caused the glass to stick to her and there were several pieces that felt like they were deeply embedded in her foot. Symone's lamp was only a few feet from the door but it seemed to take forever for her to reach it. She sensed that she was within reach of the sofa so Symone bent down, swept the debris away with her hand and stood in the safe spot. Painfully, she bore down so that she could jump the few feet to the sofa, landing in an uncomfortable heap.

"You make it, Babe?"

"Yes," Symone answered reaching for the lamp. "What the hell is this?" She asked incredulously.

There were hundreds of mousetraps placed all over her floor surrounded by sharp, broken pieces of glass and thousands of thumb tacks.

"Who the fuck did this?" Symone screamed. She sat on the couch and looked at her bloody feet.

"The fuck you looking at me like I know? Hell, I was out with you all day."

"Whatever. Call 9-1-1. We need the police and the ambulance. My feet are fucked up."

Donnie did as she was asked and made her way back to the tiled foyer. As usual, there wasn't a scratch on her. She waited by the door and texted her friends until the police showed up. Symone could tell by the hard, aggressive knock that it was the police.

"Police," the cop announced. Donnie opened the door.

"Da fuck you doing here?" Donnie said, recognizing the officer. "We called for a regular cop, not no big time detective like you, Blair."

"Funny that you should call us. We were just about to come see you," Detective Blair said. "What the hell is this?"

"Duh, that's what we called you guys for. We came home and this is what we found. My girl's feet are fucked up and shit."

Detective Blair looked across the room to Symone and could see that she was in need of medical attention.

"The paramedics are on their way. Hold tight, Ms. Morrow. Until then, Ms. Stone, I'm going to need you to come with me."

"I ain't going nowhere with you. Matter of fact, you need to tell me why your ass is here anyway."

"Donita Stone, you are under arrest for conspiracy to commit murder" he began snidely. "You have the right to remain silent. Anything you say can and will be used against you."

While Detective Blair read Donnie the rest of her Miranda Rights, he was turning her around to place the handcuffs on her wrists.

"Murder? This is bullshit. My woman ain't hurt nobody," Symone defended.

"Man, let me outta these cuffs. I ain't done shit. Y'all not gon' pin this shit on me," Donnie said. She was scared shitless but put on a brave front. Inside, she felt like crying though.

"We've got DNA and that's all that matters."

Chapter Twenty-Six

Dana Don't Lie

As happy as Detective Blair was to finally have Donnie in custody for Morgan's murder, he was devastated at having to tell his cousin Randall, that his ex-wife had been murdered. His instincts told him that it was her but for once, he wanted to be wrong. His cousin Randall was a good dude who didn't deserve this. Even though Morgan and Randall were divorced, Keenan knew his cousin still had a soft spot for his ex wife. After all, she was his first love. Keenan's assistant, Kimmy had long since stolen Randall's heart and he was debating whether or not to have her break the bad news to his family member.

"Keenan, you're awfully quiet. What's up? You and Zabria argue or something?" Kimmy asked.

"Nah, nothing like that."

"Good. 'Cause I like her. Don't screw that up. I think she might be the one for you."

"Hmmph. I think that, too. Kim, listen, now that we have Donita in custody, we're going to have to tell my cousin about Morgan.

"Fuck!" Kimmy said, taking a seat across from her boss. "He's going to be so hurt. How're you going to tell him?"

"Uh. I was kind of hoping that…"

"Coward. No worries. I'll do it. I'm seeing him tonight."

"Okay. Let's get in here and talk to this murdering dyke. I

can't believe that Morgan went that way."

"Hell, we're in Atlanta. Homosexuality and Lesbianism runs rampant in the black community here. This is San Francisco of the South," Kimmy accurately stated.

Homicide detectives were in the interrogation room questioning Donnie who was crying and sweating bullets. Keenan and Kimmy watched through the two way glass as they relentlessly questioned her.

"So, you mean to tell us, you have no idea how your blood came to be on a ring that Mrs. Calloway was wearing the day before she disappeared?"

"That's what I said. Why would I hurt Morgan? I loved her. She was looking out for a nigga like me," Donnie said.

"I notice you keep referring yourself as a "nigga"," the condescending black cop began. "Do you think you are? My friend down in property said they had a blast laughing at the strap on you wore in."

"Man, fuck all of y'all. Where my lawyer at? I ain't saying shit else to y'all pigs!"

The officer laughed. "You don't have to say shit. Just listen, as we speak, my friends are at your brother's house and your fiancé's house, ransacking the place, coming up with even more evidence. The deck is already stacked against you. I hope your bitch loves you enough to pay for a good attorney. You're going to need it."

Donnie got out of her chair and flung it against the concrete wall. She was praying that between Symone and her brother Damon, they would get her the best attorney money could buy. The detectives had pictures, phone texts, and voice mail messages of her and Morgan. Shit she had no clue even existed. The attorney that Symone and Damon hired finally showed up and sat with Donnie trying to get to the bottom of things.

"They have some hard evidence, Ms. Stone. Right now, things don't look too promising. In order for us to have half a chance, you're going to have to be honest with me," the attorney said.

"What the fuck you think I been doing? I didn't kill Morgan. Yeah, we had some fights. I fucked up and hit her a few times but what couple you know don't have their ups and downs?"

"This is about way more than a few ups and downs, this is about Capital Murder. You could be facing the death penalty. It's time for you to start taking this seriously."

"Dude, I am. I'm telling you, I was set up by Charmaine. I swear!"

"Ah, yes. Ms. Franklin. Are you aware that the police did a background check on her? The only Charmaine Franklin that came up in the system was of an 80 year old black woman, who died five years ago?"

"Yeah, yeah. They told me that. But check it, talk to my brother and his wife. They will tell you that I ain't making this shit up. I dated Charmaine Franklin for almost four years. She was psychotic. Every bitch I fucked with ended up on the receiving end of some foul shit because of her."

"I already spoke with your brother, sister-in-law, your friends; even Ms. Morrow. All of them substantiate that Charmaine Franklin is the name of the young lady you were seeing, but the prosecutor is going to spin this in an ugly direction. How is it that you dated someone so long and didn't know what her real name was or even what she really looked like? You don't have one picture of this woman."

"I know it looks bad, but I'm innocent. I didn't kill Morgan."

"I believe you. Unfortunately, I'm not the one you have to convince."

Donnie was escorted from the attorney booth to a holding cell to wait to go to court that was set up inside of the Fulton County Jail.

"Damn, they do everything in this damned jail. I just knew I was going to get some fresh air," Donnie griped.

"You only go to outside court after your bond hearing," a female inmate said. "Hopefully, they'll release you today on your own recognizance. The last thing you wanna do is fight your case from inside the jail. This ain't no place for nobody to be."

"Shit, you ain't gotta tell me. I only been here a few days but I'm already tired of that damned thick ass, cold bologna and those soggy ass cookies. I mean damn, can't a nigga get a hot meal, or something? What happened to three hots and a cot?"

"I need Kennedy, Lowe, Green, Stone, Crenshaw, Pinkney and Young. You all have a bond hearing at 9 am. Let's go," the detention officer said.

The women filed into the courtroom and sat quietly waiting for their names to be called. The judge seemed very nice and every person who was called was either released on time served, their own recognizance or a low bond. Donnie's name was called last. She figured the way things were going she wouldn't have any issues either.

"Donita Stone," the judge began. "You're charged with capital murder. Prosecutors recommendation?"

"Your Honor, the people are requesting no bond be set at this time. Ms. Stone is a menace to society. At this time she is unemployed, and other than a brother, she has no solid ties to the community."

"Do you believe this shit?" Donnie whispered to her attorney who shushed her.

"Your Honor, although my client is unemployed, she was born and raised here in Atlanta. Her brother is willing to be a signatory on the bond as well as Ms. Stone's girlfriend who is a popular radio show host. My client is not a flight risk. Please grant my client a reasonable bond," Donnie's lawyer pleaded.

"I see no reason why Ms. Stone should be held without bond. Bail is set at $250,000. Next case." And the judge smashed the gavel.

"A quarter of a million dollars? Where in the hell are we supposed to get that kind of money from?"

"Don't worry. We'll petition for a bond reduction hearing. We can set a court date in a couple of days."

• • • • • • • • • • • • • • • • • •

Two weeks later, Donnie was heading to Fulton County Superior Court for her arraignment. She was tired from tossing and turning all night. The detectives found some damning evidence at her brother's house in the attic which put a few more nails in Donnie's coffin. The detectives brought Donnie back in for questioning and she insisted she had been set up. It was a horrible night.

As Donnie sat quietly in the courtroom while she was being arraigned, hot tears streamed down her face. The list of charges seemed to grow by the minute. And to make matters worse, Symone wasn't there. Someone sent Symone a video tape of Donnie in their bed. Donnie having a threesome in their bed. Donnie knew it was Charmaine. Symone was so angry she stopped accepting Donnie's calls and didn't show up in court today. Just like Charmaine said, Donnie would remember the day she fucked her over. Late last night, while Donnie lay on the hard metal bunk on top of a green plastic mat, she thought long and hard about what the detective asked.

"Who would really go through so much trouble to set you up?"

Donnie knew the answer; Charmaine. The last time they were together, Charmaine told Donnie she would regret the day that she broke Charmaine's heart.

"I gave you the best I had Donita, and all you did was shit on me. After all the bullshit I took from you, you went out and chose to make the next bitch your wife, instead of me. You hurt me to the core, Donita Stone. But trust and believe, you will pay. You have no clue who you're really fucking with and by the time you find out, it's going to be too late."

221

Chapter Twenty-Seven

The Real Psycho

Cha-Cha and Devine were finalizing the preparations for Jynx's bachelorette party. The hotel suite was booked and all of the invitations had been mailed out. The duo had sent them out over a month ago. Devine held a clipboard in his hand with a checklist on it as he was systematically going through each task to make sure that each one was complete.

"Cha-Cha, I have a question about our guest list," Devine began.

"What's up, Diva?"

"You know we mailed these invites out a long time ago at a time that we were still cool with Ms. Symone. Now that she's all but said 'fuck us' should we uninvite her?"

"Chile,' I doubt if she shows up. I mean, why would she? I wouldn't wanna be around people who I didn't like," Cha-Cha said.

"True, but this is Symone we're talking about and real talk, we're the only friends she has. And you know Donnie has been locked up for a few days now so she's probably lonely as hell."

"Well, if she does show up, I just hope she doesn't try to cause a scene because you know Lil Ms. Domynique is going to be there and her belly is getting big. I know we've been knowing Symone longer but I'd hate to have to kick her ass if she tried to set it off with our new friend."

"Cha-Cha, you ain't never lied. Well, if Symone does decide to grace us with her presence let's just make sure that we keep an eye on her sneaky ass."

Devine poured him and Cha-Cha a glass of wine and they got back to the party details. There were a few last minute things that needed to be handled and the two of them were frantic. It was crunch time. The party was in less than eight hours. The phone rang and Devine sprang across the room to answer it.

"Hey, Diva. What's up?" It was Kimmy.

"Oh hey, Boo. Not shit. Finalizing a few last minute party details. What's good with you?"

"That's the reason why I called. I wanted to know if I could invite a new friend of mine. She's Keenan's new girlfriend. Very down to Earth and sweet as hell. I promise you guys will like her."

"Sure, Sweet Tart. I'm sure she's cool if you hang with her. The party starts at 7:30 sharp. Please be on time," Devine admonished.

"I will. I'm leaving the station at six and heading over to pick my friend up. We may be early."

"Cool. See ya' soon." Devine hung up the phone and went back into the room with Cha-Cha.

"Who was that, Devine?" Cha-Cha asked.

"Kimmy. She asked if she could bring a friend of hers. Keenan's new boo. I told her yes."

"Hmm. 'Bout damned time he moved on. That last little chicken head ran a number on him. I hope this one is different."

"You and me both. Come on, let's hurry up because I have to go and get my hair done."

A few hours later, Cha-Cha and Devine walked around the impressive suite that they booked at Atlanta's upscale hotel, The Georgian Terrace. The penthouse boasted two levels that had two bedrooms, two-and-a-half baths, a den and magnificent views of Midtown Atlanta. The room was almost 3000 square feet of pure luxury.

"We did good, bitch," Cha-Cha said, giving Devine a high five.

"Yes, we did. I give this place two snaps up in a circle."

"Yesss, honey."

There was a knock on the penthouse door and Cha-Cha went to answer it. It was room service bringing up the food and liquor selections that Cha-Cha and Devine ordered. A few minutes after the wait staff set everything up, there was another knock on the door. This time is was Kimmy and her friend.

"Heyyy," Kimmy sang, walking in and hugging her good friend Cha-Cha.

"Hey, Boo. How are you?" Cha-Cha asked.

"Girl, I'm good. This is the friend I was telling you about. Zabria, this is Cha-Cha and Devine. My day ones. We go back like four flats on a Cadillac."

"Right. Welcome, Zabria. I'm Devine," he said, introducing himself, "and this beautiful specimen right here is Cha-Cha."

Introductions were really unnecessary. When Zabria lived as Charmaine she knew all about Symone's friends. They were all on some of her surveillance footage at various times. Yes, she knew exactly who each of them were and what they all had going on but she wasn't going to bust herself.

"Hello. I've heard so much about each of you. And Cha-Cha, I happen to frequent your boutique all of the time. As a matter of fact, the dress I wore for New Year's was one of yours. It was the black, tiered off the shoulder dress by Herve' Leger."

"I was wondering who bought that dress. It wasn't even in the shop one day before it sold. You must have some serious loot to spend $1200 on a dress, huh?"

"Girl, her grandfather invented the Hoveround," Kimmy answered for Zabria.

"Not the Hoveround itself, but he holds the patent for the motorized wheelchair. Everyone who makes a power chair has to get written permission from him in order to use the motor," Zabria clarified.

"Damn! Well, all right then, Grandpa. Good for him," Cha-Cha said. "You'll have to come in next week. I have some one of a kind pieces coming in from Hermes that you may like. We can have lunch afterwards if you'd like."

"Sounds great. Thank you."

Guests began to arrive and Cha-Cha and Devine gave each of them instructions. This was going to be a surprise bachelorette party for Jynx and they wanted to make sure that everyone was on the same page. It was Domynique's job to get Jynx to the hotel without letting on that anything was going down. Devine got a text and looked down at his phone.

We're on our way up. It was Domynique.

"Okay, ladies. They are on their way up. Now, we have to be very quiet. Hit the lights, Cha-Cha."

Everyone got as quiet as a church mouse.

"Domynique, why are we here? Devine and Cha-Cha are going to be angry if we're late for dinner."

"Oh my God, Jynx. I told you that I have to pick up something for Grandma Steele that she wanted from the gift shop. It's only going to take a minute. You could have stayed in the car," Domynique said, pretending to be exasperated with her friend.

"No. I hate being left by myself."

Domynique and Jynx made their way to the suite. Once inside, Domynique pretended to grope in the dark for the lights.

"I'll be right back. I gotta find a light."

Jynx stood by the door in the dark room and almost jumped out of her Giuseppe Zanotti heels when she heard people scream.

"Surprise!" Everyone yelled as the lights came on.

"What the hell? I can't believe this," Jynx said. She looked around the room and saw her closest friends and family laughing and smiling.

"We wanted to do something special for your last hurrah so we decided on a surprise party for you," Domynique said. "I almost let the cat out of the bag a few times."

"I know you did. Your ass can't hold water," Devine said.

The party goers laughed loudly at the same time someone knocked hard on the door.

"Shit, we better quiet down before we get kicked out," Domynique said.

"May I help you?" Cha-Cha asked the very handsome man at the door.

"I'm the manager of this here establishment and we got a

call that there was a loud ruckus coming from this room," the man said.

"Uh-oh," Jynx said.

The man was dressed in a nice black suit and had on a badge. Jynx thought that it was going to be a stripper dressed like a cop coming to tell them to keep it down. But this man was not a cop, at all.

"I'm sorry, Sir," Cha-Cha said. "It's our sister's bachelorette party and we got a little carried away. We'll keep it down."

"Please do, or else, I'll have shut this party down."

"And how do you plan on doing that?" Devine challenged him.

"Like this." The man in the suit opened the suite door and five fine ass men strutted into the room and began to take off the expensive suits they wore.

"Take it all off!" one of the ladies yelled.

Jynx stood dumbfounded as the sexy, chocolate men gave her the show of her life.

"Now, you know we shut this whole floor down for you, don't you? We go hard or we go home," Cha-Cha said.

The party was in full swing and all of the ladies kicked off their heels and let their hair down. An hour after the exotic dancers got there, Symone arrived. Neither Cha-Cha nor Devine knew who let Symone in. All they knew is that she was there. The only reason Symone came was because she knew that Domynique was going to be there and she had unfinished business with her.

Cha-Cha and Devine watched as she scanned the room. They watched intently as Symone stared at Domynique with an angry scowl on her face and a flared up nose. Bile rose up in Symone's throat as she looked down at Domynique's stomach. The last time Symone saw Domynique, she wasn't showing. Now she looked like she was at least six months pregnant.

"Get your girl," Cha-Cha told Devine.

"I got her," Devine said. He walked over to Symone and greeted her.

"Hey, Lady. We didn't expect to see you here tonight," Devine said honestly.

"I couldn't miss my best friend's party, now could I?"

"Yep. Especially since you told us all that we were not your true friends and to kiss your ass. We figured that you meant what you said."

"I was angry, Devine. I'm sure you all knew that. It was hurtful to me that you all knew that Keyon had moved on and didn't tell me."

"Symone, you moved on too and we'd been trying to reach out to you for ages but you kept blowing us off. Hell, you probably only fucking with us now because your stud is locked up."

"That's not fair, Devine. You all know that I love you guys."

"Symone, you always try to play the victim. We love you too but you ma'am have a funny way of showing your friends love."

"I know, but I'm not going to be acting like that anymore. You know me and Keyon have been talking more lately and I think that he wants to work things out."

"Keyon?" Devine was perplexed. The last time Devine spoke to Keyon he was talking about killing both Symone and Donnie because Donnie had threatened Domynique and Keyon felt like Symone had something to do with it. But Devine was going to allow Symone to live in her fantasy world for tonight. Anything that would keep the peace.

"Keyon loves me, Devine and has for almost six years. Do you really think that a video vixen can come between that? I think not."

"Okay," Devine said, letting it go. "Well, welcome. You wanna get something to eat?"

"Sure. Tell me how you and Jynx ended up dating twins and not knowing it."

"Well, it took Jynx a minute to introduce us to Jonathan. By the time she did, I had already met his brother. I ended up seeing the brothers together and that's when Charles explained everything to me. Jonathan wanted it to be a surprise for Jynx so I promised my man I wouldn't tell her. You know how hard it is for me to keep a secret. I swear I almost died a few times holding it in."

"I heard about the fight on New Years. Was it bad?"

"Symone, you have no idea. Jynx was going crazy. It took three strong men to get her under control and once they did, she was so confused we had to explain to her what was going on a few times before Jynx understood. She thought that Jonathan was cheating on her. It was a simple misunderstanding."

"I understand how things can look one way and actually be another. I'm glad that things worked out. For both of you."

Devine and Symone went to the buffet table and fixed a plate of food. Every where Domynique moved, Symone's eyes followed and Devine's followed Symone's. He knew that his friend was not okay with Domynique being there and he wanted to make sure that Symone didn't fly off the handle. Jynx, Domynique, Cha-Cha, Zabria and Kimmy danced the next five tunes that the hired D.J. played. Even from a distance, Devine could see that Domynique was tired.

"Whew, girl, I have to go lie down for awhile and put my feet up. Do you mind if I crash upstairs for a bit? I'll be back down but this little man of Steele in here is giving me the blues," Domynique said, patting her stomach.

"Sure, go on upstairs and rest. This party ain't ending no time soon," Jynx assured her.

Symone followed Domynique upstairs with her eyes. She was going to give Domynique a few minutes and then Symone planned on going up to talk to her. All she wanted to do was talk. Symone noticed that Devine was sticking to her like glue. Clearly he was trying to keep her and Domynique apart. *His ass ain't slick*, Symone thought to herself. In order for her to talk to Domynique, Symone was going to need Devine to go somewhere else. The perfect opportunity came when the D.J. played *The Cupid Shuffle*. Devine loved that song and loved dancing.

Cha-Cha came over and grabbed both Symone and Devine and they all got out on the dance floor and started jamming. As their line dance shifted, Symone made her way to the back of the formation. Before anyone noticed, Symone slipped out of the line and crept upstairs. But Zabria was watching. She was always watching.

The light was off in the room that Domynique was lying in but Symone could see that she had a towel over her eyes. Symone turned up her nose as she walked over to the bed. She turned on the light and sat on the bed next to Domynique.

"Wake up, Bitch," Symone snarled.

"What?" Domynique said, taking the towel off her face.

"I said, wake the fuck up. Bitch!"

Domynique rubbed her eyes, trying to focus.

"What are you doing here, Symone?"

"Hmph, so the Bitch knows my name, I see."

"I'm not a bitch, Symone," Domynique said quietly. "And yes, I know who you are. Keyon showed me pictures of you and your brother, Shymon. He told me all about you."

"Did he tell you how much he loved me and how he chased me for the longest trying to get with me?"

"Yes, as a matter of fact he did. There's nothing we don't talk about."

"I'll bet you didn't know that he came to my job and we talked. Or I bet he didn't tell you how I was in your bedroom with his dick in my mouth, now did he?"

"He told me that too, Symone. Keyon and I don't have any secrets. I know about your pathetic attempts to get him back and even slobbing on his knob didn't work. You could lie in the bed with a wet pussy and legs wide open, and Keyon wouldn't fuck you with a ten foot pole."

"Shut the fuck up!" Symone yelled, slapping Domynique across the face. Domynique tasted blood in her mouth and spit it in her hand. She didn't want to ruin the comforter in the luxurious suite.

"Why are you doing this, Symone? Keyon and I are going to be married. I'm carrying his child. We are going to be a family. You're with someone else. Build a bridge and then get over it. Keyon has moved on and you need to as well."

"Bitch, Keyon loves me. The only thing standing in the way of me and him getting back together is you. That's why, you gotta go."

Domynique gasped when Symone pulled the gun out of

her bosom.

"Symone, listen, we can work this out. You can have Keyon. Just let me and my baby go. I promise you don't have to worry about me again."

"Ho, I ain't worried about you or your bastard ass baby."

Downstairs the music blared. Everyone laughed, drank and lived it up. Cha-Cha was the first to notice that Symone was not among the other party goers.

"Devine, Symone is not down here. Go check upstairs," Cha-Cha urged.

"Damn. I'll be back, girl."

Devine ran up the stairs two at a time. The music was so loud that Symone didn't hear as he opened the door.

"What the fuck is going on?" Devine asked.

"I just needed to talk to her, is all. That's all we're doing."

"If that's true, then why is Domynique bleeding and crying, Symone?"

"Because she's a hateful, deceitful bitch and she's going to get what's coming to her."

"Symone, Domynique didn't come between you and Keyon. Let her go. She hasn't done anything to you," Devine pleaded for his friend.

"This trick gotsta go, Devine. She's trying to steal Keyon from me and trap him with a baby that ain't his."

Symone turned around and showed Devine her gun.

"You gotta gun?" Devine yelled at the exact same time that the music stopped downstairs. Kimmy heard Devine's shout and motioned for the other women to be quiet. She walked over to the D.J. and told him to play some music. Whatever was going on up-stairs, Kimmy didn't want to alert them that they knew about it downstairs.

Cautiously, Kimmy made her way upstairs until she reached the room where Devine and the two women were. The door was wide open. Weapon drawn, Kimmy stepped in behind Devine who was talking.

"Symone, please don't do this. You're right, Keyon loves only you. Put the gun away and let's go to him." Devine was crying now. He saw that Kimmy had her gun drawn and knew that this wasn't going to end well.

"Fuck that, Devine. I'm tired of people taking what's mine. She took my man. The baby she's carrying is supposed to be mine. My brother. Everything I had, she took."

"That's not true. Please. Put the gun down."

"Yes it is. She even took you guys."

By this time, guests had made their way upstairs. Zabria was able to get a front row seat of the action.

"Symone, I'm a cop," Kimmy began. "Put your gun down and let's talk this out. Domynique."

Domynique cried harder.

"There's nothing to talk about. It's over," Symone said, squeezing the trigger. She turned her head quickly towards the door and faced Kimmy. The music died downstairs. Two gunshots pierced the air followed by screams.

Epilogue

Zabria looked at herself in the mirror and thanked God for delivering her from her old self. Charmaine was dead and gone and Zabria couldn't have been happier. So much had happened in the past 18 months. It was hard to believe that a year had passed since Donnie's sentencing. The judge had thrown the book at her. After she was arrested, tons of evidence was introduced from an anonymous source that irrefutably proved that she had murdered Morgan Calloway, Kelly Vanderbilt and Nina Carter. The D.A. also obtained the video footage from Houston's restaurant that showed Donnie driving off in Keyon's car. She was charged with grand theft auto and felony destruction of property.

Video footage, journals and damning text messages showed how Donnie had set up women and harmed countless others. All because they no longer wanted to fund her lifestyle. There was even evidence that showed Donnie setting up an ex-girlfriend, planting drugs in her car. The evidence exonerated Tranice Rice. A young lady who had been sentenced to 15 years in Gwinnett County for drug trafficking.

During Donnie's trial, the prosecutor portrayed Donnie as an opportunistic, money hungry gigolo who showed no regard for the people in her life. Even though Donnie's family had paid for one of Atlanta's best defense attorney's, there was no way he could get her off with all the chips stacked against her. He couldn't explain away how police found Morgan's decapitated head, hands and feet in a bucket in Donnie's attic. Hell, Donnie didn't know herself. Donnie told the jury that she believed Charmaine was the culprit but no one believed her.

. And why would they? It was hard to believe that Donnie had fucked with a woman for over three years and did not know what she really looked like or what her real name was. The prosecutor was able to use those facts to their advantage, proving how self involved Donnie was. They even subpoenaed Angela Duke, a young lady who was held hostage for two months as a result of her affiliation with Donnie. The judge asked Donnie for her final words before sentencing.

"I know I am innocent of all these charges. I didn't kill Morgan, Kelly or Nina. I was set up and one day you all will know the truth, hopefully. The only thing I'm guilty of is cheating. If I would've stayed faithful to who I was with, then maybe this chain of events wouldn't have occurred." Even still, she rubbed her thigh like she still had the dildo strapped on.

Donnie didn't show any remorse during court and the judge was livid when he sentenced her. She hadn't even shed a tear or made a scene.

"Ms. Stone, I've never seen anyone so incredibly callous or stupid in this regard. You madam, in your pursuit of happiness are criminally negligent and culpable in the matter of the kidnapping of Angela Duke but I can't charge you with that. Thankfully, a jury of your peers has found you guilty of three counts of capital murder, one count of evidence tampering, three counts of drug possession, one count of conspiracy and 23 counts of malicious mischief. You should be on your way to death row now. But by the grace of God and the mercy of the jury, I hereby sentence you to two consecutive life sentences without the possibility of parole. One day soon, Ms. Stone, you will find yourself lonely, scared and even hurt in prison and it's at those times I want you to remember why you're there." Then, that's when she lost it. Anyone who knew Donnie could tell you she was ruthless, but at that moment, she wailed like a baby. As she was escorted out by the deputies, some families of the victims yelled obscenities and laughed at Donnie.

After the ordered the courtroom quiet, he read the sentence. Cries of outrage and cheers of joy rang out. Emotions were strong from all families in the courtroom. Zabria, who sat in the back of the courtroom the day of the sentencing, was happy that Donnie got life and not the death penalty. She just couldn't get over Donnie's reaction. There was a time in her life that Zabria wanted Donnie dead but not any longer. Being with Keenan and experiencing true love had changed her. Hopefully, Donnie would choose to change as well.

• • • • • • • • • • • • • • • • • •

"It's almost time. Are you nervous, baby?" Zachary Moreland asked his daughter.

"No, daddy, I'm not nervous. I've dreamt of this day since I was a little girl."

"Well, I'm nervous," Kimmy said. "Who would've thought that I would be having a double wedding with my best friend?"

"I know right? I love you, Kimora Lynn Bradshaw, and I am so glad we are friends. Who better to share this special day with than my ace boon coon?"

The two friends hugged and tried not to cry. Zabria did both of their makeovers and they looked fierce.

"Well, I'll let you two finish up here and I'll go check on your mom. I love you, Bria."

"Love you too, Daddy."

Zabria was happy that her mother was well enough to come see her walk down the aisle. She loved her mother and over the years, Melissa Moreland had been the only person Zabria could confide in. Melissa was the only person who knew of *every* dastardly deed and murder that Zabria or rather Charmaine had committed. Zabria wasn't worried about her mother saying anything because her mother didn't speak to anyone but Zabria. It was on the last visit to the mental hospital that Zabria told her mother that she was getting married. Melissa got a look in her eyes that Zabria had never seen before. Excitement. Melissa was excited to see her only child get married.

Greater Elizabeth Baptist Church was packed. Atlanta's elite milled in and were ushered to their seats. Kimmy's husband-to -be had just been nominated for another Oscar award and the paparazzi was out trying to snap photos of the star-studded double wedding. Friends and close family sat on the first ten rows on both sides of the church.

Keyon and his wife Domynique sat on the third row. He held his one year old son, K.J., Keyon Jr. in his lap. Domynique, who was more beautiful than ever, held their one year old daughter, Britain in her lap. Domynique kept the fact that she was carrying twins a secret from Keyon, only telling his mother and his grandmother. He looked at her and rubbed her pregnant belly and kissed her on the cheek. They were expecting another, already.

"Have I told you lately that I love you?" He said.

"This morning, but I can stand to hear it a few hundred times a day. I love you, too."

"You are so beautiful pregnant. I didn't think you could look any better but you do."

"Thank you. I hope it's not your plan to keep me barefoot and pregnant our entire marriage?"

"Meh. I don't know. I'm off to a good start, wouldn't you say?"

"A very good start. Since your parents moved into their new home six months ago, I think you've tried to sex me silly every day. I'm worn out."

"You telling me you don't like it when I make you cum?" He whispered in her ear.

"Keyon, we're in church?"

"And? You're my wife. God knows I be putting it on you. He sees all and knows all."

"Ooh, you're bad. Stop talking like that in front of the kids."

"Hmmm. I know that look. You're getting wet, aren't you? Don't worry, all this'll be over soon enough. And then it's on like Donkey Kong."

Domynique shook her head, "What am I going to do with you?"

"Love me for the rest of your life, I hope."

"I will."

Keyon leaned in and kissed Domynique. Every time he thought about how close he came to losing her, he was humbled.

With Big out of the picture, he was able to breathe a lot easier. The police still hadn't found his murderer. Keyon didn't think that they were looking very hard either. It was reported that Cleophus 'Big' Abignol, was under investigation by many law enforcement agencies including the FBI. For Keyon, it was good riddance to bad rubbish. Domynique handed their daughter Britain to Keyon, interrupting his thoughts and she leaned her head on his shoulder. She was five months pregnant with another son and she tired easily. Keyon ran his fingers through his wife's hair and listened as Shymon began to sing 'You and I'.

Never in a million years did Keyon think that he would be the only family Shymon had left. Symone's death had rocked them all to the core. Keyon didn't want to seem insensitive but if Symone hadn't died after Kimmy shot her, he was going to kill her himself. After the shooting, the police had searched Symone's house and found the lug nuts from Domynique's car. Never in a million years did Keyon believe that Symone could kill. It was obvious that Keyon didn't know Symone as well as he thought.

Keyon looked up at the grooms and smiled, noting that they both wore nervous expressions on their faces. The same look that Keyon himself had on his face a year ago. Marrying Domynique had been the best decision of Keyon's life. He didn't care how they met. What Donnie meant for evil, God was able to turn around for good. Domynique was everything that he had ever wanted and he was determined to make her happier than she had ever been.

Devine sat next to his new, very handsome boyfriend, Peter. The two hadn't been dating long but Devine was happy with the way things were progressing. He wanted a relationship like Cha-Cha had found with Michael and Keyon with Domynique. Hell, even Jynx had found Jonathan and now the two of them were expecting their first child. The past year had been hard for the friends but they were all doing great and moving forward.

The organist began to play the wedding march and the guests stood up to see Zabria and Kimmy walk down the aisle. Love was in the air. The two grooms smiled at their brides-to-be as they slowly made their way down the aisle. Randall was one of Keyon's good friends and Keyon knew that he had never seen his friend happier or more excited. *That's what the love of a good woman will do for you*, Keyon thought.

Melissa Moreland looked at her daughter, Zabria. She was the only one who knew of the true evil that lied within Zabria's soul. An evil so pure it could kill without remorse. Not once. Not twice. But three times. An evil that would allow a mother to sit in a mental institution for years for a murder that she did not commit. Only God, Melissa and Zabria knew the truth of what had happened that fateful morning when Jean left.

The night before, Jean and Melissa had a terrible argument. Jean wanted to leave. Melissa begged her to stay, threatening to end her own life if Jean left. Zabria had been livid. She couldn't believe that Melissa would choose a dyke over her and she told Melissa that.

"You got me fucked up and so does Jean so I'm gonna put an end to this dyke shit once and for all, *Mother!*"

Melissa had seen her daughter do mean things to other kids but never thought that her daughter could kill. When Jean got up to leave the next morning, Melissa had already made peace with her lover's departure. Jean wanted to say goodbye to Zabria because she really did love the little girl as her own. But Melissa thought it would be best if she left without seeing Zabria because she knew that Zabria would take it hard. When Jean went into the living room, Zabria was there, waiting. She told Jean that she loved her and asked the woman for a hug. When Jean leaned in to hug Zabria, that's when Zabria plunged the butcher's knife into Jeans back. She took it out and stabbed Jean fourteen more times after the woman hit the floor. Melissa was so shocked, all she could do was stand there.

Zabria took the knife and placed it in her mother's hand before she called her father, who in turn called the cops. Melissa was catatonic and didn't speak. Words no longer formed; she became mute. Because of his wealth and connections, Zachary was able to have Melissa committed instead of sent to prison. The judge swept the incident under the rug. At fourteen years old, Zabria had gotten away with her first murder and by the looks of things, history would repeat itself.

Melissa looked on as the two women finally stood next to their men. Zabria saw her sitting there with the same zombie look on her face. She could never figure out what she was thinking, or if she was even paying attention. The father's gave their daughter's away, proudly. Vows were read as friends and family looked on. When the preacher asked if anyone saw a reason that either couple should not be wed, no one made a sound. At last, it was all over. Randall and his new bride Kimmy turned and saluted the crowd first. Kimmy's mother stood up and hugged her daughter before Kimmy walked out of the church. Melissa followed suit. She stood up and walked slowly over to her daughter with a bouquet of flowers in her hand. The same bouquet she held throughout the ceremony. Zabria was smiling the most beautiful smile ever.

"I love you, mommy. I am so glad you were here to share this special moment with me."

"I love you, too, Bria. I always will." Melissa reached around her daughter and hugged her. Keenan was receiving well wishes from guests and no one paid much attention to the mother-daughter exchange of love. Melissa, holding a bouquet concealing a knife, pressed it against Zabria's lower back and pushed in with all her might.

"Mommy, no!" Zabria screamed but it was too late.

Keenan turned just in time to see his wife of ten minutes slither to the floor. A pool of warm blood spreading underneath her. Helplessly, Keenan watched the life fade from Zabria's eyes.

"No!" He screamed in agony.

Everyone stood around in shock. Zachary frantically tried to revive his daughter but it was too late. Zabria was dead.

"Why?" The father yelled in anguish.

But Melissa didn't answer. She just stared off into space withholding the truth. And six months later, in a mental institution in Savannah, Georgia, the truth would die with her.

For more information visit us online at:
www.lifechangingbooks.net
Twitter: @lcbooks
Instagram: @lcbooks
Facebook: Life Changing Books and LCBooks

LCB BOOK TITLES

See More Titles At
www.lifechangingbooks.net

CHECK OUT THESE LCB SEQUELS